Other Published Works by the Author

Parthian Stranger 1 The Order
Parthian Stranger 2 Conspiracy

Parthian Stranger 3

SUPREME COURT

STEWART N. JOHNSON

Order this book online at www.trafford.com
or email orders@trafford.com

Most Trafford titles are also available at major online book retailers.

Printed in the United States of America.

ISBN: 978-1-4907-3261-9 (sc)
ISBN: 978-1-4907-3263-3 (hc)
ISBN: 978-1-4907-3262-6 (e)

Library of Congress Control Number: 2014905893

Trafford rev. 04/01/2014

 www.trafford.com

North America & international
toll-free: 1 888 232 4444 (USA & Canada)
fax: 812 355 4082

Thank you, to all those that have helped me in the past, present and in the future, with a guiding force and assistance from: Breanna Gibson, without her contribution, support and help, this book would not be here, she is such an inspiration to all of us, thank you for believing in me. For my wife, Penny, your assistance is so invaluable, if it weren't for you this book would have been difficult to make this book be possible.

CONTENTS

Chapter 1   Orgy at the spa; Bella Haven 1

Chapter 2   Carlos & the Cuban Warriors 18

Chapter 3   Back to the Spa, with guests 35

Chapter 4   The new beginnings 46

Chapter 5   The vortex of water 67

Chapter 6   The wedding to Sara 94

Chapter 7   The Honeymoon 114

Chapter 8   Annabel Ryan the Damsel in distress 135

Chapter 9   New team, New tactics 145

Chapter 10 The day that the men had court 159

Chapter 11 The Supreme Court 182

Chapter 12 Sam is on the fight for her life 198

Chapter 13 Death becomes her 218

CH 1

Orgy at the spa; Bella Haven

T he landing was soft as the helicopter shut down on the luxurious spa. The grass was finely cut, large walls surrounded the spa. Outside the outer gates, a sign above read, "Bella Haven." It was like a little city, with agents running around and off in the distance, was their location. Jack stood by, as a long stretch limo pulled up, all the girls piled in. Jack took his time to assess his surroundings, and to think to himself, "This is going to be nice and well, remembered."

Jack got in, to sit next to Cody, who was on Mitzi's hip, whom was more of the mothering kind, other than all the rest of the girls. Each girl having a specific beautiful quality that sets each of them apart, all were considered extremely beautiful, except to Jack, who see past that and sees them as just his little helpers, at best. The short drive was over before it began, Jack saw the gates open up, as the limo drove in, went around the pool area. Jack stepped out to see, Robert the manager for the Pine Acres spa, to say, "Welcome back Jack, the spa is all yours, as each girl exited from the limo, Robert personally met each one. Jack led the way inside to front desk, to see a ripe peach, to say "Is it Tami", said Jack.

"It is how did you know, you actually remember me, speaking of remembering me, there is someone wanting to see you, I'll send her to your room" said Tami with a smile, "Here is your key card." She smiles at him in a flirty sort of way, "Also any of the staff has access to your room, from 9 to 5, and then you have the night for privacy." Jack strolled down the huge hallway, seen each brightly colored number of each room. He finally reached his room number four, the door was open, and Jack walked in. Jack looked around to see a giant king sized bed in the middle, half way, pulled down, a pair of yellow swim trunks laid on the bed. Over on the night stand was a white wooden box, Jack slid it open, and carefully placed his weapon in the red silk lined white box, he felt a slight shock when he released it, down, and he laughed a bit as he closed the box. He followed the large cord to the wall, and said "Ah, its recharging itself, nice." He then began to undress, taking everything off, he dropped it where he stood and went into the bathroom and stepped into the shower, automatically it turned on, the already warm water, came down on top of him, he spoke up, "A little hotter please", the water adjusted accordingly, to his command.

Instantly he felt a soft hand on his back to say,"I'm here to make it even hotter, let's say we pick up where we left off Jack", whispered Missy the massage therapist. Jack kept his head under the hot water and his hands firmly on the walls as Missy gave Jack a wash down with her big breasts, from the back of his calf's up to his buttocks to his back then whispered again, "I will make this week the most memorable one in your entire life, you know you're the only man here, and on top of that you brought five beautiful girls with you, your quite the stud, I still owe you a mega orgy with ten of my best friends, you deserve it for saving the Governor, from our state of Alabama, you're a hero and now turn around so I may give you quite a hero's welcome."

After both Trixie and Mitzi helped Cody settle in to her room, they put her to bed as a group of doctors and nurses surrounded her. Both of the women left her room to find the maids, walking around the big horseshoe they could smell a meal being prepared, they saw the door open to number nine and both Monica and Jen were on the bed playing, Just as the two girls walked in Trixie closed the door as Mitzi began to speak, "Listen up girls, I want to lay out the code of conduct here, as a team member, chosen to protect our boss Jack, we ask that you don't hang on him, ask before taking and above all respect his space, if I or", "We feel, one or both of you is out of line, one call and you're out of here," said Mitzi.

"As I was saying, consider this a holiday for yourselves, there is unlimited things to do, swimming, tennis, badminton, the works, this resort is the Governments equivalent to have a place that is totally secure, there are literally agents of every kind here, to watch one person, and that person is Jack", said Mitzi.

"We get the point, so where is the pool?" asked Monica, the blonde.

Both girls turn to leave, when Mitzi stopped as Trixie opened the door to see two hunks walk by to say, "One last thing, whenever possible always wear a robe, except in the water" both girls left in a hurry, to follow the two guys down the hallway.

"Oh, oh, that's it that is the spot", said Jack laying face first in the bed, in the back ground his phone was buzzing, as Missy straddled him with her nude, still wet body, rubbing oil all over his back, Jack fell fast asleep.

A loud sound erupted over the speaker and a sweet voice spoke, "Dinner is ready, it will be serving for two hours, we recommend the guests to eat now, if you want it in your room, just hit the number one button on your phone, thank you", spoke Tami.

Jack rolled his head over, to see the lights coming on outside through his large window, he closed his eyes to think about how soft the bed was he was sleeping on and the reminder of once past, then he heard giggles and a warm body on his back followed by someone else touching his feet, at first it tickled him, but that went away when, the touch became sensual and warm soft strokes. Jack eyes were down and couldn't see a thing, the girl on top of him was nude as her own wetness was touching his lower back and running off, her small breasts individually touched his upper back, as she applied more lotion, instead of oil to his back and whispered, "Were you're, the night's entertainment."

"I'm Tami the front desk clerk and my friend down rubbing your feet is Tracy, Missy asked us to keep you company while she gets everything ready for tonight?"

Jack began to speak when a ghastly voice came over to announce that the meal was over and that only room service was available." Jack began to turn over as Tami rose up to let him do that, she looked down to exclaim, "Wow your enormous, but that's the way I like it, and lowered herself onto his manhood to say, "I'll be your number two, Jack laid still while the young minx went to work, she did all the work, midway she stopped to say, "Do you like this?"

"Yes, please continue", said Jack reaching up to begin to play with her breasts, again the phone buzzed off the dresser on to the floor, while she continued to do all the work, while Tracy continued to rub his feet, using lotions, and getting them extremely wet and moist. The friction from her hands, was intensifying the session, several minutes went by then Jack let loose and Tami slid off to help Jack finish up with her hand, stroking it, it went all over the both of them.

"Now that is over with, it is time for you to eat, and this will require you not to do a thing, but just lie there and we will feed you", said a defiant young Tami, taking charge. Jack lifted his head up to see another beautiful blonde at his feet, wearing an itsy bitsy little tank top and no bottoms.

"Why don't you come up here and keep me company while she gets the food", said Jack motioning with his hands, she left his feet, midway she pulled off her tank top to reveal, two nicely shaped orbs, with a pair of stiff nipples, she slid up on him and inserted him who was already to go again, into her, while it was his time to do most of the work while Tami stood by and watched, for a split second, then went to the other side of the bed set the platter down, then got up on the bed, then straddled her feet on both sides of his head and knelt down.

Jack slowed his momentum to focus on a new task at his mouth, and began to lick something that was very wet as it was, it took but a mere moment and Jack received a wet surprise as

Tami showered his face. Tami was out of breath as Jack paused to absorbed most of the shower, then went back more eagerly than the first time and again she erupted, Tracy switched her position, off of him, to using her mouth and hands to get Jack off, but Jack was a study soldier, and Tracy quickly grew weary, so she remounted him the opposite way, much more to her liking as she heard Tami erupt again, each time a bigger more pronounced scream of excitement and a wetness she could feel at her knees. Jack just continued to lick and taste those sweet juices, that he was loving it more than her, and eventually Tami released the last time, let go of the head board and fell over onto the platter of food, exhausted, as Jack released himself all over Tracy, her two exhausted, and fell next to Tami and falling fast asleep. The next morning came, Jack awoke. Jack was re-energized he slid off the bed and went into the bathroom, to take care of business, then a quick shower, to step out to see both girls gone, as was the red silk sheets and now a new bed spread, all in green, Jack walked over in the nude, to the remaining platters and began to try something different, like this oily thing on a cracker. He then bent over to pick up his phone to see he had missed ten calls.

"That's an oyster; they say it's a good aphrodisiac."

Jack turned to see a tall, picturesque beauty with long black hair and some really big knockers, wearing a chef's jacket and white pants, to say, "Were the feeders, we will do what the nymph's were unable to do, over there, is the spa director, her name is Debbie." Debbie set up the portable table, as Jack watched, as his manhood twitched, as Debbie came closer, wearing that business suit Jack could see she was top heavy.

"Please come over and have a seat please", said Debbie.

Jack picked up a few more oysters.

"Don't worry, every two hours I've arranged to have this platter refreshed because it will be a long night for you." "Who says?" said Jack.

"Why of course Missy, she was the one who arranged this get together."

"Oh", said Jack thinking back to what he said to her the last time then running out, not this time he was in it for the long haul.

"So, here it is, on one platter is French cold cuts, with slice cheeses, and next is yogurts, creams and butters."

"To spread all over your body," said Jack.

"If you like, maybe later, as I was saying, on this platter is artichoke leaves and hearts, caviar, roasted vegetables, plenty of pastas and most importantly plenty of champagne, let's eat." "My name is Tanya, I'll be your chef while you're staying here."

"Please feel free to take off whatever you would like, make yourself comfortable" said Jack.

With that Tanya began first, by unbuttoning her jacket and letting fall to the floor, to reveal a pink camisole, then she slipped off her pants to show Jack her purple panties, she leaned in for a kiss, as Jack slid his hand into her panties she French kissed him as he stirred up some unexpected trouble, the more he worked the longer the kiss lasted, the wetter she become and the harder he was, she pulled back, long enough for her to get out of her panties and pull off her bra to see Jack move the chair back, so she came over to have a seat on his lap, she eased down on his already stiff manhood and proceeded to do all the work, while Jack played with her breasts, and the two of them, French kissing. The whole entire time, Tanya whispered in his ear to say, "You can come inside of me I have my tubes tied."

Jack needed no more words of encouragement and let loose, as the two of them rode it out to hear that Tanya herself let loose, almost as if it were the first time.

Tanya got off of Jack to say, "My work is done here, good luck with this one", said Tanya as she kisses Jack, then says "You can have me anytime you like, bye" she waves, then gets dressed and leaves. For Jack to say, "Hey, then where are you going?"

"Oh, I can't stay; you fulfilled me to last the entire week, thanks."

Jack continues to eat, to look over at his remaining companion, who briefly spoke, "I am here for the ride, although we can't do anything", she said.

"Ok "said Jack looking over at her.

Jack continued to consume food quickly and drink the remaining champagne.

"Aren't you going to ask me why, I won't have sex with you?"

"Nah, it's up to you, you know, personally I like to watch, a woman take off her clothing than the actual penetration."

"Really that's a relief, I guess it wouldn't be to harmful if I did that, it's not like, were doing anything right?"

"Yeah, if you feel comfortable with that" said Jack.

Debbie got up, placed her napkin down, and began to unbutton her business suit, she moved closer to Jack as she let it fall away, to expose a large bra, barely concealing that King Kong sized tits, as she asked, "What do you think?"

"From what I see, it looks spectacular?"

"Really" she said as she moved a little closer to him, as she unzipped her skirt, and then let it fall away, Jack turned in his seat to show her how he really liked the view, she reached down to touch it, as Jack placed both of his hands on her large bags, and began to get her excited, he unhooked her massive bra, to let the bags be free, while she bent down to work on his manhood. Jack got up and led her to the bed, where he pulled down her panties, bent her over the bed, and inserted, himself, quickly building up momentum, she began to scream, and in that instance she released, as did Jack all over her butt, he collapsed on top of her as the two crawled on to the bed.

Debbie whispered, "I needed that, thank you, it has been so, so long, I'm married."

"So am I, what is the big deal?"

"What do you mean; don't we have to be faithful to our spouses?"

"Who said that?" asked Jack, now looking at her; he began to stroke her face, to wipe away the tears.

"I feel so guilty now, I've cheated on him."

"Cheer up, think of this as a break in your marriage, you needed some attention, and you had the desire to be here, so what's the big deal", said Jack.

"Well, you could be right, oh what the heck, if I did it once may we do it again.

"Sure you begin this time", said Jack watching her go.

Jack awoke to see his eyes open, with both of his arms around two smaller framed girls.

Jack was looking to his right was a dirty blonde, small chest girl to whom he used his hand to stroke the fine hairs on her arm, on his left side was a long haired brunette, with a cute smile, and big breasts. Jack put on a smile, when all of a sudden the door flew open and in the middle of the room stood Missy who said, "Alright girls the party is over, get up and get out of here now."

Jack watched as one by one they gave him a long kiss to say, "That was the best night I ever had, call me, my name is Brita, I work in the laundry room, come and see me, lover."

"And my name is Kari, Missy and I go way back, so call me", as the brunette gave Jack a long kiss then swept off the bed. Jack sat up to watch them leave past the waiting Missy with her arms crossed watching, to say, "Now get up Jack", as she came to him, picking up a robe, and helping him into it, to say, "I've got your day planned out, let's go, into the dining room, she led him, he wore his robe and flip flops, to take a seat, where Missy watched him eat a hearty meal, then she led him out down a corridor to the first room, he remembers this well a large black mud pit, Jack stepped out of his flip flops as Missy took his robe, Jack slowly walked into the fiery hot mud, and sank down to his chest, then laid back, into a stone chair, with his head firmly resting onto a head rest and letting the mud come up to his neck.

"I'll check on you in about one hour," said Missy.

Jack closed his eyes to relax, some time past . . . .

"Jack wake up, it's been one hour, come on let's get you out of there."

Jack woke up to view Missy still dressed in a see through short dress, holding a hose in her hand.

"Get up and get out ", she demanded, Jack slowly moved, and climbed out, as Missy turned on the hose, and sprayed him off, both back to front, she placed down the hose, and turned off it, to help Jack into his robe, he slipped on the flip flops, and Missy led him to a refreshment table where Jack drank a glass of lemonade and a then ate a couple of nutritional bars, then Missy led him to the next room, to say, "This room is called the butter room, the red clay is from Egypt, but will end up here, our next stop is the wet room, go ahead and hop up on the table, minus the robe please."

Missy watched, as Jack lay onto the table, in one instant Missy removed her dress, to reveal nothing on, and to join her was another friend, Jack watched as a platinum blonde, with a perfect body stepped in wearing only a bra and panties carrying a bucket.

"Turn over Jack, face down" said Missy.

Jack felt the searing heat of the wetness of something slimy on his back; he squirmed around while they applied it.

"Don't worry honey, this is an herbal seaweed pack, now turn over."

Jack saw another helper at his feet, he remembered her name it was Tracy, back on his feet to say, and "How about after this I give him a pedicure?"

Missy shook her head yes, to say, "I think he would like that as the other girl spoke, "Hi Jack, Its Caroline, I want to take you out and teach you some water sports, I hope later you want to go out onto the lake and go jet skiing?"

"Sure", said Jack lying his head back to absorb the three pairs of, make that four sets of hands as a hot washcloth went on to his face, then a head massage began.

A voice spoke out, "It's me Jack" Tami, she said, Jack reached out, with his right hand to feel her firm body to reach between her legs to feel no clothing, then relaxed as they all massaged him, to the point that he went to sleep, they wrapped him up in cellophane, then a blanket, and then a hot tarp, while Missy performed a facial, while Caroline held one foot and Tami the other so that Tracy could give Jack a pedicure, she even painted his newly trimmed nails with a clear coat. Then they let him be and left the room.

Several big black Suburban were coming close to the gate when a voice spoke out, "How long till we get there, are you sure, why isn't he picking up his cell phone, what is he doing?" asked the fiery red head.

"Ma'am, maybe he is in the mud pit pool."

"Shut up Stevie, you're not helping here," said Lisa.

"Fine, remember you're the one who sent him here, besides the rumor is there was a big party last night and he was the main target of the party," said Stevie.

"Again you're not helping here, what have you been doing while you have been down here?"

"Well for one, last night almost all the men were asked to leave out of the spa, and the women took over, so I took a detachment to the airport, to secure it for you."

"That was good thinking, thanks," said Lisa.

"No problem" said Stevie.

"Now when we get there, show me who is in charge."

"Well, Ma'am, her name is Missy, or I guess you would say she is the Colonel, Melissa Adams, a fiery girl who ensures, everyone has the best time when they stay there."

"So what you're saying is that, Jack is probably being well taken care of."

"That's exactly what I'm saying," said Stevie.

Their vehicle approached the spa gate, as they motioned there vehicle to move slowly through the bridge, and the x-ray machine, two guards followed the vehicle with it, a gate lifted they drove on, down the street to the spa. Lisa watched all the skimpy clad girls of extreme beauty walking around, only to see several nude ones, as they drove past a tennis court, to say, "Since when did they choose clothing optional."

"Since Colonel Adams directed it."

"I'll have to meet this woman," said Lisa.

The SUV came to a stop, a dapper gentleman stood as Lisa exited, to see him.

"Welcome to the Pine Acres spa, my name is Robert, and I manage this place how I can help you Ma'am."

"My name is Lisa, Lisa Curtis, I have a room." "Yes Ma'am, we have been expecting you."

Lisa strolled in from the hot sun into a well-lit entryway and to see a bright young and pretty face girl.

"Hi, how can I help you?" said Tami.

"My name is Lisa, and I'll be staying here, but first I need to see Jack, is that possible?"

"I don't know about that, but I can get you settled in your room, and call on Missy to visit with you."

Lisa nods in agreement, behind her five husky men carrying huge metal suitcases, which followed her in to her room.

"Put those over there and please leave."

Lisa closed the door behind them, and began to undress, taking everything off she stepped in the shower, after a long hot shower, she toweled off, wrapped up her hair, then placed a towel around her, stepped out of the bathroom, to see Missy, to say,

"What kind of place are you running here?"

"Only the one where you would be the center of attention, now come here and give me a kiss", said Missy, as the two embraced and kissed, to say," It's been a long time friend" said Lisa.

"Yes, and now, let me have that towel," said Missy, pulling it from her as the two began to explore each other.

The next morning, everyone slept, except Jack, Caroline, woke him up early, and led him down to the docks, it was cool, at the dock, sat several pairs of jet skis, for Caroline to say, "chose whichever one you want, do you know how to ride?"

"Yeah, sure, I have a pair of my own." "Not like these you don't."

"How so, what makes them better?" asked Jack, getting a life vest to put on, while he watched her, undress, down to her one piece, for her to say, "That show is over mister, now you're on my turf, that one over there is the fastest, it is turbo charged."

Jack jumped on it, stuck the key in turned, hit the switch, it roared to life. Jack kept turning the accelerator, revving up the engine, waiting for Caroline, who was slow deliberate, bending over, teasing him, only to turn to see, Jack placed it in gear, and off he went, leaving her in his wake, the lake, opened up, to see a dam of sorts on the south end, reaching for his phone, only to realize it was in the room, trying to think where he was at, on the other side was a hill with houses, and to the north was the base, he slowed, to stand up, to see the base was actually, for women, some marching, some running, others in formation, a combat training course, was off to the left, where he could hear drill instructors yell out commands. A wave of water washed over him, as Caroline, sprayed him down, instantly, it was on, Jack chased her around the lake, for a good hour, till she led him in, whereas, he came to a stop, next to the dock, she was there to tie him up, to say, 'Let's go sailing?"

Jack shrugged his shoulders, as Caroline led him over to a pair of small boat's, instantly Jack had a flashback, to his youth, and sailing on the lake, he went to his boat, pulled up the sheet, tied it off, climbed in, and took, a seat sideways in the boat, with one hand on the mast and the other on the rudder, he pulled out, that was with Caroline's help, she pushed him off, he turned, and off he went, while Caroline shouted, "wait for me?", she was fumbling around her boat, while Jack caught the current, and worked his way back over to the north side, where drill instructors were all over their female charges. Jack slowed the boat, enough so to allow Caroline to catch up, it was a lazy day, except for the sun beating down on him, his legs and arms were getting fried, even the lotion, Caroline earlier applied was gone, he continued to watch the women, being yelled at, to remark, "I like that course, it looks fun."

"Hey mister what cha doing? Said Caroline, while she was catching up with him.

"Just looking at the course"

"Why don't we go back, looks like your getting fried." "That's an understatement, so, where are we at anyway?" asked Jack, turning the boat around.

"Sorry can't divulge, it's somewhat a secret." "Alright, then what about that course."

"Sure, you can try it."

"You say that kiddingly" asked Jack.

"Well actually, that course is more of a test, you see once a recruit passes it, they graduate, it's really designed for you to fail."

'I'd like to give it a shot, you know to see if I pass or fail?"

"Sure, you can try, actually, you can do anything you want, you have total access to everywhere, she said as he was off in a distance.

Jack caught up with her, and was the first to the dock, he jumped into the cool water, and then scrabbled up to tie off the boat, then, climbed out of the water, and worked his way back to the spa.

It was all quiet as he made his way in, only to the smells of the kitchen, where Jack stood at the door, waiting an invitation to come in. Tanya saw him, lit up, and said, "Sure come in, what would you like?"

"A heavy carb load."

"Nah, you don't need that, how about a perfect omelet?" "Sure whatever you think, I don't want to put you out." "Oh you're not, have a seat, I'll bring it out to you, in the meantime, choose a drink."

Jack went over and chooses milk chocolate and whole white, four cartons each. And then took a seat facing the door. In walked Lisa, with a smile on her face, she said, 'How has the spa been treating you?"

"Oh fairly well I guess."

"How can I make your stay better?"

Jack just looked at her, as she said, "Besides that?"

"Oh I don't know, how about a ride into town, for some night life."

"Sorry can't do that either, you know this place is a secure facility, you know that this is a place for the military to relax, thus the name, "Bella Haven, literally means safe spa, but it is also a code word for rest relaxation and sleep, soundly, without the worry of being attacked."

"That's nice" said Jack, to add, "So what's the story with the base next store?"

"Well it's a training base for future recruits, why do you ask?"

"How about a visit?"

"Sorry no can do, it's off limits to all men, imagine, what those girls would do to you?"

"I'm thinking and can't imagine what would happen to me?" "They would literally attack you, rip off your clothes and then have their way with you."

"You're dreaming, why would they do that?"

"Just kidding, if you want to go over there, I'll get you an escort."

"Thanks actually I was more interested in the combat course."

"They call it the confidence course, and I'm sure the drill instructors would love to show a spy around."

"So you're saying, I can't complete the course."

'No, what I'm saying, you'll encounter a little resistance, up for the challenge?"

"Sure why not."

"Great I'll set it up, in the meantime, you should go to sickbay, and have those burns looked at."

A plate of food was delivered to Jack, who thanked Tanya, and then consumed the meal. Jack then went to sickbay, and his condition was cared for.

Late afternoon, they all waited for the sun to set. Jack dressed in an outfit and a pair of gloves, and running boots, no weapon on him so to speak. He was asked not to wear one. Jack was led over by Special Operations Group, all dressed in black, with weapons, showing, and the gate was opened, between both bases.

By now all the girls, heard the news, and a cheer was growing, just for Jack Cash, "He can do it, so can you."

Caroline was by his side, as all the attention was on him now, and along the course was the imposing drill instructors, a Black Ops guy stepped in and whispered, "Do some damage to them, one of them hurt my girl."

Jack waved him off, as emotions, wasn't his cup of tea, he was ready, as everyone took their places, for one of the drill instructors to yell,"Let's get this on, go whenever you're ready."

The senior drill instructor just arrived, he was last to hear about it, a bit out of breath to say, "Warning Mister, you're going in Marine territory" said the Gunny Sergeant, Chad Turner.

Jack looked at him to say, "What does that mean?" as he went for it, the first set was bars, he caught hold of the first set, only to have the guy above, Sgt Wes Moore, step on his fingers, and Jack went down in a thump, on his back. In the crowd was "Ahs, and Oohs", as the Gunny, helped Jack up, whereas, Jack pushed him away, to say, "Let's do this", as Wes was above laughing, and said, "Leave him alone Gunny, he is some smart aleck spy, let us have some fun."

The Gunny began to chant, "No, No, No, He will kill you, you idiots," soon realizing it wasn't just a game anymore, as other units came out to support Jack Cash.

The Marine was distracted, as Jack made another attempt, this time; it was quick movements, with his hand, as he raced past the Marine above, to the other side. Leaving the marine cussing.

For the second part, Jack was moving, quickly to a ladder, as soon as he touched the first bar, he slipped off, on to his back, as a Marine from up above, laughed, as Wes egged on his fellow marine, he yelled out, "Get em good, Sergeant Green." and for Jack to say, "Greased pole", Jack cleared the cobwebs out, and got up, to see the first Marine, mouth some death threat on his way past, Jack got up, took off his gloves, now his mind was racing, he decided to use some help, and put up his watch, instantly those that were cheering, ran for cover, Jack just spun the top, and instantly shot a line out, and upward to a rung which it wrapped around, exactly where he aimed, and reeled him up past the mess, he reached it, unhooked, it, allowed it to reset, and worked his way up where Sergeant Green await, ready to push Jack away, instead, Jack showed his agility, and side stepped, and went upside down, locked a leg around the top, and in one motion, swung around and swept off Sergeant Green, who, went down, hit the bars below, snapped his neck, and landed in a scorpion position.

Jack was on the move upward to the high platform, where the next Marine was screaming,"You just killed my friend, Die you bastard." ready for Jack, he was saying, "You won't get me, come here bastard."

Jack reached where the Marine was at, and out of the blue charged him, Jack hit the big guy, and in that moment, the big guy fell back, and with the momentum, both Jack and Steve, cleared the platform, and down to the next, the impact broke Steve's neck. Jack slowly rolled over on his back, he hurt, I mean it hurt, his hands were shaking, that impact really stunned him, but was able to get up, for those below to see he was the victor, a loud cheer went up. He dragged his left foot, as he was beat up, above him, was a handle, no safety harness, he reached up, and took a hold of the handle on one side, and reversed his hand on the other side, below he saw what was ahead, another Marine, all he could hear was 'Fisher, Fisher get em." The Marine held a board of some sort, Jack hoisted himself up, which released the catch, and off he went, down the zip line, instantly, he felt his hands slipping, he knew if he let go would be some complications, as he traveled down, he began to rock back and forth, so when he reached the Marine, he was in his own full swing, and impacted him, in the head, knocking the board, out, and sending the Marine into a giant telephone pole, he hit with a thump, rolled back, and over the edge, where it came to an abrupt end. Sergeant Fisher hit the sawdust; a cloud of dust could be seen. Jack was now weary, in front of him, was a rope, looking up, it was connected to a tie line, and another Marine, was yelling at Jack,

"Come here and I'll kill you." Jack hoisted himself, up and getting his bearings on the platform and instantly, went back to the gloves, with them on it aided his ascent up, he used his ankles to bind the rope below, he went up quickly, all the while the rope was being pulled on from Sergeant Murphy Jack was swinging, it was a distraction, but not enough to rattle him, as he went right past the guy, and onto the next platform, it was the Marines who were reeling, as Jack was gaining momentum, up a pole, to the top platform, and now down, platform, at a time, to the ground, and to a tall wall, which was at least ten foot tall, he went back, and gained momentum, jumped, and snagged the top, with his fingertips, only to slide off, and fall back, he promptly took off the gloves, and took another run at it, just on the other side, all the rest of the Marines got together, and hoisted one of their own, on the wall, Jack leaped, snagged the wall, reversed his body, and with his leg, swiped off the Marine, who hit head first, in a thump, standing on the wall, Jack saw the remaining Marines, as some were assembling, he reached up in his pocket, where his wallet was at, inside he pulled two credit cards, all the time waiting for the rest of the Marines to assemble, as Sergeant Moore yelled out, "Mister spy, you ain't getting past us, looking around to see nine others including his self, at the ready. Jack, removed the end caps, and put his wallet away, as he held onto the cards, like ninja stars, and leapt off the wall, rolled, as they rushed him, it was cut and slash, for their throats, and the first wave went down, two by two, all the while the Gunny, watched in horror, as Jack was cutting up his men, to see the last guy standing, Sergeant Moore, who held a K-bar out, and egging Jack on, who simply decided to walk off the course, and then Sergeant Moore charged him, as those in the crowd, yelled, "Watch out."

Jack turned, side stepped the advance, and slit his throat, the Marine went down, holding his throat, as Jack went over to the finish line, and rang the bell, like it was a statement to all those that want to mess with him, they would have hell to pay.

The Gunny looked up at Lisa, to say,"Who was that guy?"

"His name is secret, but you should know him as Jack Cash, International Bounty Hunter."

Caroline was first to help Jack limp off the course, Emergency help was on the way, as base ambulances were dispatched.

Jack limped back to the spa, where he needed immediate attention.

CH 2

Carlos & the Cuban Warriors

J ack stood at the door to the gym, watching a woman work over another woman with some slick karate moves and outwitting her every move, a lot has changed since that night, the gate to the base is always open, evidence came out about the abuses, and Jack was the hero, so he had complete access to their base, a new guard was set in place, and real training was underway. Jack was still healing, but was an avid fan of watching, especially this girl, so when they were finished, they both just smiled at him. Both dressed in a traditional white jacket, and hair pulled back, Jack watched in fascination with the way they moved, the grace of their execution, and their precise arm motions, they bowed to each other, they notice him to say "Don't be shy come in, you must be Jack, my four o'clock, my name is Blythe, so what can I teach you?"

"I don't know, it's been a while since I have had any hand to hand combat."

"What just last week?"

'Yeah, that was different, that was for survival." "Then come on over here, and we will tussle a bit."

Jack made his way over towards the mat, when all of a sudden, Blythe, jumped at him, with her foot extended, knee bent striking Jack in the knee, as he swung down to catch her and the two tumbled together, with him being on top, holding her around her neck, choking her, as she rolled, Jack went with it, still holding his position, she started to knee him in the back as Jack tighten down the grip.

"Let her go" spoke a command voice.

Jack looked up to see it was Lisa, and let her go, "You're a hard man to track down" said Lisa, moving in as Blythe got up with a smile on her face to say, "I want a rematch Jack."

Jack laid on his back to see Lisa standing above him to say, "I guess your vacation is over, there is major trouble brewing in Cuba, they have taken, your wife Maria and Carlos captive and is seeking 10 million in U S cash, for their return and safety." "How does that affect me?"

"She is your wife, don't you want to save her from the Cuban Warriors, and who have her."

"How do you know it's not a scam, besides I thought that was a fake wedding, for international relations?"

"It was not," said Lisa.

"I have no feeling for her or her family or even Carlos, if it were up to me I would have taken him out," said Jack.

"I know, well here is your chance, I'm sending you in there", she looked hot when she was getting angry, for Jack to counter, by saying, "Since when are you telling me where your sending me, instead of just asking, how don't I know that this is a trap?"

She looked at him, to say," Your right, I was wrong, I was asking you for the International sake, nothing else, but let's restore some peace in that area", she looked at him to further say,

"You have a choice; go or either don't and I will send someone else down there, to extract Carlos and your wife Maria, then we can relocate them to America if you like."

"I don't know, let me think about that", said Jack, playing with her.

"Also Sara is here, with her two friends, and is waiting for you," said Lisa.

"Thanks" Jack rolls away from her and gets up to say,

"You know you can count on me." He trots out of the gym, past a building, and through the gate, towards the spa, down the hallway, to the left in the third room down, was Sara, standing there with Leslie and another girl.

"Jack my, my what have you done, you look so handsome", said Sara, as she ran to him and jumped into his arms in the hallway as the two kissed passionately, Jack carried her in, and set her down, as she spoke first," Honey, this is beautiful here, thanks for inviting us up."

Both Leslie and Tabby move in to share in the ceremony, I'd like for you to know, Tabby, will be my maid of honor, and she was the one at Sam's wedding, she has decided to want to spend some time with you."

"As you can call me, anything you like," said Tabby, with a huge grin on her face, looking over the man in front of her.

Jack held her trembling hand; it was moist and still shaking to say, "It is a pleasure to have you, thanks for coming to our wedding" said Jack.

"I'd like to be one," said Tabby. "One what", said Jack.

Sara stepped in front of Jack to say, "I told both of them, about us and our arrangement, you know with Sam, you and I, and Leslie and Tabby want to be a part of it."

"What get married to me?" said Jack caught a bit off guard. "That's about it," said Sara.

"Where is this coming from?" said Jack pulling her away from the others to talk privately.

"Well I told them about the money and the security," said Sara.

"And what you didn't tell them is a lifelong commitment to me, and lots of babies each?" said Jack.

"Well no, I don't think that mattered, look we're all having fun and I thought what better way, than to have all my friends around me, was this way."

"That is happening now, fine let's just ask them, shall we", said Jack as she diverts Jack out of the room, they were in, to hear,"Sara, there is the responsibility of having children, is that what they want, the last time Leslie and I spoke, she was nowhere close to having a baby, so what has changed now?" Said Jack.

"I don't know, I guess the money," she said.

"That's fine too, but, once they decide to be my wife, it will be a lifelong commitment, I know you understand about how all this works, but for those two girls, don't have the real understanding at what this means, let's go in there and ask them." Jack who walked past her to see them standing, waiting, for Jack to say, "Let's talk, are you aware that once you chose to be my wife, each of you will be solely committed to me, and that means for the rest of your life, and that also includes that you will be to me, exclusively, that's it for the rest of your lives are you ready for that type of commitment?" Leslie looked at Tabby, who looked at Sara to say, "I say No, I thought it was for a short time, till we get on our feet."

"Not only is it for the rest of your life, but if I were to die inadvertently, that you would still be committed to raise the children I have provided for you, well past when I'm gone, is that what you want Tabby?"

"No thanks, I didn't know, Sara didn't make that perfectly clear."

"Personally, I don't care who I marry, yes there is benefits, but also there is some risks, like I get shot at everyday of my life, one of these days I may not be as lucky, don't get me wrong I like the pair of you, but I just don't think you're ready, for that type of commitment and four kids per each of you."

Jack began to lecture the two girls, to say;"Besides each of you needs, has to be as strong as Sara's, for me to consider taking you as my other wives."

Jack left the room, with Sara tailing behind him, as Sara pulls his arm, to say, "Wait, I was under the impression, that you wanted, multiple girls, and I just thought that both of my girlfriends, who do you suggest?"

"Wait, are you saying you want more girls around, I have more choices that I would like, and I want to let you know about, as Jack veered into his room, with her.

"What do you mean?" asked Sara, very intrigued.

"Well on my last mission to Cuba, I thought I was marrying a women for the mission, but as it turns out, she and the country of Cuba, is upholding the union, so what do you think about that?"

She seemed coy, to say, "Yeah, I'm O Kay with that, when can we meet them?"

"Well about that, they want me to go down there and rescue them from the Cuban Warriors and bring them back."

"So what are you waiting for?" asked Sara. "What do you mean?" asked Jack.

"Why aren't you going down there and helping them out, and bringing them home."

"Who are you, so you're O Kay; I'm married to another woman."

"You already have Sam, what's a few more, yeah sure, how is she in bed?"

"I don't know, I was drugged, by some agents that double-crossed us."

Jack began to get dressed and she was undressing him, for Jack to say, "Yeah I believe her family is connected to the spy I was chasing."

Then Sara said, "Then you better go get her and her family." "You're not the least bit curious who she is."

"Nah, I think I know the type of girl that turns you on, just like you said, a girl just like me, a girl who wants that long term and lifelong commitment, so I trust you'll bring home a keeper."

"Yep, she is that and much more."

"Well, I know you must go, there is so much I need to talk with you about the wedding, finances and Sam."

"What about Sam?" asked Jack, she looked amused when she said her name?

"Well I haven't heard from her in a while and, well, I was concerned", asked Sara.

"The last I heard anything, was that she was moved to a private hospital in Virginia."

"Do you think after you get back, that we may go up there?" asked Sara, still watching him get dressed, and finally leaving him alone.

"I think you and your friends could go up and see her, I will meet with my boss and set it up with Lisa, oh by the way how is the house coming along?"

"The builder just finished a high speed express elevator." Sara stopped what she was saying to stare at him, "Now we have access to the new boat dock and buildings, down below, that the Parthian Stranger will lay to wait, one side is the dry dock and the other is wet. A steel building encloses the entire thing, the dock runs to a large house on the water that will serve as a shop and ticket sales also several holding cells for prisoners, I need help in the office, so Leslie and Tabby agreed to stick around till after the wedding, and if you don't want to marry them, then what should I say to them."

"Listen, it's up to you, if you want me to marry them I will, but I won't allow you to say who I will marry in the future," said Jack. "I'm fine with that, you can marry whomever you want, I know as a spy you need to keep up appearances, so in order to do that I'm prepared for whom ever you bring home, all I know is that you have me forever, and that is all that matters."

"I don't know what to say to that," said Jack. "Just say yes."

"To who?"

"You mean whom, you know Leslie and Tabby." "What's her story anyway?"

"Well after college she went to Seattle and met a boy, who took her life savings and ran off with another girl, so she owns a flower store now, and she said she would move out here and live with us, besides her family lives here."

"How much did she lose?"

"What do you mean?" asked Sara not really understanding the question.

"How much did that guy take from her?" "Oh around twelve thousand dollars."

"Give her hundred thousand and see if she just wants to get on with her life."

"I know her, she won't take it."

"While you're at it give the same offer to Leslie and see if she takes it as well, if they return it then we will talk, if not, we know, it's either money or love, don't we", said Jack.

"Yes your right, love isn't all about money, and I know my friends and they are not money driven", said Sara, and then says,

"Then it should be about supporting each other and how good our sexual chemistry will be together."

"Hey speaking of sexual chemistry, I know a guy who would be perfect for Tabby", said Jack as he pulled out his handgun and holstered it.

"Who is he", said Sara.

"Let me introduce you to him" said Jack dialing up his phone, to say, "Yeah, I need at least ten more clips can you bring them to me."

"He will be there in a moment", said Jim.

"So do you want to walk me out", asked Jack.

"Of course, in six months you will be my husband, are you still changing your name to Sanders."

"Nah, it will be Cash, until I find out my real name."

In the hallway, was Lisa and Brian, who hands Jack the magazines, Jack puts them in his pockets to say, "It would be nice if I could have that vest I had in Cuba."

"I'll pass that along to Jim for you," said Brian.

"Hey Brian I want you to meet a friend of Sara's, her name is Tabitha, she is the one over there, what do you think?"

"Yeah, she is", said Brian who looked at Lisa, then walked away.

As Jack and Lisa talked, Sara went in to talk with the girls, to say,

"Hey Tabby what do you think of the guy next to Jack?" "Seems nice looking, what's up, what did Jack say?" "Alright, he said he felt bad, that your savings was wiped out, so he wants you to decide, either be committed to him for the rest of your life or take a gift from us, Jack wanted to give you a gift, of over hundred thousand dollars which will it be, for what you lost, and the freedom, you seek."

"Really, he wants to do that for me, well O Kay, thanks," said Tabby.

The two embraced, as Sara whispered in her ear, Jack wants four kids with you, and he wants to know, if he gave you one hundred thousand dollars, would you take the money and run, or give it back and be his wife."

Tabby looked at her friend, to lower her eyes to say, "I'll take the money, sorry."

Sara smiled and the two broke apart to address Leslie, to say, "What do you say old pal, do you want Jack and have four kids with him, or take one hundred grand?"

"I'm with ya all, but wait you said four kids a piece." Jack yelled to them, to say, "Make it ten kids, apiece."

"I'll take the money; too," said Leslie then leans in to Sara, to say, "Are you going to have that many kids with him?"

"As many as he wants, for as long as he wants, you see girls it's not about money for me it's all about true love, I love that man, like no other woman will, so you girls get ready were going to the spa and relax."

Jack waved good-bye and left as awaiting helicopter landed outside, Jack raced to get on it, and it took off and left.

Lisa waited until Sara, stepped out to the hall to say, "Sara, can I have a moment with you?"

"Sure, do you know how long we can stay?" "As long as you would like."

"And my friends?"

"Them too, come on in my room" said Lisa, Lisa closed the door, to say, "I talked with Jack and told him what I knew of your friend Samantha, she has weak blood cells and is dying, inside she is fragile, but has survived the surgery."

"When can I go visit her?"

"After your stay here, I'll arrange a flight for you, but more importantly, Jack has asked me to let you know, he has those cases over there to go home with you, that is payment for his last job." Sara looked them over to say, "What did he do?"

"Sorry I can't tell you, but I can say this."

"He is the best agent I have ever met, and I'm the lucky one who gets to watch over and take care of him, also I will have a security detail go home with you, when you're ready, can I ask you something?" said Lisa looking at her.

"Sure", she was looking over at the huge cases.

"What's your connection to Jack, I know he says he loves you and wants to make you his wife, but."

"It's simple really, he saved my life and scared me straight, and I've never met a man who could have ever done that for me." "How do you cope with his other wives?"

"Well with Sam, I understand his compassion for her, and I will accept any one he chooses as one, I'll just see them as sisters and work together to make Jack the happiest man in this whole world, by the look of those cases, I'm sure he has done something pretty spectacular to deserve that."

"He did, he saved a Governor of a state" said Lisa, to add,

"Some say, he was a hero for what he did."

"According to the papers, I read, it was his Mistress and the Super Model, that is why I love him, he is the protector", said Sara, countering back a shot.

"I must commend you on being so loyal and understanding, what about him being with other women?"

"Jack is Jack, he is his own person, if he feels the need for additional companionship, then I will accept them, however many they are, because I am Jack's closet friend, best friend and companion for life", she said, as she looked around, to say, "Can I go now?"

"Sure", said Lisa watching her walk away.

The short flight to Andrews, Air force base, helicopter took a slight turn, as it was near the hanger, Jack got out, and entered the hanger, Jim was waiting, Jack went up the ramp, Jim fired up the plane, the hanger door, opened, the Brian raised the ramp, as the plane went forward, it taxied, then, off it went. Jack relaxed in his new room, a well stocked refrigerator cabinet, drinks from all over the world, he loaded up on protein bars, as he stuffed them into his windbreaker, the flight was over quickly, as Jim circled the hillside, once in Cuba, as Jack was at the ready. Jim took it to the airport where he landed, taxied, and went to the UN hanger, and drove in, turned and shut it down. Jack opened his door, to see an old friend, Jim, the two shook hands, for Jim to say, "I have your car ready for you, here is what we know, Carlos went in to negotiate the

release of his wife Rose, and that was the last we heard from him."
Jim continued to say, "The two agents assigned to your wife Maria,
had been killed, and their bodies have been discarded, Maria's only
surviving brother escaped and is waiting outside."

"Was it Hopi?"

"It was, he said that you told him what to do, so he fled at first
trouble. He reported that Carlos had something to do with it." "It
figures, I should have taken him out when I had a chance."

"You'll have another shot," said Jim. "How many in the
compound?"

"Hopi reported that there is a older man, his younger Son, a
couple of body guards, and a couple of men around the girls, Hopi,
had made a list out of girls being held, here it is" Jim handed it
to Jack.

Jack scans the list, from top to bottom, he sees some familiar
names and of course Maria and Alexandra, thinking to him, "Why
is she on this list?"

"Some are on that list additionally because they had a party,
and the Elders were off on a vacation to an undisclosed Island."
"Yeah, courtesy of Carlos", said Jack.

"Yeah how did you know?" asked Jim.

"That's what he said to me, for my wedding to Maria, he was
going to do."

"So do you think it was a set up?" asked Jim.

"Yeah, maybe, maybe, they wanted to get them out of here,
why don't you send some troops down to that island and free
them."

"You know we can't escalate this to be a National incident
without you being there, so how do you think you want to handle
the siege?"

"Head on, in their faces; probably by the sea, up the bank
through the village and drop as many as I can, no I take that back,
why don't I go in there like in stealth mode, and subdue those in
charge and diffuse the situation."

"If you plan on going in through the water, at least let me help
you out" said Jim

"Don't you have a high speed boat, you know the one I tested?" asked Jack, sounded excitedly.

"No, I don't, that turned out to be a bust, but I can lend you a Black Ops raft?"

"Nah, I'll find something at the harbor" said Jack, to add,"Aren't you suppose to be the gadgets guy."

"Not really, that's not my title, I'm more of just the hands on support guy, but from this point on, I won't let you down."

"Don't worry, let's go see Hopi", said Jack, as both men walked together down the ramp, Jack saw Hopi, as the two embraced.

"Good to see you, my friend", said Hopi. "Are you O KAY?"

"Yeah"

Jack leads Hopi away from Jim to say, "What's going on?"

"Well after the elders left on the trip. some of my brothers went to guard them, as of this morning they are fine, then the Cuban Warriors stormed the fence, and after several hours we lost control of the compound, so I left, all the girls are safe in the panic room, Carlos went in to negotiate their release, a good portion of his wife's were in there", said Hopi.

"Do you think he was involved?" asked Jack.

"Nah, he has turned a new leaf, he pays us the appropriate price for our gold and gemstones, and he even had the panic room installed, so that the women and children would be safe during something like this."

"So they are safe", asked Jack.

"Yep, you know all they want is that gold, to fund their operation, after they are done they probably will leave", said Hopi. "There done now, and yes they will pay, for what they're doing", said Jack, to say to Jim, "Lets hold a meeting, as the SEAL teams from Virgin Islands, were at the ready, Jack said, "Team one, from the East, Team two from the south, and as for me, well I'm coming in by the sea."

Jack watches the teams via his phone ready themselves, as they would go in by helicopter. As for Jack, and with Jim's lead, goes to see his car, for Jack to say, to Hopi, "Can you get me a boat?"

"Follow me friend", said Hopi, trying to get Jack to go.

Jack thinks and the doors open up they both get in, he thinks start up, Jack puts his phone in the dash, the car peels out, as Jack throttles it open and out of the hanger through the gate and down the road, hugging it close to the edge as he made his way down into the Marina, on the outskirts of the city of Santiago, quickly taking a sharp left turn to the docks, and as he drove Hopi spoke while holding on to say, "Down on the end, over there."

Jack continued to the middle of the dock and stopped, they both got out as the big engine shut down, Jack looked on the inside part of the dock, where a big cigarette looking boat sat.

"Whose is that?" asked Jack.

"That was Carlos's drug running boat," said Hopi.

"Good, I'll let him know were borrowing it, unhook the lines" said Jack, who went to the controls, looking around to see where the key was.

"Check under the seat" yelled Hopi.

Jack found the key, inserted it and fired the twin 750 hp engines, it idled, it was moving forward, Hopi untied the lines and got in, to hear Jack say, "Hold on", Jack eased the throttle forward slowly, and those transmissions enabled that power, sending Hopi back to the rear as those props propelled that boat forward, in that instance, that boat was out of the harbor, and on the open seas of the Gulf of Mexico, Jack did a wide arc, away from the beach, and down past the south cove, right north of Guantanamo Bay and the U S naval base, Jack slowed the boat down, riding the wave into the new dock and boat ramps, the sun was burning them up. Jack left the boat in idle mode and hoped out of the boat, to say, "Take the boat back and get in touch with Jim, and tell him I've landed."

"I want to stay here with you", said Hopi.

"You can't, it's too dangerous, now get going" said Jack. Jack watched as Hopi turned the boat around and slowly took off, as the engine noise died down, he was on the move, he climbed up the stairs to the upper level of the ground and made it to the gold shack on the southern most part of the compound, he peered out to see a guard, walking in front of it, Jack pulled his fighting knife, held it close, stepped out and pulled the guard back, and slit his neck and let the guard go, picked up his weapon, and jogged down to the next building, deciding to either go up or down to the beach level, he choose the beach.

Jack was moving in the soft sand with no resistance, the high bank disguised him as he ran next to the wall on the semi-wet sand, as he continued he was heading further away from the houses as the beach and the wall tailored down. Jack crotched down, to scope out, the wet lands of the field to the big main house, he admired, Jim's work, and that of the Army Corps of Engineers. Jack could see his shadow on the ground, then decided to make a run for it to, so he held his gun out, with all his mite, he ran inward towards the barrack type two story house, with each step in the open, workers, began to stop what they were doing and watched the sole figure, just as they realized, Jack was still on the move.

The Cuban warriors picked up their weapons, the sounds of gunfire erupted, as Jack did a zig zag pattern, as bullets peppered where he just stepped, moment by moments went by, Jack was still a ways a way, but kept on going, he looked off to his right to see half of the workers heading his way, the building was getting closer with each step, Jack held his hand gun and began to fire.

Each intended target dropped, one by the nearest window, as each bullet penetrated it was still intact as he emptied his weapon, ejected the clip, and reloaded a new one, and he started to fire at a window, as he dove through the window. Jack used the dive and roll method, he turned over once to a sitting up position, to be on the solid wood floor.

Waiting a moment, he heard voices speaking to say, "Go get 'em." Jack changed clips to realize he was bleeding, from his head, arms hands and his legs. Jack got up to his knees, waited to see who was coming, a tall guy poked his head over the desk, Jack looked up and pulled the trigger, pulled back and watched as the big guy crashed down onto the desk. Jack was on the move, past the big guy along the hallway, with the weapon ready, out of the corner of his eye he caught an older guy, who was about to leave through the front door, Jack waited, till the door was closed to move. Jack stepped out to feel his arm get hit, as his weapon took off and hit the wall, Jack reacted by grabbing this guys arm, and away he went, lifted off his feet, a big hulking figure, started to punch Jack, and drug him down and continued to throw punches, Jack was quickly running out of energy. Jack used one arm to block some of the throws, Jack brought up his knee and hit home, causing this hulking figure to let loose of his arm, he pulled out his knife, and began to slice and stab, catching everything, drawing blood, as the big guy backed away from Jack with his hands and arms bleeding.

The Madman was literally upset as his stomach was in his hands, blood was pouring out.

Both of them noticed Jack's hand gun, and the big guy was closer, he watched Jack still backing up, the guy reaches for it, while Jack watches, the guy picks up his weapon, begins to shake, and gets off a shot as Jack dives away, then the guy short circuits and falls forward, releasing the gun and it firmly burned into his hand as he shakes to death.

Jack gets up, walks over to that mass of a big guy and turns him over, to see the gun did its job and burned a hole through the guy's hand. Jack picks up his weapon, prying the dead man's hand from the gun, wipes it down with his t-shirt, then moves to the door, peers through the glass, and decides what to do, Jack decides to go down, he reaches the main set of stairs, he takes them downward, to reach the bottom, he see Carlos tied up in a chair, looked like he had been beaten. Then a guy came out of the bathroom as Jack hit him, knocking him down, the guy lay motionless, as Jack use some zip ties, from his jacket, to tie both ankles and wrists, then he pulled out his knife and cut the bindings off of Carlos. Then he pulled the duct tape from his mouth to hear, "Thanks my friend, now let me have my way with him."

Jack left to go back up the stairs, at the top of the stairs to hear the screaming from behind him, he shakes his head, Jack continued, on to the front door, looking out through the window he saw, and the old man was in the open, who was barking out the orders, so Jack opened the door, to see the SEAL teams were advancing from the east, through the fields, and the south, as the village was secure, as Jack put his gun away and pulled his knife, then ran out into the open field, to the old man, who's back was to Jack.

Jack caught up to him, put his arm around his neck to hold him from the left and the knife was at the guy's liver.

"Listen up" yelled Jack, moving the old guy around to ensure no one was behind him.

Jack reiterated his position to say "Stop what you're doing" at the top of his voice, he finally got their attention, instead of listening the last of the Cuban warriors rushed him, they started to rush Jack. Shots went off, and all those went down.

"Kill em Jack", yelled Carlos standing in the doorway.

Jack turned to see Carlos with a big knife in his hand. When all of sudden an explosion went off as Jack gutted the old guy, and let him drop as he ran back towards the house.

"Jack watch out", exclaimed Carlos.

Jack felt a twang in his arm, realized he just got shot at, but the bullet went to his heart. Jack, turned and threw his knife at the figure who was screaming, "You killed my father."

The throw hit home glazing the neck of Junior.

Jack turns, pulls out his gun and shoots Junior in the head, and then goes to him and stands over him, while the soldiers secure the remaining.

Jack heard over the loud speaker say," Cease fire, cease fire, this is Carlos, I command you to put down your weapons."

Silence spread over the compound, as the SEAL teams had secured the compound.

The old man and his kid were dead. Jack stood and pulled Junior over to the senior.

"Now one by one, come to the man in the middle, place your weapon down, and empty out your pockets "commanded Carlos.

Behind them was a convey of trucks, led by a monster looking truck, Jack watched as the remaining soldiers laid down their weapons and cleaned out there pockets, while Carlos, opened the gates to allow the trucks to come in, in a instance Jack's team surrounded him, to help out, both Mark and Mike in the Monster truck took over for Jack, as Devlin coordinated the surrender of the remaining Cuban Warriors, while Trixie and Mitzi went down to the basement to see that the women were safe.

Two men met in the middle of the compound, Jack limped, realizing he must have turned his ankle, to have help by Carlos.

Carlos swung his arm around his brother in law, to say, "Thanks for rescuing us, your injured, let me help you, boy you got some balls", the two walked together to see Jim, with phone in hand, to say,

"You're on your way home, your ride should be here soon, we located your relatives, there fine."

Just as the door flew open and the girls came to them, to surround them both, they all helped Jack to the steps where he took a seat, as Frieda, Carlos's oldest wife, began to go to work on Jack's ankle, standing in front of Jack was Maria, tears in her eyes, dressed in traditional wear, behind her stood Alexandra, which Jack smiled when he saw her, then Maria came to him and hugged him around the neck, Frieda said something, and Maria backed off, as hot water and bandages arrived.

Frieda, quickly putting on some solution, and then wrapped a bandage on it, while another girl worked on his back, trying to loosen him up.

It was Margarita; she leaned in for a kiss on the cheek.

Just as a Helicopter came in slowly and landed in the field, and shut down, they helped Jack up, Jack saw his team gathering to say, "It's time to go home."

Hopi came up to Jack and gave him a hug, then a kiss to say, "You O-Kay?"

"Yeah, I'm fine, just a few scratches", he felt his pocket, on his heart, to realize his wallet was missing. He frantically was looking around for it, for Hopi to say,

"You're hurt, are you staying around, what are you looking for?"

"My wallet, I think I might have lost it on the run from the beach up here."

"I'll find it, said Hopi, going back to the beach, while Jack is being cared for. Inside one of the girls found the wallet, and brought it out to Jack, which he reinserted it back in its slot.

Jack turned to see both Maria and Alexandra standing together, as Alba was a helper, almost forgotten, for Jack to stand up with some help, to say, "Let's load them up, everyone, and you too Carlos, and bring your wives, and Alba too."

Carlos was at Jack's shoulder helping him, while Mark was on the other side, as they walked to the helicopter, they helped him into the back, as he passed on the co-pilot seats, to the back seat, both Maria and Alex got in, followed by Alba. Carlos said, "Thanks again, I owe you one."

"Get in, up front so that I can keep an eye on you", he said jokingly.

"I think I will I won't bring all my wives but how about this group?"

Carlos begins to yell, "Come on girls."

CH 3

Back to the Spa, with guests.

The girls sat with Jack, Carlos took the co-pilots seat and gave the thumbs up and the helicopter started up and took off. To a short flight to the airport, where everyone got out, and into the plane, for a flight to Andrews, once there they were shuttled to Bella Haven by helicopter.

The entourage was loud on the flight, noises and women shouting, it was chaos.

At the Spa, people were running down the hall, getting to a room, a light switch went on, several burly men rolled out some equipment and opened up Jack's room, to wheel it in as all the doors opened, and those that were still there were moved into specific rooms, to see Lisa come out to say, "What's going on here?"

Robert approached her to say, "We just received word that Jack is enroute, with an entourage, to include another spy, named Carlos." "Carlos the killer, oh my god, you're kidding right, how long before they get here?"

"About a minute, Jack has requested three ladies himself, and one of them is his supposed wife", said Robert.

"On the ground, the team called to say, he was injured twice?"

"Who ordered that he come here rather than a hospital?" "Jack, himself said he was fine, he was patched up, and now wants to rest."

"When he gets here, we will have him checked out, as directed by the order of the President." said Robert."

Lisa was on the phone, confirming the order, and she went to see Sara who was out at the pool with her two friends.

Lisa came out to say, "Sara and friends, Jack is on his way, and should be here in about a minute."

She was drowned out by the sounds of helicopters, as each one lands, another takes off, one by one, people and parts were being taken into the spa.

Lisa got a hold of the situation, and coordinates the event, instead of relaxing in her room for her much needed rest.

"Look the spy is coming in" said Robert, waiting to welcome him in.

The helicopter was on a beeline to the spa, with its landing, and then shutting down. Limos were in place, to receive them.

First out was Carlos and his wife Frieda, followed the two dark haired lasses Alba and Margarita, the very tall Rose was helping Jack who had a limp, followed by Maria and Alexandra. The ride over was short, everyone got out and the succession proceeded up the side walk, to a couple of men dressed in white, with gurney in hand, waited till Jack met them, then he laid down, they adjusted a pillow for him.

The rest of them past, Robert making his announcement clear, Carlos had a smile for Lisa as he walked by her, all three of the girls got out of the pool to watch, Tami was ready for them to say,

"Please follow me to your rooms" she led them straight down the hall, past the laundry to the first room, to say "This is your room Mister Gomez, and the next three is for your party to divide amongst your self's.

Next in was the Princess Maria and Alexandra, to whom, Sara remarked, "Wow she is pretty, I wonder, who she is with?" "Which one are you looking at?" asked Leslie.

"The one who was wearing all black" said Sara. "Maybe that's Jack's new mistress," said Leslie. "Nah, really, then I want to go meet her," said Sara.

Just as the gurney came in, and took a sharp left turn right in front of the three girls, long enough for Sara to catch hold of Jack's hand and away she went to say, "Are you alright?"

"Yeah", he was yelling to screaming at her, to add, "It was no major wounds, just a couple of scratches" she caught up with the moving gurney, trying to kiss him to no avail.

She let him go as he was wheeled into his assigned room, where the double doors closed, and a burly guy stood.

Jack was taken off the gurney, to the bed, whereas, doctors checked Jack over and as two beautiful nurses stripped him down, carefully not to touch his weapon, as told by Brian who was carefully helping Jack out of his vest and holster, then Brian used special gloves to pull the gun out and placed it into the box.

Brian left the room, to hear one of the doctors call the nurses back in.

Jack was resting, as he saw two beautiful nurses, the brunette was named Jessica, very young, strong and confident, the obvious leader, then on the other side was nurse Amy, a stunning blonde, equally beautiful. They both smiled at him, as the doctors finish hooking up the leads, then given the O Kay, both girls went to work washing Jack from head to feet, then dressed him in a gown, as the two doctors left, they helped him to the bathroom, then back into the bed, then one said to the other, "Alright who wants to go first?"

"I will ", said a commanding voice behind them, they turned to see it was Lisa, who said, "Leave us, please, you can have your way with him after I'm through."

"Yes, Ma'am", said both Jessica and Amy, and heard from Lisa who said," I want you two to guard the door and keep Missy and her friends out of here."

Amy covers up Jack, who has pulled a pillow in tight as he closed his eyes, as the medication was kicking in; he was waiting for Lisa to speak. Amy went to the blinds to close them, then the curtains, to make it semi dark.

When all of a sudden the door crept open, Sara peeked her head in to hear.

"Visiting time is over," said Nurse Amy as she opened the door to look at her.

"Well that is my boyfriend."

"That doesn't matter, you could be his wife, lover or whatever, he is on a military base, thus he is under the base Commander's laws, which states he will have no visitors, till he awakes and asks for you personally", as she was to finish she heard a voice speak deeply "Ma'am, I have to ask you to back up and leave this secure area immediately or we will take you into custody."

"On who's authority" said Sara turning to look at them, pausing she looked up at two of the tallest men she had ever seen, and tough too.

"By order of the base commander, now go back to the pool and relax, you'll see Mister Cash when he is ready."

Lisa looked Jack over to say,"So what happen?" "What do you mean?"

"Your injured and wounded how did this happen?"

"I guess when I was running my wallet fell out, is that what you mean?"

"Part of it, that is something I'm going to have to fix, as she was on the phone to Jim, and told him what to do, for her to say, "Is there anything I can get you?", she said with a smile.

"Nah, how about my wife?" "Which one?"

"How about all of them?" said Jack looking more annoyed with her, than she was with him, to say,"Alright it shall be done." With that she turned around, went out to the hallway, to say, to the husky men, "Go round up his wives, and bring them in here for a visit."

"Yes, Ma'am." they said in unison. Sara who stood in the hallway while waiting for the okay, and she was motioned in.

"I may reconsider, what I said earlier," said Leslie, seeing Sara go in, from behind her the two guards were calling out, for all of Jack's wives to come to his room.

The two guards made it to the pool to announce,"Jack would like his wives to come and see him, so if you please", one of guards was waving at all the smoke. Almost everyone was smoking cigarettes.

Three girls got up, Alexandra and Alba, off to the right by herself was Maria, they went inside.

Sara was lying next to Jack, harassing him, when the three of them, was at the door, then one by one they came in.

"My name is Maria, said the girl beside Sara, who extended her hand to say, "Are you his American wife?"

"You could say that, we are engaged to be married, my name is Sara."

The other two was on the other side, the tall one, who was quite beautiful said, "My name is Alexandra, I'm from the Dominican Republic, I was a princess there", she extends her hand to Sara to take and shake, for Alexandra to say, "This here is Alba, she is shy, but she is a gift from Carlos, this is his sister, for which she said,"Hi." It was awkward for all of them except Sara, who went back to what she was doing, working Jack over, much to the surprise and delight of the others.

The girls watching didn't have to take any more special cues, as they all began to undress, Maria was the slowest, as Sara watched, thinking of her friends, but now her attention, was on the women, as Alexandra was first, to be nude, and take a place next to Jack, and her right hand joined in on the fun Sara was having, Alba was next, and immediately Sara saw something she liked, her big boobs, as she got on the bed, and worked her way up to Jack's man hood that was fully erect, and that she was the first one to claim it, the smell of smoke was intoxicating, as it mixed with the fragrance of the different types of perfume, but that all changed, when the Cuban princess, was nude, and climbed on top of Sara, to begin to kiss her body for her to say,

"Oh yes this is going to be fun."

For the first time, Sara was getting the attention she so desired, and that from a real woman, not her play friends, as Sara and Maria were locked in a long kiss, Maria's hands were all over Sara, and Sara had her hands all over Maria.

Jack continued to kiss Alexandra while Alba continued to grind it out, she was screaming in ecstasy; Sara had reached up and was massaging one of her huge breasts.

Everyone had heated up the room, and when Alba was finished, she went to Sara, then it was Alexandra's turn, she slowly slid back, down, and allowed him back in, and liked to rub her body back and forth, while Maria, went around to Jack's right, and curled up next to him, and began to kiss him.

Sara was in a lip lock with Alba, her fingers found Alba's wet spot, and kept it going, till Alba let loose, and Sara was hot and bothered, that Alba helped her get undressed, and the two of them watched as Maria was next to take that purple thing and move forward slowly, squeeze, and then back again, while Jack played with her tiny breasts. Alexandra was exhausted, but went back at it as Sara and Alba was working on her, when Maria let everyone know she was through, she slid off, for Sara to be last, she too was ready, hot and wet, she stood up on the bed, then, quickly went down on him, for him to jump, as she was getting physical with him, and the others were enjoying the show, especially Sara, who finally found the place she really wanted to be, riding Jack to the finish, which he let out a roar, and let loose and deposited his load, she continued to ride the wave out, till she got off and they were through.

Jack opened his eyes, to see that Sara was still on top of him, next to him on his right was Maria, who had her arm pinned by Sara, and next to him on his left was Alexandra, equally turned in, with her hand pinned under Sara, and finally, Alba, who was resting on her big tits, all were smiling, awake, Jack said,"Are we ready for round two?"

The girls said in unison, "Aah, Ooh, Eeh."

Jack smiled, and was back at working his magic.

The next morning was getting to know each wife, and their story. Sara was the most fascinated, like for instance, how Carlos, once controlled the lower part of Cuba, and in one day, her soon-to-be husband, changed all that and Maria's life, as she was given to Carlos, who then turned her over to Jack, she was used like a pawn, to satisfy each mans needs, only it was on her wedding night she actually lost her virginity. The act was not a success. When there was no baby, as a result. It was a family failure; she was disgraced, within the family, and had since then lived with Carlos's harem. She had taken up needlepoint, and sewing, as she likes to design clothes, and garments, her specialty is rugs.

Sara kept looking at Alexandria, Alex for short; Jack called her the sophisticated sex kitten. and she could see why with how her body was built, her arching back and all the right curves. But just like all the island girls, they all smoked, those awful cigarettes, for Alba, she was somewhat out of place, a girl just above Timmy's age, she was young. But was the first to be ready for sex, just the mention of it and she is ready, but other than that, she was very quiet and reserved, with no hobbies, other than watching TV, is all she would rather do. Sara noticed, two new girls in the picture, from Jack's last big mission, Jen and Monica. Two super sexy sex machines, eager to please anyone, anywhere, turns out, they may end up being the nannies. As Jack had requested, they help with Sam's baby, Sam Jr. Sara has yet to decide that and who does what. After they were all separated, Lisa came into the room, and said,"Alright ladies, I need some time with Jack."

Lisa closed the door, and turned to say,"Jack we got a problem." Jack was still forging from the countless platters, of food, to say, "What is it?"

"I'm having difficulty getting your wives through immigration, and naturalization."

'I thought you said I could marry whomever I want?'

"You can, but now is the mountain of paperwork, plus each is suppose to have an agent assigned to them."

"So assign someone from your huge resources." Said Jack. "It doesn't work like that, besides, we need to clear it with the

Pentagon, and then it will be alright, so in the meantime, they can stay for up to 90 days. I have their visa's right here, in the next couple of days; I'll need one at a time, and get them tested." She continues, to say "Do you have any preference on who goes first?"

"Nah, you choose, how long do you think it will take?"

"Who knows, it could be a week, a month, six month's or up to a year."

"Even with the Presidential seal of approval."

"I think he would want you to be happy, but even he doesn't have any pull for this, it is what it is, in the meantime, Secret Service, is now assigned to watch over them, you won't see them, or hear from them, just as long as you obey, and they go home safely."

Jack gets up, and sets down a drink, to say, "Fine, allow me to check with Sara, and see when the wedding will go off, and I'll get back with you on the when's and where it will happen."

Jack left his room, down the hallway. And out to the patio, where Carlos, held court, smoking a Cuban cigar. Jack was out of place, but not for the girls, they were all playing, water volleyball, they were egging him on, to join. Jack waved them off, to take a chair next to his brother-in-law.

"So Jack when will we kick this bucket?"

Jack looked over at him, the fragrance of the Cuban was intoxicating, but distinctive, even for Alex, who got out of the pool, took the cigar from Carlos, and took a huge drag, held it in, then blew it out in front of Jack, she whispered, "Let's go to your room lover."

She led the eager Jack, back in and past Tami who smiled at Jack, as Jack took another look at her. Once in the room, Alex closed the door behind them, as Jack was loosening his swim trunks, he turned, to see she was just standing there, for Jack to say,"Come on let's go?"

"Wait, I want to talk with you." "Sure go ahead" said Jack.

"How can I put this, I don't wanna leave, the D, R, I have a growing business there, and if you allow me, I can send money back to you."

"It's not about the money; I married you for the sex." "Fine I accept that, but that's it, I know what you said to those two young girls, four babies, please, you're not getting any, do we have a deal?"

"Sure, whatever you want, so come over here and give me pleasure." Said Jack showing her what he was working with.

"Wait, one more thing, you can't tell anyone about our agreement."

Jack raised his hand to say,"I promise."

"You promise, she said, as she came to him, peeling away her sleek thin swim suit, to allow him the opportunity to feel her fun bags, as she stripped out of her suit, and pushed him onto the bed. And quickly took his manhood, in her mouth, and spent time enjoying herself, doing what she does best, give pleasure. It was a fight to the finish.

The next morning all was asleep, except that of Jack and Carlos, who had a late night, lying in wait in the mud pool, each relaxing in their own chairs, all the while two young attendance waited on them, each dressed in a super sheer clothing. Carlos continued to puff up his Cuban cigars, while Jack had his head back, and a warm towel was wrapped around his head, when he heard, "So my brother, I want to give you a present . . . . there was a pause by Carlos, then he continued, "In my country we have our annual Miss Cuba competition, to see who will represent Cuba in the Miss World, it's usually held later in the year, but I could make special arrangements and in two weeks, say on your honeymoon, you can have first choice from fifty of the most beautiful women in the world, what do you say?" . . . . Still no response from Jack who was sound asleep, and every fifteen minutes a new hot face wrap Up was applied. Carlos finally had enough, and called out, "Could I get some help", he stood, and exited. Some time had passed, when Jack heard a whisper, "Jack, Jack your time is up, you need to get out."

Jack came to, as the towel was unwrapped, to see it was Tami, the cute front desk clerk, who wore nothing but a sheer body suit, for which she said, "Come on let's get you out of there, you must be a prune." Jack awakes, turns, and slowly climbs out, of the warm clay, to stand up both ways, for Tami to smile and said,"No, I'm not using the hose on you, come follow me."

Jack walked behind her, to the steam room, which she held the door open for him, as he made it through, as she escorted him, to a step down, into a square pool, the water was warm, about ankle deep, for Tami to say, "Have a seat, and I will turn on the steam." Jack sat, with his back against a wall, instantly the steam came on, and it was a fog of steam, at head level, instantly Tami appeared to say, "Come in the middle I'll bathe you." She proceeded to wash his back, using several sponges, he continued to sit, while she worked around him, she was wet, and well exposed to him, but Jack had other idea, and kept his eyes closed and allow her to do her own thing, listening to her commands, until, she said,"Alright I'm finished, is there and thing you would like to do to me?", Jack opens his eyes, to see, her waiting for a response.

He didn't have to say a word, as he turned her around, and bent her over, and was ready for, when he heard, "Jack, Jack are you in there, It's me Missy, your family is assembling in the dining room, if you're in here, finish up and", the door closed, as Jack was feeling his own pleasure as Tami, was using her mouth to its fullest potential, much to Jack's happiness, she did things that was new, exciting and in that instance he erupted and she finished him off, cleaned him up and wiped him down.

Jack left the steam room a very happy man, into his room, where he dressed, with holster, and windbreaker, and down in to the cafeteria, for breakfast, it was announced, by Jack, "Listen up, I think we need to go down to Mobile, so let's finish up breakfast, then we will shuttle to the airport, and down to the house we have in Mobile." Jack sat down. They all finished eating, each went to their specific place, as for Jack, he was late, but was surrounded by all of his wives, and two potential mistresses, they waited while he ate, then disbursed to their own rooms, leaving Sara alone with Jack. Sara spoke up first, to say,"Have you received any word, on when the other wives will be permanently?"

"Nope, but we have ninety days, with them, and I think, we could all be at the wedding, then we could go to Cuba for the honeymoon, how does that sound?"

"Fine, I guess I should go pack?"

"Yeah, what about Leslie and your other friend what was her name?"

"Tabitha,"

"Yeah, where are they at?"

"Gone, I gave them the money, except that they both returned it," and said, "They were sorry."

"That's alright; they could have had the money."

'It wasn't about money for them; they were ready for a threesome, like the wives and I had with you."

"So make it happen." "I can't they left."

"Maybe a rain check" said Jack finishing, to say, "Let's go."

CH 4

The new beginnings

"Dear diary, I think I made a huge mistake, and now what do I do to get out of it. Let me explain, I gave my address book to Alexandra to type up and to sort, to have for my wedding party, then invitations were sent out, on that list was my two ex-boyfriends and that psycho 'Steve' that got away, now he knows when and where I'm getting married. Everyone said it would be fine, there will be plenty of security, but deep down I know something's going to happen, I just know it, anyway it's been two months since the spa, and let me update you on what's going on. Jack surprised us all, Sam will be home for the wedding, and for Jack's other wives, there here to stay, until we all go to Cuba. Carlos, has turned out to be a fairly nice guy, he is slightly older than Jack but in many ways a bit more mischievous, Samantha who took a turn for the better, called to tell us she will be home in a couple of days for the wedding, and her Baby is fine, she has finalized the name, for it as it will be, Sam. Samantha is here now, she looks weakly and is bed ridden, and Alba has taken on the job of her assistant. Maria is two months pregnant, with a boy, her brother has been flying in from time to time and spends most of his time with Jack, I'd sure like to know what happen in Cuba, everyone's been hush, hush about the details, I'll I know was that Jack was the one who saved them all. That is what he does saves people from danger, as for Alexandra, she is staying child free for as much as Jack and her do it, well actually I do it more than her, he sleeps in my bed every night, and they know that I'm number one. Jack married them for diplomatic relations, which I'm sure there will be more weddings in the future, although he has said he was done with that, and that having the five of us is taxing on his mind. However I know he has his mistress's, like Debbie at the hospital, then there are the two nanny's he hired before the babies are even born, whom he picked up when he saved the Governor, the blonde is Monica and the brunette is Jen, he has this theme going on, blonde and brunettes, but all the other wives have jet black hair. The more I become accustomed to how all this works the more I understand the life of a spy, he has the toughest job in the world, just last week . . . ."

Sara put down her pen, closed her book, in her mind she knew that this was a mistake to write down what she was feeling, she placed the book in the wall, in a safe. and closed the safe door, and then swung the picture to hid it.

"Sara, I finished the corporate paperwork, and I want you to look at it" asked Alex.

Sara reviewed the documents and signed off on them, to say, "Do you want me to get Sam to sign as well."

"No, I will have all the sisters sign, then present it to Jack, is it you and I this morning going in?", said a very confident Alexandra. "As far as I know" said Sara.

"Oh I was going to tell you that my parents will be coming back this in this evening, and Jack asked us if we would pick them up."

"That's fine, let me finish getting ready, can you have Mike pull the Suburban around to the front" said Sara.

Sara finished getting ready for work, Alexandra, visited with Maria, who was the household chef, house keeper, to sign the documents, then onto the bed stricken Samantha, who was lying in wait, as she lay still in her own bed, but could still talk, as Alexandra entered her room.

Sam smiled at her as she heard something, then signed something then closed her eyes. She saw her best friend Alba, who signed her name as well.

Alexandra felt sorry for Samantha, as she really cared for her, but no one could do anything now, in her heart, she really longed to see her get better, she knew that this experience was like no other, as she remembers Carlos's palace was a constant sex fest, living with Maria was tame, now Jack is a bit nonexistent, as her day to day operations have switched from every day sex orgies to real business and commerce, and to herself she thinks "This is perfect, this is what I've been trained for, and Sam left me a great model for in which to continue and make it better."

Alex had the truck keys in hand she picked up off the kitchen's table, as she called out for Sara, the bride to be, this weekend's the wedding, her and I will go out and make the last minute preparations.

"Sara come on lets go" said Alex, with her set of keys in hand.

A guard watching the girls opened the door for Alex, who really does feel like a princess now, the days are behind her for whom other men will abuse and use her, she knows that now, and only one man will have her from now on. She sees her sister Sara, and the two get into the Suburban and the driver JJ drove off.

Alex was in the back as Sara rests, with the baby inside of her to say "I think I made a huge mistake."

"Why do you say that, I thought you and Jack were right for each other?"

"I don't mean that, what I mean to say is, remember the address book you copied and made out all the invitations for?"

"Yes, it was about two hundred." "Well it was on that list" said Sara. "Who do you mean?" asked Alex.

"I was talking about the single men, or a family connected to a single man" said Sara.

"Yes I remember now, I set out a list of all single men, and a list of all single women as well, do you remember?"

"I don't think so, I just could have, well anyway, I don't know" said Sara a bit confused.

"What is the issue?"

"I think my ex-boyfriend, received an invitation, actually I know he did, and now he knows where I will be."

"What's wrong with that?"

"He is a psycho, and used to stalk me."

"Oh dear I'm sorry, should we tell Jack" asked Alex.

"I think we have to, I'm really fearful for my life with this guy."
"You have nothing to worry about, I'm here to protect you, now go in there and get your dress. As the vehicle came to a complete stop and Sara got out.

Mark was piloting the Parthian Stranger, along the coast line, picking up the pots they dropped, earlier, on the boat, for the bachelor party for Jack was the four girls from the Pine acres spa, Blythe and Jack had been practicing martial arts on the deck, Caroline and Rob the builder were on some jet skies, Tracy has spent most of her time with Mark, in the pilot house. Brian and Jim have been fishing on the deck with Tami who was flirting with Brian and Timmy, but they kept their distance.

Carlos has been resting in his room, due to a little sickness, well actually, he and his two wives Sara Maxwell and Margie, to whom he brought for Jack's entertainment along with the five other ladies, who are all sick now, and are in there rooms.

Jack would ready his stance then Blythe would attack, she was relentless.

The two fought each other for several hours, then took a break, when Carlos came to the deck, to see Jack to say, "It's your turn, they are waiting for you."

"Nah, not now, I'm working out, you should try this one." Carlos shook his head, yes and Blythe and Carlos went at it, when all of a sudden the horn went off, and the men went to the railing. The winch line became taut and each pot was hauled up.

Jack, Mike and Timmy, was at the rail, pulling pots and emptied the pots and unsnapped them and pushed them against the wall, they did that for all the rest of them. On the table was a collection of fishes. Jack fired up a long grill, as Timmy broke out some stock pots; he then filled them up with fresh water, about half way, while Jim, Brian and Mike carved up the fish and lobsters. Caroline had chosen to help Timmy cook, she brought out some elegant salads and some roasted corn on the cob, Carlos had both of his wives Sara Maxwell and Margie, break out a case of some Cuban wines, Rob got involved with the cooking and the spa girls were the servers, led by Tami and Blythe, the plates went on the table, along with the silverware, as Jack took the head of the newly set up tables, to say "Thank you my friends and guests for coming out to help me celebrate my Bachelor party, it had been suggested to me, by my Best man Carlos that he fly me to Cuba for some Wine, Women and Song, but I refused him, I love this boat, I miss this boat and what better way to enjoy this boat, is to use the boat, so here's to you my friend and brother, let's raise our glass and toast, to a great evening of fun, entertainment and drink"

"Here here" said the crowd.

The girls served the platters of cooked foods to the table where Jack sat, he had his brother Carlos next to him on the left and Jim on the right, then it was girls in the middle followed by men towards the end, once everyone was eating, Blythe took a seat by Jim who actually shifted so that she could sit by Jack, who looked over his plate, of mashed potatoes, and white gravy, a slice of his favorite, Jellied cranberries, a mixture of grilled vegetables, a lobster tail, sitting in a hot bowl of butter, and two long crab legs, over the top, Jack watched as Carlos poured some ketchup into his lobster bowl, so he tried that and it was good.

"Jack you ever try, a spiky globe of a thing called artichoke?" "Can't say that I have" in between bites as he gobbled it up. "It is but a delicacy" said Carlos.

"I'll call Trixie, and tell her to put it on the menu".

"I'll show you how to eat it then".

Jack nods his head as he continued to enjoy the meats and seaweeds from the sea, as he lastly finished a seaweed salad of fine green and herbs, with fried bacon pieces and walnuts.

Jack tasted a light vinaigrette sauce.

They completed the meal as Carlos stood up to say "In my country it is common for all of us men to enjoy a cigar after the meal, and I have brought another two gifts, first an after meal drink called Lambrucio, a nice port wine, and there are now several cigar boxes to chose from on the table, inside is two types the darker the cigar the heavier the flavor, the lighter one the more mild.

The men and a couple of women chose one, as Jack chose a darker one, "Now, next to enjoy the flavor, there are three degrees, with this device, you can clip off the closed end, or simply not for those who have never smoked before, for those who want a medium flavor clip in the middle, if you want full flavor, clip at the top"

Jack clipped in the middle as Carlos lit him up; Jack took several long drags, and then began to cough, several times till he gained some momentum and took smaller more pronounced drags.

Jack went to the rail to watch the sea, and smokes when Carlos joined him to say, "My friend what are you thinking?"

Jack turns to see Carlos with his two hottie wives Margie on one arm and Sara Maxwell on the other, and in the back ground was Blythe, to whom he had grown quite some feeling for, there daily workouts have been inspiring and get exercise, even when he mentioned for her to become his wife, she said she would consider it. Jack spoke to Carlos to say, "Oh nothing, just wondering what is your next gift for me is?"

"Well now that you asked, why my three wives, take them do what you want with them, then send them back to me." "Is that one at a time or all at once?"

"That is your choice my friend", said Carlos patting Jack on the back.

"Is this the last gift you're giving to me?"

"Nah, this is only the beginning, as my brother, you will be receiving constant gifts for the rest of your life, my friend, my brother" Carlos kissed Jack on the cheek, to whisper, "I owe you my life, and in the future I will show you how grateful I really am, so enjoy."

Jack tossed the cigar over and placed his arms around the two willing girls and went into the boat's cabin, he led them to his room, opened the door.

Jack turned on the light, to take a seat on the bed, while the two girls undressed him, they in turn undressed themselves, both got Jack excited, and slid on protection, each one of them mounted him, while the other sat on his face, as each girl got off, they would switch, for the other, then Jack let loose and it was over, as the entertainment left.

Jack pulled back the covers and slid into the sheets, put his head on the pillow, closed his eyes, only to hear a knock on the door.

Jack looked up to see Blythe standing in the doorway to say, "Can I come in?"

"Sure, come in and lock the door."

Blythe walked in she wore a white blouse and jean shorts, to show off her long legs.

"May I join you for tonight?"

"Sure, but wait you need to take off what your wearing."

But of course, shall I go slowly, to give you a show or fast and just jump right in there with you."

Jack sat up on the edge of the bed, exposing himself to her, for her to say, "Looks like your happy to see me, now where did we leave off with this afternoon, as I recall, you said if I could pin you, you would lick me out, so I want to take you up on that, so for that I need to remove my shorts like this."

Jack watched, as Blythe took her time, turned around to face the wall and pulled her shorts down, she bent over, and spread her cheeks, for Jack's viewing pleasure, slowly she pulled her panties down so he could see it all, then she backed into him. Another knock at the door, as Blythe opened it up and Tami the minx with the hot body, walked in to say "Can I join in, and serve you, Jack?" Jack nods his head as Tami begins to undress, right in front of Jack, then turns and bends over, Jack touches her perfectly round butt, then goes to the inside, to feel her wetness, as Jack lays back, Tami, turns around and gets up onto Jack and kneels down at his face, in one last move she pulls off her blouse, Jack pulls her down and the two wrestled around, Tami takes control, and stays onto of Jack as the two of them kiss, as Jack is feeling her up, eager Jack waits no longer, as he slips on some protection and Tami slides down onto him, while Blythe watches from the door, secretly she exits with her clothing.

The next morning was a bit different the young minx from the night before, stayed and her infatuation with him was apparent, for her to open her eyes to say, "Your quite a handsome man, what would you say, If I told you that I wanted to be your mistress?"

Jack looks at her to say,"Then I'd say you would have some options, what did you have in mind?"

"Well since the spa, I've been thinking, what would it take for me to get to know you a little bit more?"

"Other than this?" asked Jack massaging one of her perfectly round boob.

"What I meant was, maybe I'll come work for you?"

"In what capacity, it seems like I'm doing fine the way it is, but what do you have in mind", he was working his way down, between her legs, she parted them to allow him access, to say,"

"I don't know like maybe a secretary?"

"Tell me more," said Jack as he was working his way over, and back on top of her, she was more willing than ever, as he was ready, he slipped on protection, and then it went in easily, his strokes were intoxicating to her, as she closed her eyes, and took up the breathing with his, her legs were up, and rocking to allow him, a better entry, his hands were all over her breasts, he was comfortable just where he was at, and she stayed there exactly where he wanted and the hour had past and they were still going at it, the concentration ever so much more present as he was doing all the work, as she reached climax and let everyone know about it, that signaled Jack to let loose, calming down, he collapsed on top of her, as she held him in her arms, for her to say, "I know a man like you need this kind of loving, intimacy, be still and rest, when you ready to go again, I'm here for you."

The boat was in cleanup mode from the party before, while Mark and Mike were hauling fish line, and with Timmy's help they were hauling, big eye tuna, huge ones at that.

In the wheel house, Blythe, sat across from Mark, as he kept the boat in line and on track, looking over occasionally at Blythe, who looked back at him, to say, "Did you have fun last night?"

"I have fun everyday", said Mark.

"Do you know what the plan is today, or for the rest of the week?" back."

"As far as I know, I'm fishing till I'm full, then were going

"Isn't Jack getting married this weekend?"

"Yeah, he is?" asked Blythe questioning Mark. Mark looked at her suspiciously.

"What I meant was doesn't he need to get back, for the wedding and all that?"

Mark just looked at her, as she also realized he was the wrong person to ask, got up and left, down to the galley, where Carlos's women, were at, Margie in particular, gave her a dirty look as she past. She went onto the deck, to see a full scale fishing operation was underway, Ice was everywhere, and while she was there, Tuna and some shark were being pulled in, the shark were let go, she turned back around, and went down, to the cabins, she past Carlos's room, it reeked of cigars, alcohol and perfume, lots of noise was coming from his room, she went to Jack's room, waited try to listen, when she heard a voice, "It's not nice to ease drop?" said Brian.

She turned to say, "I'm not, I forgot something in there and was ready to go in, when you saw me."

"Sure, do you have a moment?" "What do you have in mind?"

"Come here and I'll show you, said Brian. Brian led her to the scuba room, and pulled out gear, to count out six, to say, "Will you be going?"

"Going where?"

"Were all diving, to check out a wreck off the Florida coast." She looked at him, thought a moment to say,"Nah, I'm kind of afraid of deep water?"

"It won't be that deep, maybe twenty feet, it's in a shallow pool, but there is a catch, is in a tidal pool, meaning, that there is a vortex of water, that surrounds it, so if you're not a really strong swimmer this may not be for you."

"Then I'm not definitely going out." "Good then you can be a spotter." "I'm fine with that, who is all going?"

Mark thought about it, then said, "Jack, I, Mike, Caroline and Rob." "Oh, which one is Jack's?"

"I have it, but I'll be the one checking his canister, check those three and let me know if they need filing, check cracks, then hold the air down, and put the mask on your thigh, to check for leaks, you'll hear a distinct wine."

Jack still laid on Tami, who was smiling at him to say," I can feel like you're ready to go again, I'm waiting?" "Alright, you can have the job."

"I already knew that, silly, I meant continue where we left off."

Jack was checking his nightstand to see that all of his protection had run out, to say, "Looks like I'm out."

"That's alright, I'm sure your fine, I've only been with three men total, and that count's as you're number three, I don't care if you don't, go ahead stick it in, I want to feel it again and again and again, please Jack give that to me."

Jack obliged, and in he went, as it felt different, more sensual, rewarding, it felt like he was stretching her out, like it was wrapped up and she was clamping down on him, she came and he followed right behind her, he was still inside of her as he continued to throb, to say,"Yeah, I like this too", he pulled out, to see her smiling, to say, "You have nothing to worry about?"

"Worried about what?"

"Like if I was to get pregnant, or a STD?"

"I don't know anything about that, what are you saying?" "Oh nothing, all I want you to know, is that I'm here to service all of your needs anytime", she said that as she came around to straddle him to say," tell me when and where and if not, I'll be the one, who initiates it", she kissed him, then got up, went into the tiny shower, turned it on, then filled up her bucket, turned off the water, and bathed standing up, then rinsed off, stepped out to see Jack was gone.

Jack stood on the deck, looking over the last of the fishing, Mike told him that they were nearly full and steaming for New Port Richey, Florida, for an offload, Mike pointed out the scuba gear was ready, each had a dive kit with it, to say, "Mark said we should finish this string soon, then we will offload, then set up for that spectacular dive, can't wait actually, hey I want to let you know, Mark had mentioned to me, that he felt Blythe was acting a bit suspicious?" "Really, why do you say that?"

"Just asking questions and I don't know?"

"She is a girl right, they ask questions, besides leave her to me", said Jack sounding a bit angry, for Mike to pull back to say, "Sorry, I wasn't trying to offend you."

"No worries, thanks for the Intel, I know your looking out for my best interests."

"That I am", said Mike going back to work.

Jack went up to the bow, to find Blythe, she wasn't up there, however the view was spectacular, dolphins off the port side, kept up with them, behind him, the crew was cheering as the fishing was incredible, Jack turned suddenly, to think it was Tami, only to see it was Blythe, for her to say, "You look disappointed in seeing me?"

"Well I was wondering what happen to you last night; you were there to help me celebrate my bachelor party."

"Yes, at first, then Tami came in, I felt, a bit out of place."

"I see, all those month's of sexual tension, and you give up at the last moment?" said Jack.

"It's not like that at all, I was just a bit intimidated, about her." "Don't be, so are you going to dive with us later?"

"I wasn't planning on it, but do you want me to go?"

"Sure the more the merrier", said Jack ready to leave as she holds his arm, to say, "I have to tell you, I'm a bit afraid of dark water."

"That's alright, that's what flash light are for, besides there will be six others down there, what do you have to worry?"

She looked at him, with a frown on her face to say, "Well alright, I'll go."

He looks at her, to say, "Well its actually too late, we have only six dive gear, but if you're really interested I'll have Mark buy one just for you."

She looked at him to say, "Yes, I do want to go."

"Then you shall, do you want to go to your cabin and make up for last night?"

She shakes her head, to say, "Yes, that would be fine." "I hope you have protection, I'm out?"

"Really, I might, I'll go check, meet me in my cabin?" said Blythe.

"Yep, be there after I visit Mark and have him get us another dive gear."

She kissed him on the cheek, as she went back towards the cabin; Jack crossed over, the bow, and up a ladder to the second level, opened the door, to see Mark to say, "How are we doing?"

"Were all finished, will place the drum back in its carrier, clear the deck, and get ready for the offload, then set up for the dive."

"Is it off the stern or the bow?"

"It will be the bow, I'll have Jim, push against the wave pool, and we will jump into the vortex, I did this one other time, its cool."

"Right on, thanks for recommending it, sounds fun, hey can you get one more dive gear?"

"Someone can have mine, what's up?"

"Nah, I want one more to go with us?" said Jack.

"Alright, I'll call it in, there is a Coast Guard base nearby, and I'm sure, they will be, sending one or two over, unless you want another to add to your collection,"

Jack shrugs his shoulder, in thought, to say, "I don't know?" "Well what we have, is all blue, a specialist set, designed especially for you, a girl, or a wife, smaller, which Caroline wanted, and five others for us, now don't get me wrong, I'll buy one, this minute, it's your choice, If I were you, and I'm not saying that, I'd ask the Coast Guard to lend one, and by the way, their usually red, so we can see where she is at?"

"You mean the target", said Jack.

"Listen, don't get me wrong, I like the girl, she seems a bit sneaky."

"Well I'll get to the bottom of that here in a moment."

"That's a good idea; we need to see if she is on our side or theirs."

Jack shook his head, to say, "Make the call." "Will do" said Mark.

Jack went down stairs, to the cabins, up to his room, he opened it up, to see the bed was made, and pillows were aligned at the top, he turned around to say, "She isn't in there, and went to Blythe's suppose cabin, knocked on the door, no answer, he peered in, to see the bunk was empty, it was quiet, so he went up, to the galley, still she wasn't to be found, so Jack went out onto the deck, and grabbed some gloves and helped out Jim and Mike stow the rest of the gear.

A newly refreshed Blythe, opened the door, to peer out to say, "Jack is that you, I'm here in the restroom?", she further went out simply wearing a robe, she checked her room first, opened the door, to see he wasn't there, then, doubled back and went to the Captain's quarters opened the door, to see that the bed was fully made up, to hear, "He isn't there, he is out on the deck, but you can wait in there if you like?" said Tami.

Blythe looked at her rival, Tami, who smiled back at her. Blythe past her, and went to his bed and laid on the bed, her robe was slightly open exposing her intentions. Tami said,"Shall I tell Jack you're ready for him?"

"Yes, you don't mind?"

"Nah, I'm his new assistant, I'd love to do it." "That will be great thank you."

Tami left the cabin area, went up on deck to see Jack, she met up with him, to say, "Wow look how beautiful the city is?"

"Yeah it's quite something?" said Jack checking her out, in her itsy, bitsy two piece bikini, barely hiding her assets. She leaned into him to say, "Are we going on shore?"

"Perhaps, why do you need something?" "The store, it's that time of the month." "Oh for you, that's a shame."

"No, No not for me, Blythe mentioned it to me." "Sure, we'll wait; I'll send Mike in with you."

"Thanks, she reached up and gave him a kiss on the cheek, then she left as everyone watched her move, for Jack to say, "That why you're doing what you're doing."

The boat steamed into New Port Richey, with a purpose, its brilliant blue and white color scheme showed proudly how beautiful the Parthian Stranger was, the crew was on the deck ready to secure the lines as it was positioning itself for market. Ships and boats were all around, especially the Coast Guard presence, right across the water way, stood several large Cutters, the action was at a feverish pace, as Helios were taking off, planes took off and were landing.

Jack was at the starboard side, admiring the Cutters when a familiar voice said, "They are sure quite lovely", her hand touches, and his back, for her to come next to him at the rail.

"Yeah, their alright."

"What's wrong, you seem down?" asked Blythe.

"Oh nothing", said Jack as the boat did a complete one eighty, for Jack and Blythe to see the fisherman were all scurrying about, but also a lone powerful figure stood dress in military uniform, he saluted, then, helped with the lines, as Mike and Jim threw them out, Mike also helped him, to secure the boat. A line of helpers formed, as the Fishing market manager appeared to say,"

Welcome back Mister Cash, permission to come aboard?"

"Granted", yelled Jack back, as the workers scurried onto the deck, as Mark was on the crane, and the panel was lifted out and moved away, as the Market's brailler, moved into position, and the workers were at it loading up the fresh Tuna. Jack saw that Tami had Mike with her, as they disembarked, only to see a sharply dressed Coast Guard Officer, salute and ask to come aboard, Jim waved him on, the man appeared to Jack to say, "Mister Cash, I'm the Commander of the New Port Richey coast guard base, my name is Juan Alvarez, and I'm at your disposal, we received the call from Mister Reynolds, requesting additional gear, where do you plan to dive?"

"I don't know really, Mark mentioned a ship sunk off these waters, in some tidal pool, do you know of them?" "We do indeed, however they are off limits."

"Then I won't need that dive gear" said Jack, as Blythe was backing away from them, and back into the cabin.

"Well let me clarify that, they are off limits to others, but not to you, you can go anywhere you like, regardless of its dangerous or not."

"How so, it's really not a big deal", said Jack getting a bit annoyed with his, line of talking, turning to see that the workers were still at it.

"Mister Cash, it's not that their dangerous per say, it is just that there are over two hundred."

"Really, yeah, I can see a problem with that."

"Yeah, so what we will do, is lend you a very qualified diver, and guide you to the exact spot to dive, and we will go out and support you out on this dive."

"Whoa, that's not necessary, we should just be fine?"

"It's not about that, I have an order here, straight from the President himself, that says that above all else we are to support you and whatever your doing in any capacity, do you see what I'm talking about?"

"Yeah, sure, then alright, how will this work then?"

"It doesn't, you're in charge, and you command me on what you want to do?"

Jack looked at him, then turning around to see the base and the activity, to say, you mean I have access to all of that too?"

"Yes, would you like to come over and spend a few days on the base", said Juan realizing he needed to back down, because Jack was getting a little overwhelmed.

Jack looked at him then back at the base, to say "Alright, I could use a tour", said Jack looking how long it was going to take them. The two went to the ladder, Jack said to Jim, "Can you secure everything, and hands Jim a credit card, to say, "Have them put the total on this card."

"Yes Sir."

"I guess, I'm going to the base, if you need me I'm a phone call away."

Jack followed the commander off his boat, to an awaiting vehicle, whereas, the commander opened the passenger side door for Jack, who said, "No thanks, I know what you said, but you're their boss, I'll take a seat in the back."

"Thanks", shook his head in respect and acknowledgement. Jack sat in the back, for the commander to say, "On to the base, have those tournaments started yet?"

"No sir, their waiting your arrival, and your guest."

"Hear that Mister Cash, the base is awaiting your arrival?"

"Sounds fun", said Jack, with his hand on his weapon.

The vehicle, took a right and went over a very large bridge, and back down, it took another right, as they stopped at the gate, they were waved on, immediately there was a huge difference, everything was nearly immaculate, newly painted houses were white with a red trim, and even the large ones, for the commander to say, "What first the swimming pool or the boxing tournament?" Jack said, "You choose, it doesn't matter to me, he said more quietly, looking out at the base housing system, wondering what it would be like to be one of them.

The vehicle stopped by a huge building, they got out, the hot pavement was evident, as they went in, to hear, "The commander has arrived, with a VIP, please rise, a huge noise was heard, as everyone was at attention, the Commander and Jack took a seat, in a box of sorts overlooking the four rings, a platter of refreshment was set down, next to Jack, to hear, "On the right is the women, and the left are men, three, three minute rounds." Jack was more occupied by the five different choices, bottled water, a orange drink, a grape and some red stuff, Jack looked up to see a stunningly beautiful blonde that had the name of GOODS, printed on the back. Jack smiled at her, she did nothing to hear, and "She is our best."

"I imagine she is" said Jack quietly.

"She holds all the base records, said she wants to go pro, when she is through with the Guard", said the commander. The bell

sounded, and GOODS went right after her opponent, throwing
precise punches, and then a straight uppercut and the other girl
went down. She was dancing with her arms raised, for Jack to
think, "I bet Blythe could give her a run for her money." Next up
was a super hot brunette, cute face, she actually acknowledged Jack
presence, to smile at him, the bell sounded for her, she too was a
warrior, stepping in and out as she threw, landing and connecting,
striking with good intentions and accuracy, for the Commander
to say, "She is with JAG, our base Attorney, she seems to like you."

Jack was clearly distracting her, as she was getting hit back,
the next round it was more of the same, she was eyeing Jack, he
motioning for her to get going. Then it was the last round, it was all
that uneventful, as they both were just slapping each other as both
were gassed. It ended and she won by split decision, she somewhat
motioned for Jack to come to her, but he stayed put. Some time
and other fighters had come and gone, Jack was easily tiring of this
non eventful tournament, to see a Seaman stand present to say,"
Mister Cash, Colonel Brian's request a visit, she said something
about signing official documents."

"You should go if it's coming from her, then it must be
important", said the commander, to add, "Take my vehicle it is at
your disposal."

"Alright", said Jack looking at all the bottles he had sampled,
thinking, that red stuff is pretty good."

Jack follows the Seaman, out to the Commanders vehicle, he
takes the passenger seat, with the Seaman, and off they went. The
ride was silent, till they reached a huge state of the art building
that read, "Judicial Attorney Group", the vehicle stopped, Jack got
out, followed by the Seaman, who led Jack into the building, using
a key card, he swiped at all the door, even the elevator, up to the
tenth floor, he had to swipe it to open the elevator doors, then at
another door, then another door, to finally a somewhat silent wing,
as they came to a huge door on the end of the wing, whereas the
Seaman knocked on the door, then quickly left, as Jack waited,
then the door opened, for Jack to see a transformed beauty, dressed
in a pristine uniform, a smartly looking makeup, a name tag, that

read, "Brian's, for her to say, "Come in Mister Cash, this won't be long, I need you to fill out some forms, while you're a guest on this base, come in?" Jack walked in, to a spacious office, a huge desk, two comfortable chairs, for her to say, "Have a seat."

Jack obliges, sits on the edge, as she pushes up the documents, to say, "Sign your name at the X, and you'll be official.

Jack read slowly, then pulled out his phone, he scanned the phone over the first page, to hear, 'Wait what are you doing?"

"Making a quick copy, to translate what you're having me sign, so far it all seems to be in order."

She sees the gun butt, and backs away, as he went over the rest of the documents, to see that the phone summarized the documents, to say, "They seem to be in order, there is a lot of responsibility here."

"After signing this, I'll give you an official military ID, to use as you see fit, on any base in the world, let alone, there is a code that renews itself every minute, something to do with GPS and the spy satellite, you use it to authenticate your position and needs, whatever that may be?", she said with a smile. Just then the door opened without noticed and Jack turned to see it was the mean looking girl from the fights, who like Brian's she was dressed up, and with a smartly face covering, to say, "Sorry, I didn't know you had company?"

"Instantly Jack realized what was going on, as GOODS, moved around to face her partner, to say, "When do you think you'll be done with the VIP?" smugly.

"Soon, I need to give him a few things, could you wait outside, and this is top secret and private."

"Yes Ma'am", she said in a huff, and left the room, for Brian's, to go to the door, and she locked it down, to say, "Now we have some privacy."

Jack was looking at her, as she began to unbutton her outer Jacket, she took that off, to say, "Isn't it getting hot in here?", for Jack to see that she wore a white blouse, buttoned up to her neck with a bow tie, she took off, she took a seat on the edge of the desk, to begin to unbutton, he blouse, he saw she was sweating a bit, had formed, even with the room being air conditioned, she went down to open it up, and pulled it off, to say, "What do you think?"

Jack looked over at her, as he finished signing the documents, to see, she had just popped off her creamy white bra, to expose her lovely looking breasts, huge nipples, she grasped them to show him, to say, "I think they need some attention."

With that Jack sprung into action, and smothered his face between her breasts, as he pulled her towards him, in the chair, her skirt was hiked up, as she straddled him, she allowed him to pleasure her, all the while she was feeling his manhood rising, and she was benefiting from it.

She pulled back a bit, to lift off her skirt, to show him, she wore no underwear.

She grinded on him, while holding onto the chairs tall arm rests. Jack was trying to undo his trousers to allow it to play, in between her strokes, he undid them, and tried with both hands to force them down, till it sprang up, she was far but right as she continued the pace, as she continued to smash into it, rather than slow, to allow him to enter her, as Jack was trying to stop what she was doing, for her to say, "No, No, No, I'm not going to allow you to put that huge thing in, you can stop right there, besides my girlfriend won't be too happy knowing I screwed you without her."

"So call her up and have her join us." she stopped realizing it wasn't really working for her now. She eased back off of him, seeing it had turned a color of blue, to say, 'Did I bruise you? I'm sorry. She backed off, to see it bobbing, she was up against the desk, looking at Jack, who said, "That's it, look what you did to me, why did you do that?"

"I was just playing around, besides you get to see me naked and touch my breasts."

Jack pulled up his trousers painfully, to realize it was time to go.

"Wait, I need to give you, your card." she said getting redressed, partway, to see Jack wasn't happy, she didn't care, but said, "Do you think you'll come to the finals tonight?"

"Why", said Jack in still somewhat of pain, trying to get it to go down.

"I'll be fighting my girlfriend, and then I'll ask her to join us" "No thanks, I'll be sure to skip that."

"Wait, what are you mad, over this?" I was just teasing you, you know give you a show, to build up for tonight." "Nice try, but it didn't work,"

"What will work?"

Jack looked at her, to see that she got to him, but she was right, she played a game, and now it was his time, to decide what to do, as she came to him, to allow him to place his hand between her legs, she was moving back and forth, to say, "You're the spy, do what you want to me, just be gentle, I'm still a virgin technically."

Jack hesitated, then he let go. "NO, no, no, you can have me honestly, I was just playing around, she showed him as she dropped her clothes, to say, "Take me anyway you want, from the front, from the back, on the side, which will it be?"

"Nothing, said Jack looking at her, as the tears were streaming down her face. He just stood there watching her cry, from the rejection, he gave her, she calmed down long enough to say," Are you just waiting for your card?"

"Yeah, how long will it take?", he had his hand on the butt of his weapon, which she knew he wasn't playing around anymore, she got up off the floor, a bit embarrassed, she began to dress as Jack waited, not really even looking at her, she buttoned up, slid on her skirt, she went over to her bookcase, while Jack had her back to him, she pulled a gun, took it, and fired off a shot.

Jack dove forward, as the bullet lodged into the wall, he turned to see the she devil coming at him, gun training on him, and she fired as each bullet went to his heart. She was screaming at him, "Die you son of a bitch." she stood over him, emptying out her gun, she smiled at him, he smiled back at her, when the huge doors were broken open, and Military police stormed her. Jack lay back, as they subdued her, and took her away. Jack said "'Hey what about my card?"

Incoherently she said,"Why isn't he dead, I shot him, he should be dead."

Special agents helped Jack up, to see Jack wipe off the four bullets, for the agent Jack recognized immediately, it was GOODS, and she was nice and caring, to say,"That is why I came up here, to see if you were alright, you must be superman, taking all these bullets"

"It's a first for me too, I had no idea either."

"Come here, let me check you out", and say, "I have been monitoring her behavior for some time, we suspect she is on the other side."

"What side?" asked Jack, as another agent, hands Jack his special code card, to say, "Looks like she was doing her job correctly, but how much does she know?"

"For as much as I know, a very limited amount, especially since I put a restriction on her level of access." said Good's.

That your real name?" "What about Jack Cash?"

"Watch it, don't be disrespectful." "Sorry, looks like your fine, literally."

CH 5

The vortex of water

Jack made it back to his boat, realizing he needed to stay on his boat, to keep away from trouble.

The commander issued a rescue swimmer to help out Jack. He sent along another kit, and since that incident occurred, there is a new attitude at the base, and all of the Coast Guard, pre screened psyche evaluations. The Parthian Stranger was parked in a slip, rented, till Jack came back, and Mark presented Jack with the total caught, Jack looked at it, to see it read, 1.2 million dollars placed on his card, for Jack to say," Are we all set to go back out?"

"Yes, were still waiting on Blythe to get back?"

"Well if she isn't here in", he turns to hear, "I'm right here I was in the galley."

Jack turned to see she was beaming, as she was trying to hold him, he allowed her to embrace him, to whisper, "Sorry I missed you earlier, why don't we go to your cabin and I'll make it up to you?" Jack nodded his head, and said out loud, "Alright, let's go, for Jack, allowed her to go, and Jack said, to Mark, "Cast off the lines, and let's get out to that site, tomorrow morning I have a wedding to attend."

"Will do Captain", said Mark, to use the intercom, to announce, "Mike, Jim cast off lines, he switched the radio frequency, to the port authority and let them know they were leaving, to back to Mobile, and then to the Coast Guard, and to the Commander, who told Mark, that they would mirror the Parthian Stranger, while they were in the Valdez Reef, and on the ship the Jupiter.

Jack was led to his cabin, by an eager, Blythe, when Jack was interrupted by, a hulking figure, He stepped out to block Jack's progress, to say, "Do you have a moment, Mister Cash?"

"Yeah, and motions to Blythe, to say, "I'll catch up with you in a minute. then looks at the guy, to say, "What do you have?"

"Well we have a problem, half of the people suppose to be on this dive are not dive certified?"

Jack just looked at him, then, he said, "Sorry."

"Sorry for what, you're here, so certify them, how hard is that?"

"It's not that easy?" said the guy.

"Sure and neither is my job, were not going to spend ten hours in a dive tank to acclimated these that are not certified, either train them till we get there or you're not going, do you understand me, Am I one, on your list?"

"No, well actually, your different, you can do whatever you want."

"Sounds like you disapprove of me?"

"No, I just want to make sure your safe?"

"Alright you convinced me, let's go up onto the stern and you teach us."

"Thank you," he said excitedly.

Jack looked at him to say, "Who's all on that list?"

"Mike Adams, Brian Burns, Blythe Serratti, and you Jack Cash."

"Alright I'll go get Blythe will you round up the others." "Yes, Sir", Jack continues on, to his cabin, when he waits then opens the door, to see Blythe, laid out on the bed, naked, for Jack to step in, close the door, he came to her, he felt her firm leg as he traced it up, to say, "You have a mighty fine physique?"

"I know, and it's all here for you now, give me a strip show, she said eagerly.

Jack put his hands up to say,"Fraid not, you need to get dressed." "What why, I've been waiting all day for you", she said getting up, re dressing, in front of him, to say, "Why the change of heart?"

"Simple, it's all for the sake of safety."

"Safety I'll be gentle with you, I'll even turn and you can do me doggie style, if you like."

"Really, I'd love to, as you can probably tell."

She came close to him, to touch him to say, "Let's knock out a quickie?"

"I'd love to", said Jack when a voice outside the door, yelled out, "We're ready and waiting on you guys, are you coming?"

"Sure, give me a minute", said Jack pushing away to the bed, he opened the door, for the guy to peer in to see Blythe topless for her to say, "Jack, how about some privacy please," trying to cover back up, for Jack to say, "You better hurry up, I don't want you to be late."

Jack followed the guy onto the deck in the stern, where Mike and Brian were at holding gear, the jet ski instructor, Caroline, Rob the builder, Carlos and some of his girls were watching, then Jack saw her the blonde, GOODS was her name, for her to smile, but more to his attention was the huge Cutter following them, for Jack to say,"

What are they doing?"

"There our backup, and afterwards, my ride home, unless you want me to join your team?" said the guy.

"No, thanks", said Jack, to announce, as he sees Blythe dressed better than she was, "I'm thinking of not going at all, you guys have fun.", Jack went for the cabin door, when the Guy cut him off, to say, "Your missing out on a great opportunity?", Jack looked at him, to say, "You don't know me."

"I know when we get there; you'll be intrigued on jumping in."

Jack just looked at him, not really wanting to be there, and his annoying voice was making it even worse, but resigned himself, to wait, he rejoined the rest, as the Guy, said his name was Tony, Carpenter, certified rescue swimmer, he went over the rules and what not to do, all the while, Stephanie was moving closer and closer to Jack, who was kind of getting into the instruction, not thinking of throwing him over, and when they were through, Tony announced, "Your all certified, now, when we dive, if you stay down past the hour, your qualified, anytime before that you're a non-qualifier, understand, now pair up", he waved his hands, to say, "He is with me, maybe you too girls could pair up, he leans into Blythe to say, "You have a nice pair of tits, say you and I go around, what do you say?"

"Leave her alone, you better watch your back, I may knife you myself?" said Stephanie, who agreed to take Blythe, who said, "Thanks, I could have defended myself."

"You know you really do have a nice set of breasts." "So do you, wanna go play?" asked Blythe.

"Sure, after this is over, said Stephanie.

The boat slowed, as it was coming to the tidal pools, the boat was turning under the force, as Mark, guided it around, the crew was at the rail, seeing the blue circular water, for each pool, the Cutter, was behind them, as Mark piloted it, around the small ones, to a spot, on the outskirts of the larger one, for everyone to hear, "Alright folks were here, don your wet suits, and grab your gear, we'll be at the bow, to jump in." said Tony, already changed and ready. Everyone else went below to change.

Stephanie was with Blythe, Jack finished quickly, with the help of Brian, he zipped up, Jack went up, grabbed his gear, and went forward, with Brian, on the bow, was some weapons laid out for Tony to say, "Each of you, take a knife, strap it to your lower leg, next is a bag, tie it to your weight belt, down in the vortex is the sunken ship, whatever you find, put it in the bag, there are four teams of two, one will collect and the other will spot, as I said before there is danger down there, watch for the sharks, both Caroline and myself will have a harpoon, take about thirty minutes and then switch, any questions?"

There was none, as those together, assembled together, for Tony to say, "Alright I got the all clear, there is no movement down below", Jack stepped up, to say, "Where is Mark, he was the one who suggested we do this in the first place?"

"He was told; he needed to be at the wheel." "Trade him out with you."

"Sorry Mister Cash, he has been instructed by the Commander, to stay at the wheel, now, if you want to do a second dive, he can come along."

"Alright that is fine then, let me tell him?" asked Jack. "He already knows did you get that Mark?" said Tony. "Loud and clear", said Mark as he waved down to Jack. "Any more interruptions,?, No, alright, first up, Is Caroline", he looked her up and down and smiled, as she positioned herself, on the front, mask on, and held it as she jumped for the opening, she hit perfectly, to spin and fight her way down, she sunk quickly, next was her love interest and partner was the builder, Rob, he was a old hand and moved away and down. Next was the two wild cards, Mike and Brian, then Stephanie and Blythe, lastly it was Jack's turn, still listening to Tony, say, "Off to the right, and swim to the dark blue, there are pearl oysters, use your knife, to scrap them off of the reef."

"Alright enough, shut up" said Jack as he jumped in, to the center, instantly the water was warm, he was on his way down, instantly Jack forgot about Tony, to realize it was all worth the wait, surrounding him was a wall of continuous water, moving at ten miles an hour or so, all the way down, twenty or thirty feet, up to the reef beds, to the east, a reef bridge to the north, behind him was the wall, it was a hole, no way out, but that wasn't his immediate worry, Jack thought about the pearls, so he went to the reef, pulled his knife, and as he used his fins to propel himself, steady, he was harvesting, every other one, to take what was needed, thirty in all. Jack then went deeper, where Caroline and Rob were at the Ship wreck, she held onto the railing, while he was visible on the deck, as Jack swims to them, Caroline points down, where Jack sees a hold, inside was Stephanie and Blythe, Blythe was collecting gold coins, from a treasure chest, Jack stayed away from them to further swim to the north, down the stairs down to see the boys, Mike and Brian, collecting hand guns, Jack see a giant hole where the reef took the ship out, and went through it to the bottom, where a colossal field of giant clams were at, Jack was on the bottom, he tried to lift, one to break it free, when Tony grabbed his arm to signal, "No, a net, and we will extract them, okay?"

Jack shook his head, only to see a predator, swimming freely, on the bottom, a huge shark, great white, it swam with intentions, as Tony had mentioned, Great Whites patrol the bottom, as it is natural, just freeze, and don't react, it will pass right by, as it doesn't like the vortex, and it's not difficult for it to pass through, especially if someone had drowned. Jack waited patiently, for it to pass, as he saw the clam open up, and tried to clamp down on his hand, luckily, he pulled it out, and swam up, to the boat, that was anchored in the stern and up in the bow, so Jack swam back in, with Tony trailing, thinking he isn't that bad of a guy. Jack past the boys, still going through, cabinets, to the stern he went, through a door, then another one as he went further to the stern he went, meanwhile, at the first door, Tony stopped, closed the door, and used a piece of bailing wire, to secure it, as he checked his time, to see the boys, to mention, "Time to go up."

Jack got to the stern, it was the stores hold, to look around, he saw his watch, he set it to count down, first to alarm the dive was near to the end, then the other one was air supply, he went back through the doors, to the outside one, tried it, it was secure, looking around, at some windows, to small, he went over his options, and went back to the window, took off his fins, to steady himself, he picked up a hammer, and busted it out, enough to remove the kit off his back, he pushed it through, along with the fins, then himself, and to the bottom, to retrieve the breather, and slip on the fins, he swam upwards, to see Tony, helping those, to be lifted out of the water, next up was Jack, as A Coast Guard, safety ring, weighted down, hit the water, he grabbed it, and up he went, swung around, and onto the deck, Jack let go, it worked Just like Tony said it would, as he was last to leave the water, to meet up with them. Jack removed his mask, and kit, and fins, as the treasures were in separate piles, for Tony to say,"Alright, we will refill the tanks, Jack did you want to go again?"

"Sure, are we going to collect some of those giant Clams?" "Yes, and there is also a lair of lobsters under the ship, so it will be you, your pilot Mark, Tony saw, Caroline, said she would help, as did Rob, respectfully, supporting Jack, who had been very kind to him, helped him with his suit, Mike raised his hand, to say, "I'll help Jack, how many do you think we can harvest?"

"Oh, there about several thousand, so probably ten or so, their heavy, and stir up a lot of sand, we'll probably need spotters, not so much muscle power."

Jack agreed, to say, 'We'll let Mark do his collecting, Jack sees him, after Brian had relieved him, to say, "Let me change and I'll be ready."

Jack saw the different stuff, and piles, to say, "So why don't we set up a rescue of the contents of the ship?"

"Sorry, it doesn't work like that, there is already a claim on it, everything that was pulled off from the wreck, will go somewhere, like a museum, or back to Spain, something, I'll see to it, that your friends will get is the cash value of what they collected, see the lighthouse, they oversee the wreck, and report any ship that is here, and then we, the Coast Guard, come and get them out of here." Jack nodded, he understood, waited for Mark to reappear, along with Tony, for Jack to think,"Yeah, maybe, I'll bring him aboard, he really isn't that bad of a guy, as he went up to the wheel house, to see Jim, who was on the crane, to say,"Can I fire my gun under the water, or will it shock me?"

"Neither, it is waterproof, and yes the bullet will go, but at about half, it will electrify anyone who still touches it, but it will turn black, as it likes to be warm."

"Alright so what do you have that I can use under the water?"

"Well right now, just the spear, but I do have a Co2 cartridge that I can add for more power, do you want it now?" "Sure if you don't mind, better safe than sorry."

Jack saw Brian to say," You know you can't keep your find?"

"Yeah, I remember what Tony said, about the treasures, but it was nice, find right?"

"Sure, why didn't you go after the pearls?" asked Jack. "What pearls, nobody said anything about that, oh well, did you get some?"

"Yeah, about thirty."

"Let me see, ah, that's cool man, what are you planning to do with them?"

"Oh make a necklace for Sara." "Nice, and of the oysters?"

"Well have them on our wedding night."

Brian shook his head, to say, "Yeah, you were asking about a gun that fires below water, you know in that huge catalog I let you look at, well there was a whole section on high pressurized pistols, when we get back, or better yet, you can use your phone, to order, anything custom, just look it up." Said Brian.

Jack looks at him, to say, "Do you see me carrying a book around?" "Well no."

"Hold on, why don't you look it up, then suggests a few for me and I'll get them, or tell Jim."

"Well, it's really not his expertise."

"What are you saying; I thought he was the gadgets guy?" "No, that is what you're saying, he really was a former spy, retired, and Lisa needed to make sure you had, some help, so be careful, he may not always have your best interests in mind."

"Thanks for the info, have you seen Tami?"

He points down, for Jack to see on the bow, lounge chair; she was getting a tan, still wearing a bikini.

Jack sees the Cutter, had a huge net they were going to use, and sent it over by cable to cable transfer, once on board, the cable was released, and the net was gathered, as it was attached to the crane hook. Jack and the others were ready for a return visit, while Jack had his oysters on ice, he wanted to be first in, and he dove in feet first and quickly over to the oyster bed.

Next up was Caroline, and Rob, then Mike and Mark, who expressed he wanted to go survey and take pictures of the dive, he sported a sophisticated camera, around his neck, whereas, Tony, had him stow it, in his bag, as he explained, so it wouldn't choke him on impact.

With the five in, Tony was last, as Brian, eased up on the throttle, of the boat, to be forced back, against the current, to stay on the outer edge of the marker, and looking at his sonar, to see more than the six small figures in the water, but seven larger one, as he clicked on the radio, to say, "Tony, this is Brian, you got company."

Tony, treaded water, as he took the huge net, and held it with Caroline and Rob, as he unhooked it, and let it go to the bottom, nearly missing the sunken ship, he looked down and saw a school of sharks that had breached the water wall, which had actually slowed, octopuses, stingray's and a sturgeon, was present, instantly, Tony knew he was in danger, as Rob and Caroline, went to the bottom, Mike and Mark at the ship, and Jack, "Where the hell did he go?" wondered Tony.

Tony watched as a huge mother shark, swam past him, as he waved Caroline, up, but she and Rob had their own problems, as, the school, was in and around them, they were sand sharks, burrowers by choice, but have known to nip, at the ankles, not bite, they were collecting every other clam, and going about their business.

Meanwhile Jack found his own bonanza, dark oyster shells, he opened one to see a black pearl, he put that in his bag, to collect thirty of them, he turned around as he felt something brush his back, he turned, to feel the pictorial fin, to see a huge great white shark, he hugged the reef, as he was inching up the spear, and still holding the knife, below him was Tony in the open, and behind him was Mark and Mike, ready to move, the shark did a figure eight, and Jack was the curve, each time the shark was getting further away, with the flick of its tail, then it saw movement down below, and made a beeline to Caroline, Rob saw it first, and lifted up the huge clam, and pushed it right before impact, and the shark, with its mouth open, took the whole thing, swung around, to knock Rob over, and hit Caroline in the head, with its fin, she immediately went limp, as she was dangling, as she was face first down, it was Mike and Mark, to her rescue, Rob, was still in a sitting position.

Jack knew this needed to be taken care of now, immediately, but before he moved, it was Tony, who took it on, as it was thrashing around with that giant clam, that was lodged in its cavity, Mike was down helping Caroline, and Mark was with Rob, they were going up, Jack swam off to position himself from the others and the shark, with his spear ready, and cocked, the others swam up to the surface.

Jack was ready, as the shark finally got that clam out, and it was angry, as it was coming for Tony, ready, with his spear, Jack was trying to motion for him to get out of there, it was hopeless, as it hit with such a force, it took, him to his shoulders, Jack was on the move, and fired his spear, it hit its side, with such a force, it opened up, and expelled, Tony, blood was in the water now, and to the attention of the sand sharks, where a frenzy was happening, and Tony was the recipient, as Jack swooped in, with knife, in hand, and sliced, the great whites underbelly, letting out her contents a mess of baby great whites, as her last ditched effort was to go down, to where Tony was swimming for his life, and in that instant he was a paraplegic, both legs were missing, as he was done for another pass, when Jack was on top of it, and stabbed it in the eye, and sent it down to the bottom to the sand sharks, as he had Tony by the arm, and was hoisting him up to the surface, where Jack, hooked Tony up, and away he went, frantic action was going on that they forgot to set the crane back for Jack, so Jack saw the bag down below, and shook his head, and decided to spin, his watch, and then sent out the wire, it raced down to the bottom, it hit the net, and he began to winch it up, it came up easily, all the while he thought, "I wonder if I can get some more oysters, when Mike had secure Tony, to say, "Get Jack out of the water?"

Frantically, motioned for Jim, to turn and set the hook, over Jack's position, just as the water started back up, like a washing machine, as he now held the net, by himself, till the hook was lowered, Jack caught it, then he hooked it up, and unhooked himself, he held on, and they were extracted up and out of the water.

As the net was lowered down, Mike had placed a tarp over Tony, as Jack got off, to unhook his watch, to say, 'how's Tony?" "He is bad, he is gone."

Some had wept, others visibly had tears, Brian, the skipper now, led as the Cutter, followed, and both were heading back to New Port Richey. There was movement, under the tarp, as Jack went to him, pulled the tarp, to help out, only to see it was nerves finally expiring, to say, "You died valiantly I will miss you, and yes, I'd have had you on any of my crews."

Jack stood, and began to drop the kit, and escape from the wet suit, with the new oysters secure, In a hold, he went to his cabin, to get cleaned up, he reached his door, to hear,"Captain, just reporting, said Brian, who allowed Mark to take over, to say,"Both Caroline and Rob, will be alright, but Tony was terminal."

"Thank you for the report, I'll be resting now. Jack opened the door, to see, both Stephanie and Blythe, naked, arms in arms kissing each other for Blythe to say, "What took you so long Captain, we both need attention."

Jack stripped. To show he was ready, and dove in between them, much to their excitement, separating, them, as he was the middle to their sandwich, he was on Stephanie, while Blythe, helped her by playing with her boobs, Jack was at her crotch lapping up her clitoris, while she had her hands on his head, she erupted easily, and began to pant, which signaled Jack and he rose up, placed on protection, and forced his way in, there was some resistance, but then it just went in, and he was doing all the thrusting, all the while Blythe was watching, realizing that, Jack pulled back, and motioned for Blythe to get on top, she did, and he reentered Stephanie who was in ecstasy and Blythe was worried, an right so, Jack had his fingers in there and it was tight, barely able to get one in, he was five times that, so he fingered her to orgasm, over and over again, till they both let out, but Jack wasn't done by a long mile, he wasn't even concentrating on that, as he kept on drilling, as Stephanie just took it, orgasm, after the other, and soon, even Blythe felt left out, she watched a bit, then left, as Jack got creative, turning Stephanie around, from behind, to having her on top, to finally, a good rhythm was being paced, she was loving the groove, as was he, she had a clamp down on him, she was actually prolonging the session, as the intimacy was gone, and now it was like a sport, for her to say, "It's about time, I met my match."

"How so" replied Jack.

"Me and my old boyfriend we could go for hours, every which way, and from the looks of it, so could you, but from the view, were back in port, so finish up and drop your load, maybe you and I could do this again?"

She let go of the pressure, and Jack was ready to release, and he did, it was an explosion, like a fountain, as she was now feeling it, to say, 'I'll take what you have left", she got off of it, and took off the protection, to suck it dry, she finished to say,"you sure have a lot, you're a mess, wanna take a shower together?"

"Sure, let's go". Said Jack, smiling.

The boat followed the Cutter in, docked and tied off; Jack was waiting as the Commander came aboard. It was a solemn time, as Tony lay covered up, as the coroner, entered, checked over the body, his team bagged him up, and was set on a gurney. CGIT (Coast Guard investigative team), took all the statements, especially that of Rob and Caroline, Then Mark and Mike, Jack was last, to tell of his story, however the female, named Peyton, wasn't convinced Jack was telling the truth, and pressed him with more questions, till the commander stepped in, to say, "Enough Lieutenant, he did nothing wrong."

"Well I'll be the judge of that, Commander, I may request an inquiry?"

"On whose authority?"

"I don't need yours, I'll call the Commanding General, he'll order it, things don't add up?"

"Like what asked the Commander?" honestly.

"Well, why was Jack at the reef and the others at the bottom?"

"And if it was like they said, they were told to be with their partner, and all of the eye witnesses expressly said, Tony was all by himself, Jack was no where around?"

"Was it deliberate or pre meditated?, there are so many more answers to be had, like if you were to ask me about Erica Brains, what she had been here what eighteen months and then he shows up and goes crazy, No Commander something is up and I say we hold him and get to the bottom of all of this."

"Hold on Lieutenant, this is rough waters ahead, He has Presidential orders and were here to help him."

"That maybe true, I'm telling you this guy has a secret, and I wanna find out what it is."

"Alright, I agree with you, on Erica, I'll invite him to stay the night, and that will get you at least 12 hours, good luck."

"Sorry I won't need it, he will pay one way or another, as she made a call, for body pick up, and left the deck looking and staring at Jack, as another man, a harden one, with a cigar, came on deck, with a mean look, as she stumbled, and went down. To hear,"Is everything alright?" said Carlos offering her a hand. She saw he was carrying a pistol, he didn't try to conceal it, as she got up, looked back and said, out loud,"Someone will pay for Tony's death." The commander approach those two to say,"So Jack can you stay the night?"

Jack looks everything over, to say,"You said I had your resources at my disposal?"

"Yes, what were you thinking?"

"I have a wedding to be part of tomorrow morning; I need a ride, say 06 hundred."

"We can do that, where to?" "Mobile."

"Sure I'll go set it up, I can actually do one better how about a helicopter, right to the wedding, or nearest to it, do you have the co-ordinances?"

"I'll text them to you." Said Jack.

"Sure, so for the time being, why don't you be my guest, and bring your crew, and enjoy the Smokers, and we'll have a celebration in Tony's honor."

"Yeah, that's fine with me," said Jack, to add, "I'll let the boys and girls know", Carlos grabs Jack arm to say,"I'll go with you brother, you don't mind, do you Commander?"

The Commander looked over at the killer, took a gulp, and then said, "No not at all, any guest of Jack's is welcome by us."

"I'm not a guest, I'm his brother", said Carlos, with his mean looking eyes, as he took a drag of his Cuban cigar, and blew it out on the Commander, knowing the Commander was up to something, and it had to do with that Lieutenant, and Carlos knew it. Carlos followed Jack in to the cabin, while the Commander was on the phone as he stepped off.

Jack slid his phone open, and dialed Lisa answered, for Jack to say,"I'm on to something, or some lady didn't get the memo?"

"Alright, I'll make a call to her, who is it?"

"Don't bother, I'm staying here till morning then flying back, be there for the Wedding."

"Alright, I can send help, or?" "Amnesty for my Brother?"

"He is there now, with you?" inquired Lisa.

"Yeah, the Commander and his first Lieutenant saw him, and I'm sure they are calling you?"

"What do you want me to tell them?"

"Place him under the protection of diplomatic immunity, specific to me."

"Alright, done as we speak, keep me informed, anything you need, you got that?"

"Yeah, phone or missile?"

"Which ever, if it's the ladder, I'll be there myself, besides I have Erica Brains to question, anything else?"

"Yeah, how much do you think black pearls are worth?" asked Jack?

"Why do you ask, their rare, is all I know." "I may have thirty?"

"Seriously, then there priceless."

"Really, I wonder, I just dove down to the Jupiter, sunken ship off Florida and recovered some pistols and coins, are they mine to keep?"

"Yes, everything you find or recover, who's saying otherwise?"

"Oh someone not here now" said Jack wondering.

"Well you can tell that person they are mistaken, don't fret, I'll be down there tonight, and we'll fly out together, understand?"

"Yeah, but wait till I discover what is going on." said Jack, as him and Carlos got off the boat, where a jeep waited for them, they were taken to the Commander's house. Juan meets them at the door, to say,"Come in and share a meal with us", he said with his hand open, as Jack is in first followed by Carlos. A beautiful lady was present holding a serving tray; she smiled upon seeing Jack then the mean looking Carlos, not so much so.

Jack took a seat, as Carlos sat next to him, while the lady said,

"Sorry about my husband he is rude, she extends her hand to say,

"My name is Lalaine, she added, I need to go change for dinner, we you please enjoy some lemonade and some finger sandwiches." She left in a hurry, as the Commander was on the phone, he put the phone up to say, "A Commander's job is never done, to add,

"Were trying to keep it from Miss Carpenter that her husband has past, she is sure a loose cannon."

"That doesn't sound like any woman I know?" said Carlos sampling Lalaine's offerings.

"That nice of you to say, said the Commander, to add,"So how long have you two been brothers?"

Jack looked at him in between bites, as Carlos looks at him to say,

"Do you have an ashtray, or shall I use this plate?"

"Well actually we rather you not smoke at all" said the Commander.

"Well that's not very hospitable, you invite us over and what you limit what we do, alright, and he hesitated, and then said, I'll be watching you."

The Commander was still waiting the answer, for Carlos to look at Jack then back at Juan to say, "Forever, and ever, till the end, forever, why do you ask?" said Carlos staring at him now, his light jacket was open, to show him his gun, he saw it. The Commander was getting nervous and began to sweat, he stood up, at the instant he received a call, to began to swear, he spoke in Spanish, which Carlos interpreted for Jack, who was already ahead of him, by using his phone, it said, "Meet me at the docks, in a hour, we need to process the body."

The Commander, slid his phone shut, turned around to say,"I'll need to be going, where is Lalaine, and that damn dinner."

"What's his problem, he sure is stressed" said Carlos, who dropped his sandwich, to see Mrs. Alvarez, Lalaine, had seriously changed, into a very revealing blouse, and skirt, beautifully dressed, Carlos was jabbing Jack in the ribs, while he was eating, he looked up to see her, to say, "Wow, your dressed up."

She leaned over, to say,"Shall I pour you another glass of wine?" her shirt was open for Jack to get a good look, while Carlos held his glass up, and waited, waited, before he realized he was going to have to pour it himself, as Lalaine, pulled back and smiled, as she went into the kitchen, for Carlos to say, "I think she likes you?"

"Yeah, so what, she is a dime a dozen", said Jack finishing off the delicious sandwiches.

"Yeah, but she is into you, if you're not going to jump on that I will? Spoke Carlos proudly.

The Commander was pacing around, too impatient to sit down, for him to say,"I don't think I can stay for dinner, do you mind I need to go to the docks to process Tony's body."

"Sure, said Jack getting up to say, "I'll go with you, looking over at Carlos who was ready, he even cracked his knuckles, to show he was ready. The Commander looked at Jack to say, "Alright, but not you, I'll take your brother, come Carlos."

Carlos looked at Jack, then shrugged to say, "Alright, can I say goodbye to the misses?" he looked over at the Commander, who saw his wife, for him to say,"Honey, Carlos and I need to go, he would like to say goodbye."

"Goodbye Mister Carlos," she said as she waved and went back in the kitchen, as Carlos slowly waved goodbye, for the Commander to say,"Jack, you'll escort my wife to the smokers later?"

"Sure", said Jack finishing off the glass, and trying to reach for the bottle, when he heard the door slam shut, and Lalaine standing there with two plates, for her to say,"Too bad for them, here is a plate of food, she sets it down, as Jack really saw that she wore no bra, and her boobs were well exposed as she bent down to deliver the plate. "More wine Jack?" She asked.

"Sure," he said devouring the plate, having waved his hand with the watch over it, she looked at him to say, "When Juan told me, that it was you, I asked him if you could come over so that I may meet you myself."

"Yes, and what do you think?" asked Jack.

"Well I want you to know, that our family appreciates what you did in Arkansas, and I want to personally thank you for your role in saving my sister's life?" she touched his hand with hers, as she began to rub it, as she worked it to place her finger, in between his thumb and forefinger, she moved it in and out, for Jack to say, "This is good, I especially love the mashed potatoes, are there some cheese in them?"

"Yes, as I was saying, I asked my husband if it were alright if I allowed you to screw me tonight what do you think?" she said honestly.

Jack kept on eating, as though he never heard the request, for her to hold is left hand firmly, for him to say, "Now you're hurting me, I don't know what games your playing, but I have to be a little safer." "I'm giving it to you, how much plainer do I have to make it?"

"Its damn if I do and it's damn if I don't is that it?" asked Jack.

"It's really no big deal, really, I bend over and you stick your big dick inside of me, how much plainer is that?" asked Lalaine. "But why are you doing all of this?"

"I told you, you saved my sister from sheer torture and a life abroad, and for that we owe you something?" "Why do you think all I want is your body?"

"Because of your reputation, so here it is, I know you like it a long time, so we have four hours, is that enough time?"

Jack stops eating to say,"Wait, are you good friends with Stephanie?"

"Well as a matter of fact, we are, and yes she did text me all the details, and I can show you I do have stamina, it has to be longer than five minutes."

Jack stood up and walked around, to say, "Alright let's see you do a strip tease, and then we'll get started. Jack took a seat, to say,

"Let it begin, she turned on the music, and closed her eyes and began to dance, and slowly unbuttoned her loose blouse, and allowed it to fall away, exposing her really big breasts, large areolas and huge erect nipples, she was playing around with them, when all of a sudden, the screen door creaked open, and the front door, swung open, and in a flash, she ran out of that living room, with her breasts in hand.

Jack waved at the Commander, who said, "I forgot my briefcase, Sorry", he went over to pick it up, to say, "Sorry again, say Sorry to Lalaine I'll see you both tonight?"

"Wait up, I'll go with you," said Jack as he was at the door, and closed it behind him.

The Commander got off of the phone, detailing to his wife of their plans, and to apologies for the interruption, as she was screaming at him back, about something her brother was going to do to him, or something, as the Commander dropped both Jack and Carlos off at the Hanger, to say, I need to go to my office, I'll meet you both back here in a hour."

Jack and Carlos waved him off, to go inside, Jack led Carlos to where he sat before, they took their seats, to see a beautiful sharply dressed woman, familiar to Jack, it was Stephanie Goods, who smile at both of them, only to see another girl, a blonde, who spoke up to say, "And I'm Bridgett, who stood at the other desk. For her to say, "So you had a chance to satisfy my friend, Lalaine, allow me have your hand, as she took it, she guided between her legs, for Jack to feel her wetness, as she wore no panties, for her to say, "You'll get your chance to redeem yourself, later, lover, she back away from Jack, to hear the Stephanie cry out, say, "Stay away from her, she is dangerous." she said in a jokingly manner.

"Who", said Jack.

"That one over there", she said with a smile on her face. "Now to redeem yourself, you got five minutes, meet me upstairs in room 3, just knock, then come in and take off all your clothes and you'll have a surprise waiting for you" said Stephanie quietly, as she left. Which left Bridgett to keep Carlos entertained, much to his liking.

The Commander made it back to his office, when he made a call to Jeremy, to say, "Are you ready?", then waited to say, We will tell her of her husband and let her do the rest, I know he was a great friend to me too, Jack Cash will pay for his death. Just then a call came in, that was more urgent than his current one, he answered it, he listened, and nodded, to say, "Yes sir", several times, then he said "Sorry."

The line went dead, as the Commander, sat down, in his chair in his office, he looked around, tears were flowing down his face, he was somber, realizing he had made a colossal mistake, he knew he was playing a game with Jack Cash, however he had no idea, the strength that Jack had, nor who he knew, nor what he just heard, was the last thing he thought would happen, has, he was told as of that moment he was relieved of all duties, per the order of the President, through the Commanding General, for not obeying the order, as prescribed and to allow a subordinate to accuse Jack Cash of Murder and conspiracy, he is the President's voice on all matters, he knew his career was over. He went to his safe, did the combination, it unlocked, he opened it, and pulled out cash, and his hand gun, pulled out the glock, loaded it, and heard some noises, then, another phone call came in, it was Lieutenant Reilly, who said,"Commander it is done, they said there sending a special prosecutor and that it would be, for me?", she said in her proud voice. The Commander nodded, to say, "Good luck", hit the button to end the call, as he saw Military police was at his door, for them to say, "Commander Juan Alverez your under arrest by order of the President of the United States, said one of them holding the official order. Two shots rang out, and the two military policemen went down, and the Commander was off.

"That was rude", said Peyton as the line went dead. She had a smirk on her face, typing the correspondence, to receive a call on her personal cell phone; she looked at it, and then answered it to say, "What Jeremy, do you want?"

"Get out of there now, the whole base is under" . . . .

The line went dead, as she continued to type, when a knock on her door, she yelled its open?"

The door opened, for her to see a Captain, in full dress blues uniform to say,

"Miss you're in trouble you have to get out of here now?" "On whose authority?" said Peyton Reily.

The Captain pulled his Mac10, to show her, to say,"Your minutes away, you want out?"

She looks at him, then says, "Alright I'll play along with you as she gets her lap top, and places in her bag, to hear him say, "Their closing in, we need to go now, he swung the gun around, and took the heavy chair, in hand and threw it at the window, it crashed through and so did they, she was cussing, and screaming, till he hit her in the head and she was out.

The Captain, carried her, the rest of the way, to a car, then drove to a boat, put her on it, and slowly, went up the inlet.

Jack, took his cue, and left Carlos for a trip upstairs, to room number 3, he knocked, he went in it was dark, and in that instant he was shoved, the lights came on, as the door shut, stood two women, both nude, Jack, saw it was Stephanie and Lalaine, as Stephanie went to the door, and locked it down, to say, "Lalaine told you once and now I'm telling you twice, strip, were both ready to give you four hours of sport fucking."

Jack smiled and obliged, only to receive a call. As he put his hand up, to slow both women's progress.

Mark, and the rest of the team, said they would continue fishing, and be back tomorrow for the wedding, Mike took it upon his self, to stow all that was collected he discovered the oysters, in Jack's bag, he opened one to see the pearl, he then made a call to Jack to ask, "What was your plan with the pearls?"

"Oh, I don't know, make a necklace for Sara, as a present why do you ask?"

"I can take care of that for you, I've done some jewelry making in the past, and I could make a matching ring, earrings and bracelet?"

Jack allowed Mike to do it, and slid his phone shut, and allowed the women to take down his pants.

On the boat, The Parthian Stranger, Mike announced to Mark,"Detour, let's go to Clearwater, I know a jewelry wholesale shop there."

Mark looked at him, thinking,"I should have been next to Jack's side, but with the over protective Carlos, he knew to back off., he steered the boat downward, into Clearwater.

Back in the Administrative building, on base, Jack and Stephanie were all over it as Lalaine took her turn on Jack's manhood. Lalaine was in ecstasy over how big it really was but took it easily and really enjoyed it as Jack took her from behind, while Stephanie massaged Jack's balls, as he played with her tits, in the background his phone kept ringing.

On the other end of the phone call was the Commander on the move, the Commander met up with Jeremy who was driving towards the hanger, said, "How do you even know he will respond to this call, besides last report we got was he was last seen with Stephanie, so you know what is going on there?"

"Yep, I can't believe he turned down Lalaine, I sure thought it was a sure thing" said the commander using his own wife as bait, telling her some story that it was Jack who saved her sister, where in actual fact it was him. The pair stopped to pick up the Captain, who said, "Yeah, we got over to the hanger and the place was empty, now what?"

"Oh, it's coming Captain, we'll get our man tonight." "What of his brother, Carlos the so called terrorist?"

"He is still public enemy number one, at least you'll get that one" said the Commander to say, "Keep trying, we got to get this working, reinforcements are heading down here as we speak, we may have about three hours tops.

Jack finally collapsed on top of Lalaine, much to his delight and hers, as he was still inside of her pulsating, a smile was over her face, for Stephanie to say, "Listen kids, I have my last fight, against Tony's wife, or ex, whatever, so afterward's, I'll come up here for my round, she was partly dressed to say, "Be sure to lock this door after I go", she left, it clicked shut, as Jack got up, to hear the phone go off again, he picked it up, and then went to the door, to lock it down, then back over to Lalaine, who's legs were spread wide, a gaping hole was present, her head on the mat, he was getting ready again, as he placed on another protection, and slid it back in, and continued to keep on thrusting, to answer the call, he answered it to say, "Yes, this is Jack?"

"Its Military police, Jack, the Commander, is escaped and is out looking for you, can we come to your position?"

"Nah, I'll be at the smoker tonight, and then we can talk. he said in between strokes, thinking, leave this or go see her husband, it weighed on his mind till he spoke up to say, "Listen up, what do you think of me leaving, or shall I just continue what I'm doing?' Jack slide the phone shut.

She was moaning, then let loose, again, to say, "Stay, why do you want to go, I still have two hours to go."

"You got a point there", Jack tosses the phone, and grabs both hips and keeps on going. As Lalaine was screaming with pleasure.

Some time had passed and the Commander was growing impatient, to say, "Awe hell, let's just get over there and all of this ends now."

The Commander and his team, with Jeremy and the Captain, and their military police loaded up and drove over to the boxing matches at the hanger, they entered quietly, as the Commander went to his box, as the military police took position at the doors, then faded in with the others, for the Commander to see it was Stephanie in the ring against a dark black haired girl and Jack was nowhere at the box except Carlos, for which in a instance Military police cuffed him, and with a gun to his back they said, "Make a word and your dead?"

'Where's Jack?" spoke Carlos, getting agitated.

"Don't know, the bathroom?" said one of the men. The Commander orders the others to search the place. Stephanie smiled the whole time to the Commander as she took care of Carla, a hardened tough Latin girl, who had a smug face, went down and was out.

The announcer said the finals would be whoever wins this next fight and Stephanie Goods, in one hour. Jack had really worn out Lalaine, who was now exhausted to say in between gasps, "Stephanie was right, I have no endurance for this, it feels like a semi went through me, I'll walk bull legged for a month." Said Lalaine, feeling good she fulfilled her obligation.

Jack was already getting dressed, as she tried several times to get up and fall flat on her face, she was done. Jack left the room, but let it shut, then pulled out his lock and pick set, he inserted it in the deadbolt, and turned, till it was set, then released it to try the door, it was secure, and whispered, "Sleep well my darling, maybe later we will go again."

Jack made it down stairs to see the Commander, who said, "Have been looking all over for you are you alright, have you seen my wife?"

"Nope, had to take a long one, sorry, when you got to go, you got to go." he took his seat next to Carlos to see what was going on, only to feel a gun in his side, he kept his hands forward, while the girls came out for another semifinals, it was the blonde Bridgett, she was tough looking, then the bell went off and it was Bridgett throwing bombs, and plummeting some ugly looking girl, till she was out. Bridgett was dancing in the ring over her accomplishment, till she saw Jack, then stared him down to give him the sign of cutting his throat, then left, for Jack to say to the Commander," She seems angry?"

"Oh yeah, wait till she finds out Tony is dead?" "What are you blaming me for his death?"

"You were supposed to be his diving partner" said the Commander, rather smugly.

"You mean she doesn't know yet?"

"Nah, it is Hush, hush, but I do know this she will extract revenge at some point, all his girls are like that, you know he was quite popular, and known as a ladies' man." said the Commander like he was a cheerleader.

Then the worse could have happen, she was told by their Military police, in the locker room, as it was purposely said to her, "Sorry to inform you, but Tony has been killed, by Jack Cash. and she went down in agony, and began to wail, as they comforted her, one of the men kept whispering, "The man who did this to him, is Jack Cash, he is sitting next to the Commander", till she finally understood, what he was saying. Then her rage kicked in, she was screaming, got up clinched her fists, to say, "Show me where he is at, so I can make him responsible for this." She said in between breathes, to say," I'll get to the bottom of all of this, that guy should be afraid, he is next."

It was intermission and Jack and Carlos was waiting for the last fight to begin, when up at the box, came a very pissed off girl, she came their way, separating Jack as he got up, and taken by surprise, Bridgett began her tirade." I'm going to sue you, your done, as she began to push Jack back, against the military policeman, he fell back, as others watched, frozen, out the door, where men waited, they jumped on him, throwing punches, only to hear, "Hold on boys, he is extremely dangerous, take him to the car, we will exact our revenge the Coast Guard way, as Jack was lifted up, and carried out, along with Carlos, Jack was being hit in the back, by Bridgett, who was crying and screaming, "You'll get what you got coming to you, as he was led to an older looking car, where he was in the back seat, flanked by two burly men, the doors shut to drown out her screaming, and two up front, Jack was trying to resist, as he was working to unlatch his watch, as they sped off, instantly just like that a trash truck, side swipes them, driving them into a wall, they were boxed in, inside the men were excited, weapons loaded and locked, ready to go, each had a camera on them, the truck stopped when five men appeared and opened up, spraying the older car with bullets, Jack could feel, pain, as the bullets were guided to his badge, the pain was intense at his heart, as he slumped over, several times, absorbing the lead.

From a monitor, a man says,"There goes our team of Exterminators, the Commander did well."

As another says, "Look head shots, he is assured dead, let's call the head seven, to confirm?"

"Wait till we get confirmation", said the man with the tattoo on his hand.

They watched as the back seat was lit up with bullets, execution style, Military Police lay scattered. Danny "the cobra" Davis, stood with both hands on a pair of mac10's, smiling as one of the men said. "Danny makes the call, confirm he is dead?' Siren's in the distance could be heard, then it was calm, it was over. Danny, went to the back seat, and pulled Jack's head back, for Jack to smile, as he flicked off the wristwatch, for Danny to say, "What the hell?" Jack forced his way out of the car, still cuffed from behind, as he dove over the wall. A boom could be heard off shore as a battle destroyer, launched a 20 inch missile, it that instant, in that moment a missile came at that car, just as Danny was the guy, the missile hit and exploded, sending the car up in the air, and the trash truck into flying debris, as it cleared out the remaining men. Just as above an F-18 super hornet flew by as Jack was down on the wall holding his position, as that signaled for the cavalry to come. As for the remaining exterminators, the searing heat done them in, as the camera for those watching to say, "Was that a missile strike, what the hell, he is assured dead now. now make that call, were ten million dollars richer, they were celebrating.

Carlos was with the Commander who were both watching the accident, Carlos was pumping his fists, while the Commander had sweaty palms, and it was like it was out of a movie just like that helicopters landed by the hundreds, and everyone was told to be on the ground, as men in black outfits, had guns trained on them. Carlos, was anxious, as a lady, came up to them she was of distinction, said, "Which one is the Commander of the base, Juan Alvarez?", the man raises his hand, to hear, "Get him up, she notices Carlos, to say, "Him too, bring them with me."

Lisa made her way down to the crash scene, there was body parts all over the place, it was gruesome, from the looks of it, the missile hit the dump truck, and the blast took out the car, about ninety feet away, up the wall she climbed to see the old car upside down, she heard a cry for help"

Instantly she smiled, to know Jack had survived, and was going to his rescue. Just as a fire truck rolls up, and burly men got out, hear Jack crying out,"Help, can someone help me out, and I've fallen but can't get up?"

"Were the fire department, we will get you out" said the Fire captain, as he looks over to see Lisa, to say "Ma'am you're going to have to get back, it could be dangerous."

"I know. I like danger. Now get my man out." "Yes Ma'am. said the Captain.

The firefighters worked to get the car off of Jack, door open, then began to pull body parts, piece by piece, till one fire fighter felt Jack's foot, to hear, "Yeah, that's my foot, the other is stuck, under the seat."

"Let's get the Jaws of Life, and get this seat out", yelled one firefighter.

They used the Jaws to pop off the driver's seat, and then Jack was free and intact. As he was pulled out, he was held up, both hands were free, with each cuff still attached, his hands were slightly burned. Lisa approached her man, he was slightly burned in places, as he was trying to get the cob webs out of his still ringing ears, for her to want to help him, for her to approach him to say,

"Looks like you just survived another one, is this what you wanted or were asked to be here?"

"I was asked to be here by the Commander and especially his wife, Lalaine."

"So essentially it was a trap?" "Yeah, you could say that?"

"How many missile attacks can you stand?" asked Lisa. "I don't know, but it saved my life, what did it do to my attackers?"

"Well from the other side of this wall, I'd say it took all of them out and everything else in a half mile radius. She wanted to go to him, but she was interrupted, as an ambulance showed up, a stretcher came out as paramedics started to treat Jack, while

Lisa watched, behind her, her two captors were being placed in a black SUV.

Just then as if it were on cue, a small old fashioned car, drove up to the Ambulance, a guy got out with a case, went over to Jack, the paramedic's stopped what they were doing, to allow, the guy, to place a new watch on Jack's left wrist. He then pulled out the pin, and said, 'Go ahead boys, help our man out." He turned, and got back into his car and left.

CH 6

The wedding to Sara

The day broke with Jack still inside Stephanie as she got her four hours in, it was now over for the three of them, Jack had another hour with Lalaine, to finish, her requirement, she had pasted out, from sheer exhaustion. Stephanie was still eager but said, "Do you wanna go get chow with me?"

"Sure," said Jack a bit hungry, both dressed, they left this time Stephanie had the key, and locked the door down, and they left.

Day broke, in Mobile Alabama, with the sun blazing through the open field as the tents were already going up, chairs set out, in the middle of all of it was Mitzi and Trixie, each taking a group of jobs and executing them with precision and expert vision, for this was a C I G operations, with the exception of the foreign guests, almost everyone there was connected one way or the other, so it was a team effort. Among the guest who wanted to come was the Governor of this state, past and present operatives, who worked with Jack, the famous Barbara Biltmore, the multi-millionaire, whose present was delivered and is in the garage. Here at the church, across from the lighthouse hotel and spa, most of the guess has been staying there and at the water park's hotel, across the street, the bride is in the basement, with her bride's maids, and the maid of honor, Tabby, her young friend. The wedding will take place in eight hours, as the boat had just arrived, according to Trixie as she just got a call from Mark the ship's captain.

Jack and Stephanie finished breakfast, for her to say, we still have an hour before your flight, how about a real quickie?" "Nah, I think I better save my strength."

"Suit yourself, but hey I have a friend in the motor pool who wants to join this club, could we go over and meet her, will that change your mind?"

"Not really, I don't need wanna-bees, I like the real McCoy, he tried to pull her in and she pushed him away, to say,"I have a reputation on this base; some might think I'm soft."

Jack looks at her to say, "Well see you then", said Jack, seeing the helicopter pad, and the group of vehicles that surrounded it.

"Wait a minute I'd said I'd walk you down there and say goodbye for now?"

"Or forever" said Jack.

"Why would you say that, I had fun and that was all I was looking for", said Stephanie.

"And so did I, but you're here and I'm everywhere."

"You'll be back to visit me, won't you, I know what you said to me, and right now I just can't, sorry." she said as she was shredding a tear, for Jack to look at her, to say, "I guess you can throw your theory out the window, your showing emotions, you're a bad girl."

"Then for last time, bend me over your knee and spank me really good."

"That's a tempting offer, but I gotta go", he began to run away from her, down the hill to the helio pad, as he opened the door, and got in, she just stood there and watched moments later the helio lifted up and was passing overhead, as she watched it leave. Just then the whole place especially around her was engulfed with hundreds and thousands of agents from all different organizations, like homeland, the FBI the CIA and the CIG, she held her hands up to think, "I was wrong, I should of chosen to be with you Jack Cash."

In the motor pool, similar things were going on, as a buff SEAL's member was waiting on Stephanie, till he saw the formation of helio's above, and knew he missed his opportunity to get at Jack, he checked his phone, and tried it, to hear, "Don't hang up, in a second, someone will be there to pick you up."

He dropped his phone and was on the move, out the back to the canal, he dove in.

The helios landed beside the church, in Mobile Alabama Jack exited, and was led to the hotel, where his partner was waiting, with a key in her hand, he takes it from her, and on to the room he went, he tried it, it was on the first floor, it opened, and hit the bed and collapsed.

"Jack wake up" said Blythe who was pushing on him, as he had his arm around her, grasping her firm body, as his head was buried in her chest.

"Jack gets up; let's get you in the shower." "Only if you join me." He said with a smile. "Of course, that's why I'm here" she said.

"What do you mean" said Jack opening his eyes to look at her as she got up from the bed. And ads, "What happen to you this morning?"

"Well nothing, you came in, took a bed to rest, I was here to protect you, and that was it, so let's get you ready." to add, as she watches him get in the shower to say, "I want to talk with you, do you have a minute?"

"Sure, fire away", said Jack washing up.

"Well I'm not supposed to tell."

"Your CIG, aren't you, do you work for Lisa" said Jack getting closer to being done.

"Well yes and no."

"Out with it" said Jack looking at her, with the door open, and all soaped up, for him to say,"Why don't you join me?"

"Well I can't and the other is, well don't be angry with me, it all started at the spa, you showed interest in a few girls, and I was recruited by Lisa to watch you as with all the other girls, there on the boat for the bachelor party."

"I thought they were into the other guys."

"Nah, that's a front, each and every one of the girls aboard that boat was for you, everything we do is for you pleasure, as told to us by our superiors, each of us is trained to handle a gun and fight to protect you to the end, our association is called "SPY CLUB" its members are of the prettiest women in the world, recruited, to serve a chosen spy, even the last women you married."

"You mean Alexandra and Alba, how do they fit into this?"
"She was assigned to you while you were in Cuba, then when you were gone they both protected Maria, I wanted to tell you this, because you asked me to be a wife, and yes I will, actually I have no choice, either way I'm yours, I just wanted you to know the truth."

"I'm listening", said Jack, who already knew about this.

"I have an opportunity either to be a spy or protect you, for me to get close to you secretly and to let you know, that when Sara came to each of us to ask us to be your wife, we refused her, so that I may later, let you know, whatever you want it is available just to you and no one else, you're the most valuable possession the U S has and they will do anything to protect it."

"So that means you'll be my wife?"

"If you like, as will all the other girls, but I will tell you that once, we become the most trusted; we will be removed from active duty, and become a permanent part of your team, if you like."

"So what does that mean?"

"Well when were not at the spa, or the job were assigned to do, then we travel around the world, assisting other spy's and gaining more experience, but once you choose us to be your wife, we become part of the group called "the most trusted" these women, are decommissioned and are assigned a handler, usually a male Secret Service agent to watch us and care for us while your away, and we are home sitters, but if you decide to add us to your team, instead of marrying us, then we would be allowed to do this more often, you know this", Jack watched as she striped, naked, and pushed him back in the shower, to help him rinse off, for Jack to say, "Why are you telling me all of this?"

"I just wanted to let you know that if anything, I would rather be a spy, first and foremost than, be your wife, but that is your choice, I may have said too much already, just let Lisa know, what your decision will be at the party, were all suppose to leave after that, now let's get you all cleaned up."

Streams of people were coming in as cars parked in the Water Park's parking lot, the park was closed to the public for the day, as the after party was at the amusement park, Trixie directed the florists where to put the arrangements, and in a box given to Trixie was the bride's bouquet.

Next was the press photographer and two federal photographers and two videographers, off to the right sat an organist playing, some intro songs warming up on the semi-warm afternoon. Mike showed up with a smile on his face to show Trixie what he had, he presented two boxes, for her to open, she opened the first box. She said, "Oh my God that is huge."

"Yep the center cut diamond, which of course is oval is four carats, and up and down the band there are over sixty smaller boxed cut diamonds", then she opened the second larger box to reveal, two pearl necklaces, one white and the other black, with a matching pair of earrings, bracelet and a ring. For Trixie to exclaim "That is lovely, she will sure love that."

"All in all Jack paid one million dollars for, the diamond ring, the others he got diving in Florida. ", for Mike to turn to see, and say, "Oh look it's the Governor." They both shook hands, he was accompanied by his wife, and children, as he Governor admired the ring, in which Mike held. In the distance was the Cuban families, all had gathered and was walking up as a force, just as the rented white bus pulls up, the boat people got off, Mark was at the wheel. Jack walked over from the hotel, with Blythe in tow. Jack dressed in his black tuxedo, followed by his best man Carlos, newly released from Lisa, who told him, him and his family was on the next flight out", all dressed up, behind him was his three wives to join the two others, to walk up the aisle through the tent up to take a seat on Jack's side, a row behind, as everyone took their seats, Mitzi directed rest of the milling people to their seats, as Jack, stood on the platform under a bridge of trailing red roses, next to him was Carlos, behind him was Mark, followed by Mike and lastly Timmy, Jack looked back with a smile on his face to see his first wife, Samantha, being pushed up by her mother, who held a smile on her face, as they all watched her push her into place on the left side of the aisle, then kissed her daughter on the forehead, and went up to Jack to say "I forgive you" Jack kissed her to say, "Thank you". Next to come up was Jack's female operatives, led by Devlin who was last to see the rest sit on the front, Devlin across and down from Jack.

Mitzi spoke, in her walkie talkie "Now" as she looked at her watch, that read four o clock.

The music started, as the organist, dealt out some sweet chords, everyone rose, to see Sara Sanders, dressed in a pink chiffon, lace strapless dress with a jeweled bust line, a diamond pendant she wore as the top half of the wrap around the neck and shoulders was lace and flowers as it was out to her sleeves, she wore a tiara on her head, as her hair was up to show off those huge diamond ear ring studs, she walked with her father by her side, behind her was the maid of honor Tabby, dressed in a dark pink strapless full length dress, behind her was her sister Kate, Leslie, Debbie, then her new sister Maria, Alexandra and Alba, took their seats on the end of the first line.

Jack looked at each girl who went by with a smile, to take their place, and his three other wives.

The music stopped, as Sara made it to the altar.

Her father, Doctor Greg, handed her hand to Jack to say, "Here she is for you."

She delicately stepped up onto the platform, as her parents took a place next to Jack's other wives and Samantha, she waited till her party got into place, then turned in to see the Pastor, who stepped up between them to say, "Dearly beloved, I stand before you as the holy figure among the sea's of goodness' and of evil, this ceremony is like no other of its kind, as most of you know, this is a union between a man and this lovely young lady, and at this time I will ask is there someone who feels in their heart that this man Jack and this woman Sara should not be bonded to together or forever hold your peace."

"I do" spoke a voice. In the back, as everyone turns to see.

"To whom are you sir and what do you say?" asked the Pastor.

Everyone turned in their chair, only to see the man waving a gun saying, "Stay where you're at or I will shoot, as he pointed the gun, unarmed Jack knew who this one was, but stood motionless to do anything, only to listen.

"You see father, this one tried to kill me because he wanted her for himself, but really she loves me, tell them Sara, how much you love me?"

"You're a crazy psycho" said Sara looking at him as the gun went off, Devlin stood up with her gun drawn, as the bullet tore through her head.

Devlin went down, as others including Sheriff John Weston, jumped the man and wrestled him to the ground, then apprehended the man, and took him away.

Jack went down to kneel on the grass to hold up the head of his partner, who was bleeding out, as Jack screamed, "Someone call for an ambulance."

A voice said "It's on its way" as it was too late, she closed her eyes, and her body went limp, as Jack picked her up, and carried her off, past the onlookers, and fellow agents, as the ambulance arrived. They helped Jack into the ambulance as Jack lied her down onto the gurney. He held onto her, thinking how good a friend she was, everyone was standing outside, while waiting for Jack. Jack heard a voice, "You killed my father."

Jack turned to see Kimberly, holding a gun for a brief moment and she too went down as both Mark and Mike did their job, of subduing her. Jack held onto Devlin's gun and placed it in his pocket, only to hear, "Jack the bride is waiting" said Lisa, as she entered the ambulance and everyone else got out as the doors closed shut.

"Listen, what she did was a service to us all, while we can't continue to grieve her loss let's celebrate, her life, and of this special moment, I feel for you that she gave her life to save yours, but where there is one I have another hundred waiting."

"Yes, I know, just let me have another moment with her." Jack held on to her, only to listen to Lisa say, "I didn't know you two were intimate with each other, or is that something new."

Jack looks at Lisa to say "neither, she just grew on me, and as she learned to be a better spy, we grew fond of each other."

"Alright, I'll give you some time, but after this I want to talk with you about a new partner and what my plans are for future field operators, by the work I'm doing with Missy, and want you to be on board."

"What's that mean?"

"I'll tell you later, but it is all about supporting you in the field" said Lisa as she opened the door, she got out to see the two apprehended go into the black Suburban, to add, "Don't worry neither of them will ever bother you again."

"Thanks" said Jack as he stood to let her go, he climbed out as the crew climbed in and the ambulance left, Jack stood to see over fifty agents in black suits, taking a place all over, Mitzi came up to him to say "Jack come over here" she led him to the church entrance, they went in as Trixie, pulled off Jack's coat. Cassandra, stepped out to show herself, and the three of them helped dress Jack, Jack said, "I want that gun back", Mitzi searched his pockets, found it, checked it, then reset the safety, to drop it into his Jacket pocket, quickly, each girl had tears running freely, Jack stood still. Mitzi finished the tie, to say "Let me help you along", as Cassandra stepped in close to say,"Hey you have some clothes to pick up, come by the shop for a special discount."

Jack followed as Mitzi walked slowly, and led him, out the side door, to a sky that was sunny, and the warm air, Jack took a deep breath. He then exited in between a line that the Governor, stood, he leaned into Jack to say, "I didn't have a chance to properly thank you" he handed Jack a thick envelop size pouch, which Mitzi, took and kept Jack moving, as she was pushing him along into the aisle. Sara was being held back by the Pastor and Carlos who had a gun drawn as well, Mitzi took her time with Jack as she passed others and the organist began again to play. Anyone could have easily jumped in to help, but waited as she did her job.

The men came down to surround Jack, as Mitzi turned to announce "Thank you for your patience, if you will allow, we will proceed in a very short moment, thank you."

She took her seat next to Trixie who had tears shown, Jack was helped up the step, to find Sara, hands waiting to hold onto his, Jack's face was somber, as was Sara's. The Pastor asked quietly

"Shall we continue?"

Sara looked over at Jack, looking for a response, and then she said,

"Let's see for right now."

The Pastor, repositioned himself, then signaled for the organist to stop, and then announce, "Let us begin, this time, from the looks of it there will be no more interruptions, first off I want to say, lets pray, Dear heavenly father, we ask that you, see to it that, you allow this man and this woman to be married together, in this moment without further delays and we ask that you bless those, that have expressed evil against us, and let us bless that young woman who so gallantry lost her live in which to save another, be forgiven and oh lord we also ask that you bless this union and to protect them in the future, we ask of you oh lord, amen, please be seated, now let us show all that is here why this man and this woman should be married."

The Pastor looked at Jack, Sara still was holding both of Jack's hands, and Sara spoke up first to say, "Father I would like to go first." She looks at him for approval, he nods, she turns to face the audience to say, "First I'd like to say thank you to everyone who has come out to celebrate this day with me, we are all on different path's and when I met Jack, he and I were on way different ends of each spectrum, I was coming out of a deranged killers love triangle, which was evident with the killing of Jack's partner, Devlin, god rest her soul, and to me for falling deeply, with all my heart in love with my protector. Who's job is to go and save people on a regular basis, and here I stand, loving a man who gives himself to all others in hopes of having a real family, at the end of the day, Jack you do have a family to come home to, you have my new sisters, Maria, Alexandra and Alba, and of course my dearest best friend Samantha, without Jack I would have never known her existence, Jack is a lot of things to a lot of people, all I know is that I have found my soul mate, and will give myself to him and the

children I bear, and will be with him to the very and lastly end."
"Mister Jack Cash, will you be my husband, continue to do your
job as a protector for all and all I ask from you is that you keep me
in your heart, for that I will be your wife, friend and companion."
she finish, looking around then re-grasping his hand, to look into
his glassed over eyes.

Jack broke the grasp, to systematically pull out a card, then
turned to face the audience and say, "Yes, I too, love you Sara, you
do have a place in my mind and in my heart, you changed my life,
my decisions and the way I look at things, I admit I was wild, with
no cares in the world, but every time I kept coming back to you,
you have an old spirit, that resides in your young body, I'd like to
thank your family, starting with Greg, as him and I are similar, and
to his wife Heidi, and to your sister Kate, for being so nice to me,
and of her friend Debbie, a true inspiration, and of your brother
Timmy, who I just can't get rid of, him and of Hopi get along so
well, and to your family's hospital who's has the best lunch buffet,
thanks. Everyone just laughs.

Jack opens up a bit, shrugging off what just happened, then
looking over at Blythe, Caroline and Tami, to say, "Sara, it's you, it
will always be you, you are my light, my everything, heck you have
all those suitcases I gave you, this is all for you, for that I truly love
you" said Jack turning, as Sara pulls out the piece of paper from his
hand to see it was blank on both sides, to let it go.

Sara reached out for a kiss, when the Pastor spoke up, "Now
who has the rings?"

Carlos says "I do," and slides the box between Jack's arm, Jack
takes it to open up the box, the reflection was fierce as the pastor
says "Now, repeat after me, I Jack Cash give you this ring as I show
you my love, dedication, devotion, through thick or thin, for richer
or poorer, till death do your part" Jack followed along" now slip
that ring on" Jack slid that huge rock on her finger, that instantly
could blind someone, to say "I do", "now Sara Sanders do you have
a ring for Jack?"

From within her beautiful dress, she pulls out a ring, to hear
the Pastor say" Repeat after me, I Sara, give you Jack, this ring to

signify my love, dedication, devotion and honor, through thick or thin, richer or poorer, till death and beyond do their part" she slid on that ring, and held onto his hand, to hear the Pastor say "With the powers vested to me by the state of Alabama and the federal government I now pronounce you Husband and Wife, you may kiss."

Sara literally jumped into Jack's arms as he held her while they kissed.

"Ladies and Gentlemen, I'd like the first to say, let's give Jack and Sara a nice warm welcome as Husband and Wife." Everyone got up, to clap and to cheer, them as Jack carried Sara down the aisle way, as the music played over to the reception tent, to set her down at the head table, he saw Lisa motions to him, so he said, "I'll be back in a moment."

The audience filed into the large tent where a band was setting up, as Jack acknowledges some of the guests as he made his way over to Lisa who stood by the suburban to say, "Congratulations."

"Thanks, I wanted to make her a legal woman."

"Your trip to the Dominican Republic has been cleared, and we have an advanced team on the ground, we have a plane for you to use at the airport."

"Sorry, don't need it". "Why not", she said.

"Tomorrow, were taking the Parthian Stranger, down there, Mark and Mike will be getting the boat ready for the cruise, besides what about that plane I was suppose to have?" "Well you're not traveling and it just can't sit around, waiting."

"Oh I see, so if I commit to all of this, then I'll have it. "Yes, I also have thirty more cases to give to you." "Can't this wait?"

"No it can't, you will get paid according to my terms" she said with a smile.

"Alright, all I have is that white van" said Jack walking towards it, unlocking it and then opening the back, one by one they loaded the suitcases, till it was done, then Lisa said "I can post some guards around it"

"It's not necessary, Tricks and Mitts will bring it back to the house later, as he pulls a white Lenin sheet over the top of it, then closes the doors and locks it down, to say "Besides all I have to do is let Blythe know and she and her team will guard it right." "Hold on Jack, you know about them?"

"Yes she told me, either I marry them or they become full time spies, things have sure changed in the last couple of months." "No, Jack that's not the way it works, it was designed that the girls were recruited, that was a sworn oath of secrecy, and for her to tell you is in the strictest confidence, you promise never to talk about this again", she said to him in a forceful tone, her seriousness caused him some anxiety.

"Come on, it's me, the one who gave you the seed money to do this."

"It was all for you, do you promise?"

"Alright, I promise, it's like I almost forgot about it." "We will deal with them." said Lisa.

"What are you planning?"

"Probably kick them out, or face jail time or . . ." "Or then I will marry each of them."

"That may work now, but I don't know in the future, that may not be enough, a serious breach of protocol, it's up to the Commander and Chief, but if that's what you want to do, then I shall allow it."

"Alright what do I have to do to clean this up?"

"I don't think you can fix this one, next time just keep your mouth shut", she said with a smile and ads, "At least you're honest, I like that that about you."

Jack walked away from her, shaking his head, as he went back to the reception, he sees Mitzi and walks up to her and whispers in her ear, "Can you keep an eye on the van."

"Will do, now you better get in there, its toasting time." Jack eased into the tent, to see everyone was milling about, the servers had a buffet line in place, and called out to the bride and groom to come first, Sara met up with Jack, to give him a kiss and to say, "I Love You" she said affectionately, Jack guides her to the start of the line, as a servers pulls back the covered lids to expose, a garden salad, Sara places a scoop on each plate as Jack holds them, behind them was Samantha, being assisted by her mother, who was all smiles. Alexandra, Alba and Maria, followed by Carlos and his immediate family, then Sara's and so forth, with each tray Sara would ask Jack if he wanted or not, overall Jack had three items, besides the garden salad, several pieces of pizza and a handful of baby back ribs, and a half dozen of a variety of deviled eggs, where as Sara, choose everything else, then said she would try what he had, then they took their seats at the head table. Jack tore into the pizza and ribs, when Mark came by to say, "Hey boss I got you and your family a case of my friends beer, it will go good with those ribs, its out in the van."

Jack hands him the key, to say, "I want that key back."

Mark looks weirdly at Jack, then leaves as one by one people swung by their table to drop off gifts, Sara accepted them on Jack's behalf as he continued to chow down on those ribs, the whole gang was there, including Red and his girl Kim, Timmy was all over Tami, Lisa makes an entrance a little later with her three henchmen, from the S I T squad, Jack watched as they came by to say, "Hi", then right over to the Spa girls, and slowly one by one they left the party, even Blythe went by saying good bye long distance, in the back of Jack's mind he thought maybe he ought to reach out, take them with him and then he looked up to see Lisa, who says, "Can we have a word?"

Jack wipes off his hands and says to Sara, "I've got to go wash my hands."

Jack leaves with Lisa, she guides him to her Suburban, and opens the door for him, Jack gets in, his hands still sticky, when Ramon, the driver says "I don't think those Kleenex will work, I have a wet wipe" and hands the box to Jack.

"Enough already" said Lisa getting in the passenger side seat, to say, "I talked with the girls, and come to find out it was a isolated incident, only Blythe is to blame, so you have three choices, the first being you marry her, she is out of the service, she will still get protected, and paid per diem, next is you say no and you'll never see her again, and option three you'll never see her again"

"What does she want?" said Jack

"To be a spy, and join your team, problem is we have only four slots available to you, we don't have anywhere to place her, I guess she told you only because she thought you would accept her as a spy, only we cannot allow her that position.

"Who came up with the four limit rule? What about her being my partner?"

"She doesn't have that type of training?"

"What are you talking about, there is no training out there." asked Jack wiping off his hands then giving the wet wipes back to Ramon, the two smiles at one another.

"Jack, you are of one of two suppose international spies, every woman, who has tried has failed, even Daphne, who has been up in cold weather training simply just quit, she is here today, but besides the point, the new training Academy's goal is to produce support candidates, not spies themselves, even Mark and Mike, have some skills but not enough, that is why I was going to ask of you to help out and design the new spy academy."

"Just as long as Blythe is in the first class, you can count me in, but I want to know when you have changed Lisa, it has only been six months and your whole design is this new spy academy, you're a closed up bitch".

"Jack I can't believe you called me that."

"Who are you to say who my partner is, or who I have on my team? What ever happen to us being equal, colleagues" said Jack.

"I don't know, maybe I was getting use to who you have been lately?"

"Do you hear what you're saying, for one mission I had over thirty, Listen I know your suppose to be my handler, but really you're my colleague, not my boss, is that true?"

"Yes, your right."

"From this point forward, if I hear see or get wind of anyone coming at any of my group, you can count on me coming to visit you personally, and then I will find the person who placed the hit, from this day forward, I don't ever want to see you again."

Jack exited the suburban, and Jack saw Mark carrying the case, stopped him and got a beer, which he opened, to taste it was sweet, then said "This is good beer" and said "Can you find Blythe, and bring her to me."

Mark went back to the van, to where Blythe was asked to hide, and came out and went to Jack. Jack saw the Suburban do a U-turn and took off, and then it slowed, and stopped, whereas Jack stood in the middle of the street, as the Suburban backed up, it stopped, and Lisa got out as Mark handed the key back to Jack, while Blythe joined Jack on his arm.

"Could I have a moment with Jack Please?" asked Lisa Blythe and Mark walked off, for Jack to see Lisa, to say "First I want to say I was out of line your right, were colleagues I forgot, I'm here to support you, and you never have given me grief so why do we need to fight?"

"You started it, by bullying me and telling me what I could and could not do, just like when you told me to go to Cuba, so that you and Missy could have the weekend for yourselves, I think you like all the glory, without getting your hands dirty.

"Well I do admit I was wrong, and your right, it is true Spy Club design is to support you can we make up?"

"If you like, your right I don't want to fight with you, I like you, why don't you come and join us for a toast."

"Alright, I will "say Lisa, as the two walked into the tent together.

Jack went in made the toasts, as Trixie and Mitzi, led Jack and Sara, to the Cakes table to cut the cake, Jack cut a piece for her then for himself, Jack took a seat, as Sara sat down on his lap whereas she began to feed him slowly, the delicate cake while all others watched the pair, at times she would tease him, Mitzi was tempted to give her another piece, because it was so sweet, Jack did the same to her, and as soon as her last bite went in and she swallowed the two kissed, the band went into a wild session, to stop and announce, "It's time for the bouquet toss, all single girls' line up for Sara."

Jack looked in Sara's eyes, as she finished off the kiss, then said "Don't you go anywhere I'll be right back", Sara went over on the other side, turned her back, as the drummer, gave her a rumbling sound, everyone counted 1, 2, 3 and she let it fly. Blythe jumped up and caught it above everyone else, immediately she looked at Jack who had Sara in his lap resuming kissing session, in the middle of the floor . . .

Mitzi signaled for the band to play, the leader said, "It's now time for the husband and wife to dance there first dance" the song started, as Sara said to Jack "I choose Love Me Tender" as Jack led her to the dance floor, him being an honorable gentleman, danced with flair and poise, with his head back, his frame straight, a smile on his face ended as Sara pulled him in and clasped her arms under his shoulders, and the kissing continued, until the song was over, only to hear the band leader announce "It's time for the single men to line up, in the middle was Carlos, as Mitzi and Trixie pulled Sara off of Jack, and led her to a chair in the middle of the room, to sit, while Jack followed, then knelt down, pulled up her wedding dress much to the happiness' of the single men, to the point past the garter so he could see her panties, then pulled it back down and quickly pulled off the garter, stood up turned around and twirled it on one finger, and let it go, several dove for it but it was Carlos snatching it. He then made an immediately look at Blythe, who turned away. The music started to play, Sara grabbed Jack's hand, Jack and Sara danced. Sara whispered in his ear to say, "Do you want to go to the amusement park or the water park?"

"The water park of course", said Jack

"Hey you know Lisa is looking for you" said Mark.

"There you are Jack, Jack turns to see Lisa carrying a large envelope.

For her to say, "Your right Jack, you need a partner, and if you want Blythe, then she is all yours, if at any time she needs some training just ask me, and this is for you."

"What about Daphne, is she available?"

"Possible, she did mention some interest, but as I told you she quit the training."

"Maybe she didn't like the cold weather training, neither would I."

"I get the point", said Lisa.

Jack stopped dancing with Sara, who went back to the table, for them to watch her, to say to Lisa, "Why don't you take off some time, and enjoy the park, we got it for the rest of the night."

"No thanks, just want to give you this, and say good luck on the trip and from this point on there will be no problems."

"What is this?" asked Jack.

"It's a present from the President of the United States, your boss. Said Lisa . . .

Jack just placed it into his jacket pocket, to say, "Is there anything else."

"No I just wanted to say I'm sorry, will you forgive me?" asked Lisa.

Jack asked, "Sure, how did it go with Helen?"

"Helen, yeah, you know who took down the Mistro?"

"Oh her, well we found out that its Worldwide." said Lisa.

"Is there something wrong?" asked Jack taking her to the side of the tent.

"I'm sorry I can't lie to you anymore, we have placed tracking devices on you and all of your wives."

"Tracking device", exclaimed Jack. "Yeah, we put it on all of our agents." "Do I have one?"

"Yes, it's on your gun, we couldn't put one on your person like the other agents, because, it could be seen by x-ray, but hidden in your gun."

"And my wives, where are they?"

"Usually on their wrists, mainly to keep track of them" Jack moved away from Lisa to see Mike, who was carrying presents to the large white van, to say "Mike you got a minute?"

"Yes Sir"

"Hey do you have a wand or something to find tracking devices."

"Yeah, down in the fishing shack, is it a priority?" "Tomorrow morning is good, just have it on the boat."

The tent was thinning down as everyone was heading to the amusement park, Jack saw Sara was talking with her parents, while

Timmy came up to him to say, "Hey Jack, what are you going to do first?"

"Probably the water park first, are you heading that way?"

"Yeah, my sister Kate wants to go swimming."

Jack took the initiative to search on his own, and went into the hotel, a card key was in his pocket thanks to Mitzi, he found his room, went in, on the bed was his swim trunks, he quickly took everything out of his pockets, and set it on the table, then undressed, then slipped on his swim trunks, then found some flip flops to wear, as he slid the card in his back pocket, out the door he went, to the elevator, inside he saw two bottom buttons, AMUS, or WAT, he hit WAT, the elevator opened on the upper level of the concourse, as Jack walked the enclosed glass, fly over to see the well lit up Amusement park below, then he saw Sara still in her dress, and her family, they all waved back at him, on the other side, he went down some stairs, to a booth, and a guy say, "Name please."

"Jack Cash."

"Ah the groom, as he held up the pass, with his picture on it, looking at him, to say, "Confirm place fore-finger into print reader please."

Jack did so, as the guy said, "Here you go Mister Cash, enjoy the water park, oh by the way if you want to go to the amusement park you need to go back to the . . . ."

Jack was through the turnstile, and amongst some familiar faces, it was a night of just fun, Trixie and Mark were having fun, while Mitzi and Blythe took the log ride down, Jack was up in line for the giant slide, which he did several times, he saw Jim and Debby together on the wild rapids ride.

Jack took a seat to see a familiar tall blonde, named Marci, walk over to him, to say, "Congratulations on your wedding, the bride was lovely, sorry I couldn't come to the wedding, it was private, and selected guests, but the after party is open to the rest of your friends, and for us lovers . . . ." She said with a smile.

Jack looked up at her thinking if she is here how many others are too?"

"Don't worry it's just me and my girl friends, Cassandra got us in, me, Terri and Claire, our husbands are out of town again." She got closer to him to say, why don't you come to my spa, and I will give you a wedding present, you'll never forget, Oops sorry", I didn't mean for that to happen" as she slowly put her right breast back under cover of her top.

Jack had a smile on his face seeing her, thinking, "Yeah, she could be number seven, where are my wives?"

She allowed him up as he went past her, to see the three foot gate, that separated the two parks, as Jack jumped over it, this side was boring in comparison to those who were having fun, it was the middle of the night, he was tired and so was the amusement park, not a person was around, Jack went into the lower lobby, everything was closed, so Jack got in the elevator to M, as the doors opened on the main floor, Jack hit the AMUS button, then WAT button, his mind was on the lovely Marci, out he went, back over the flyover, down to the ticket taker who was asleep, over the turnstile, to see that the water park was in still full swing.

In line at the log ride was the very tall Marci, Jack was several people back, till she saw him to say, "Why don't you come up and join me?"

"I don't want to cut."

"But you're the groom, that should get you over here, as she said it in such a way, the line shifted to one side, to allow Jack to catch up to her, she told them thanks, to kiss Jack on the lips to say, "So did you change your mind?"

"Sure what do you have in mind?"

"Let's do it on the log ride" she exclaimed.

"I don't know about that what it's only a two minute ride or so."

"Try five, but best, start on that, then onto something else, or I could take you into the girls' bathroom?"

"What are we teenagers? I've discovered something even better. Are you game?" asked Jack, as the line was really moving. She said "Try me?"

"Ever heard of sport fucking?"

Marci looked at him, then said "No, but it sounds dangerous."

"Well from what I know of it, it has four stages, all designed for the ultimate in pleasure and in longevity."

"You're getting me excited, alright let's do that?"

"Wait, "as holds Marci at the start of the log ride, ready to ditch her bikini bottoms.

"There is a minimum time limit?" "How long?"

"Four hours"

They were next on the log ride, went down it, got off, and she said,"No, and then it was totally weird. Jack and Marci hung out, as for the sex there was none, Jack wearily went back to his room, as the park shut down, they cleared out the park, Jack went into the lobby, then up to his room, went in, tired, he pulled his swim trunks down, and went into an empty bed.

CH 7

The Honeymoon

Jack awoke to banging on his door; he looked over at the digital clock, to see it was noon, he rolled out, to walk to the door, he opened the door to see it was Sara, as he let her in, she wasn't happy, to say "Jack where have you been?"

"Asleep"

"Alone, I thought we were to consummate our Marriage last night."

"Calm down, as Jack went back into bed, as Sara continued, Lisa gave me those tickets to the Dominican Republic, and our flight left two hours ago." "Did you go to the airport?" "Yes, with my family."

"Too bad, for them, now let me sleep."

Jack pulls the other pillow over his head, to drown out her yelling, then it all stopped, Jack looked at her, as she was undressing, he popped his head out to see that she was bottomless, as she pulled off her t-shirt, and then her bra, she was filled with excitement as she jumped onto the bed, and he let her do all the work, as he laid back, she said "I want what Maria, Alex and Alba got, three whole days to myself with you."

Jack saw her belly to say "shouldn't you be doing that?"

"Nah it's alright, my due date is a month away, and this trip is only a week, so let me have my fun, besides when we do it, it can only be doggie style."

"Just let me know when you're ready" said Jack lying back enjoying the moment enough to go back to sleep.

Day turned into night, as Jack continued on his new found discovery, and she was the ever so willing to receive it, inside of Sara from behind, he pulled himself off of her, to hit the shower, afterwards, he was getting dressed with familiar clothing laid neatly on the table, complete with gun box and his holster, he dressed, and waited for Sara, who was up, as he went through all of his messages, some he knew he missed on purpose, like Marci and Cassandra's to have an encounter with them last night, to some back from the whole Mistro ordeal, to say, "There are a lot of horny women out there, to one from two British lasses, that said that they were his next adversary, courtesy of the British Government, and if he does go down to the Dominican Republic, he will sure to see them. In addition he received confirmation that Blythe was his new partner, however she was off doing training, the latest message was some attorney for the government wanted to visit, him before he went to have him sign some new documents, and her name was Erica Meyers.

Jack dialed her up to say, "Meet you in the lobby, sure."

Jack gets up to say "I need to meet with someone, when you're ready come out and we will go."

Jack exited the room, to see a stunning short haired professional woman, with a huge silver briefcase, to say, "You must be Jack, I'm Erica" the two shook hands as she led him to a table to say, "Sorry to take up your time but I need you to sign these new will and trust forms."

Jack sat beside her to get a smell of her, as he saw huge amounts of money written, and who the beneficiaries were, he signed, then saw the release of the DOR, for Samantha. He signed but was hesitate, for Erica to say, "She went back to Virginia, as she comes to full term, which is about three weeks, they will fly only you there to be with her on her final days, and be there when the baby is born, on this form states that Trixie, one of your support members has agreed to look after the baby, he will be taken to your families hospital in Mobile, any questions?"

She held onto Jack's head as he wept, as Sara saw this she too came to his support, as Erica pulled away the forms, Sara held her man.

Jack got up to wipe the tears away as others were looking at the three, as Erica said, "You must be number five, Sara, here you go," as she hands her per diem check, which she wadded up and put in her pocket as the three walked out, Sara had her arm around Jack as Erica led them out, as she turned she said, "From now on, you'll receive that check every month, in the mail, in the advent that Jack would past, then you will see me for a restructured settlement, bye." Sara said, "She is sure cold", as Jack was getting it together, he felt a little better, with his new documents, in hand, he opens his windbreaker, to slid the package of signed papers to be with the Presidential documents, as he unlocked the van, Sara got into the passenger seat to say, "This is so big, when did you get this?"

"Oh it's a present from my staff."

Jack drove the heavy van out of the parking lot, for Sara to say, "Stop, look", she pointed to the sunset.

Jack looked west to see the sun setting, but also the grasses on the hill side on the other side, to say, "Is that our house?"

"Yep and there is more, let's go see it."

As Jack drove, Sara held on, then said, "Honey I want to tell you that the house is finished, so I will tell you how to get there, instead of the boat house."

Jack drove through the forest of the hillside, then down onto a service road, which led to a tee then by a huge mailbox, at the semi circle.

"Stop, I need to check our mail."

Jack stopped and waited as Sara opened up a large door and pulled out a hand held carrying box, and closed and relocked the door, she carried it back, to the van, to say "Do you want to see all your mail?"

"What, are you saying" asked Jack.

"Yeah, this is all your mail, some junk, some letters from grateful people whose lives are better, because of your work, and others are checks."

"Checks, like?"

"Well all four of the sisters receive a per diem check each month, and Maria's family send her checks from the gold business, to you and her and each of us, then there is Alexandra, she has a phone sex business, with over one hundred 900 numbers, with a slew of girls working for her, and Samantha, with the charter business, and the criminal business, I'd say we are doing quite well, now drive, I'm horny and I want to show you our gift to you, your House on the Hill."

Sara clicked a switch, and the large grated door swung open, as Jack slowly passed through, to read the sign etched in the gate, on the left is a guard shack, slowly he drove upward the long winding road, up the hill, to immediate turn to the right, where a newly planted field, you could see for miles", he said.

"We have twenty acres of grapes, just planted", said Sara, as Jack continued up and on the right he saw a huge brick wall, while passing the new fruit trees, as the road had another sharp right hand turn, as Sara said "Over there is the goats, four acres full, as the van was against the wall side the road went up and to the left, Jack drove around a pond, with a fountain going, to park under a columned entrance, he got out to marvel at the raised gardens, to his right and front, with a set of windows, Jack walked around, the freshly concreted surface, to see the fountain, and then he saw Sara, who said, "Alright you see everything around here that slopes down to a collection tank, is our water source, it is also filled, as needed, next to it is the newly remodeled twenty car garage, ten up front, and ten in the rear and storage, beside that is a grass field, there is the three story barn, and beyond that is a pasture with a retaining wall to catch water, come on inside the house" she leads him in to tell him, there are eight levels, you have the penthouse, so when you want a specific wife for the evening, and it is your room, as they entered the main level, it is our gathering area, a kitchen, dining and two living rooms, seven levels down each of your wives has their own level, and can be accessed either by stairs or one of the two express elevators, each has a open patio for fresh air, and windows and it goes back into the rock, she asks "Do you want to see each level?"

"No, is there a pool?"

"Yes silly I'll show you that later." "So let's off load the van" said Jack.

Jack opens the two rear doors, Jack uncovers the cases, as he grabs two cases each, to follow Sara inside, to the elevator, one level down, off the elevator, Jack sets down their cases as Sara punched in a code, and door slides open, to see stacks of money, behind a plastic wall, in the middle was a sorter/counter, for her to say "As for this moment we all have over 40 million dollars and twenty bricks of gold, and a small sack of gemstones, a present from Maria's family I had no idea how rich they were, over there, is where we stack the cases."

Jack looks around to say, "The builder did a nice job, what did it set us back?" and ads "I'll get the other cases."

"2.5 million, but Lisa told me that the Government would pay off the tab, and reimburse us".

Meanwhile Mark was getting the crew together from the water park and informing the families that the boat would be leaving in four hours, and to take the shuttle bus to the boat dock, near the house, not by the city.

Jack, and Sara finished loading the suitcases in the vault, then Jack and Sara went up to the penthouse where Jack undressed Sara and the two of them consummated their marriage again, but this time it was shorter, just two hours. Jack dressed to place his gun and holster on, then he watched Sara dress in a nice blouse and slacks, then the two of them took the express elevator down, to the kitchen level, to show Jack the pool, that led to a studio overlooking the cliff, then they took the elevator down to the sea level, to come out to a lounge, then, outside, on a dock to see some familiar faces, Mark was first, as Jack said "Mark do you or Mike have any hand held X-ray devices, I got a transmitter on me" said Jack.

Mark says, "I may in the boat house, we use it for listening devices" then up came Carlos and his family, Sara's family, friends, with Alexandra's friends and family, from the boat house, next was a huge moving van stopped and everyone helped off load all the food and supplies, the last to arrive was Samantha, mother, then Maria's family, with all on board, the boat took off at one p.m. sharp with Mark at the helm, Mike was in the engine room and Timmy as his first mate, Jack asked Glenda, Samantha's mother to come see him. Jack was in his stateroom, Glenda walked in.

"Please close the door, now let's talk" said Jack.

"First let me say something, I want to apologize, for coming to the conclusion, that you were a drug dealer, that gift of over one hundred thousand dollars was a bit over whelming, but when Lisa visited me, and told me what you did, well all of that changed. This was the first opportunity I had to say how sorry I am for treating you and my daughter in that fashion, all she ever has been is good, and one time she was bad, it still turned into good, thank you Jack for taking the time to get to know my daughter, and deciding she was the one you wanted as number one, that means the world to me." Jack sits up to say, "Why does it matter if she was number one or not?"

"Well for history sake?"

"Are you talking about the reimbursement package the family heirs receive when someone in their family dies?"

She wasn't looking at him, when she said "no."

Jack pulls out the signed package, and pulls out Samantha's will, to say, "Do you know what this is?" "No" she said calmly.

"It is your daughters will, as written and transcribed by Erica Meyers, she states that under any circumstances will Glenda, my mother, who had abandoned me at my greatest vulnerability will ever get any of my money, possessions and personal things, all of that goes to my husband Jack Cash, in the event of his untimely passing all of it will go to Sara Sanders-Cash, who I agree and allow to fully adopt and raise my child Sam Henry Smith-Cash.

Glenda was fuming, then broke down to cry, as Jack said "The government allowed one person to be there for the birth of our baby, and she chose me", as her crying became louder, in near hysterics, she was on the ground, as Jack got up, as the door opened to see Sara, for Jack to say" Have Mark get the helio ready, I think miss Smith wants to go home."

She stopped long enough to say "No, can I stay," as she paused, then collected, herself up as Jack motioned Sara in, as she came in, then pressed her back to the door.

Jack handed her the paper, as Glenda took it, Jack said "I feel you have suffered enough, I'll make the exception, and you will come with me."

Glenda stormed Jack to say "Oh thank you, thank you, as Sara watched, she too had a slight tear, she wiped away. Jack comforted her, to say "and once Sam is born, we will let you spend as much time as you want with him."

"Really" she said.

"Yes, family means the world to us" said Jack, to add "and from now on you're our family too."

"Thank you Jack you're a good man, I should have never doubted that."

"I second that "said Sara, who opened the door, to allow Glenda to leave, as she shut the door, only to hear another knock, she opened it up to see Mike.

"Here is that wand you wanted."

Mike had a green wand in his hand.

"It's about time" said Jack who was eager to get on with it. "Go slowly, and scan Sara first "said Jack.

"What is that "asked Sara.

"It is an X ray device" said Mike as he started at her head, down to her arms, then there it was on her right wrist, using his knife; he sliced her, and dug it out with her help.

"Thank god that is out, my wrists would hurt I had no idea what that was" 'then it was Jack he was clean, for Mike to say, "It was a tracking device, now he left to find the rest of the wives, Mike found a similar device, now one by one, till they were all done and the devices gone. And overboard.

Jack and Sara went onto the deck to see everyone was having fun, be it Mike and Trixie, Mitzi and Jim, then there was the newest to the team Debby, who Jack went up to say, "Doesn't look like you're having fun?"

"Well to tell you the truth I miss my old job." "How so, the pay?"

"No, not really more like the interaction with my friends, and going to the hot springs on the weekends."

"Sounds like fun, well you can leave anytime you want, if you're not happy, I'll have Mark fly you back."

Debby looked around at the guys to say, "No I'm not that home sick, besides I get to see it, once in a while."

"What do you mean?" asked Jack, to see Mark, come out to say, "Were closing in on our lobster pots, do you want to bring them in?"

"Yeah, sure, have Mike and Timmy help you." "I'd like to help" asked Debby.

"Be my guest", said Jack as he went up to the second deck via a ladder, up next to the new helio, given to him from the governor, from the people of Alabama, for saying thanks, painted in blue with white stripes. Jack watched as the three of them with Jim's help haul in four full pots, as Timmy re-baited it, his mom and dad was on the deck, with Kate and Glenda, the boat was full some seventy five, knowing tomorrow morning they would be in the Dominican Republic, as they pass by Cuba to end up in Carlos's private place by Monte Christi on the north side.

Mark and Mike would alternate at the wheelhouse, while the celebration was cooked by all, everyone got involved in the celebration. At one table was Jacks entire family and the others was his support personnel, Sara sat by Jack as was his three other wives, to make up for Samantha's absence, two new girls came along, Jen and Monica, the nannies and Jack's new partners in the new sport, Sport fucking, he so dearly loved, the two he saved, at the Manor, Sara watched everyone while they ate. Her parents were beside her, even Kate and Debbie were nice, bit envious, but Sara knew things would all change with the birth of Chelsea. Jack told me, I could name her, if it were a boy, then it would be Jack Junior. They all had shrimp, and lobster with ribs and beef brisket, two of Jack's favorites. Jack wore his light windbreaker and was armed. Sara smiled at her man, wondering how long before he would go away again.

The party died down as the support personnel started the clean up. Mark was in the wheel house as off to the south was Cuba. He stayed in to the international water lane, with all the other cargo and cruise ships, it was quite busy; each had a filed travel route plan. The coast guard was to the north and the Cuban Warriors to the south, in their little stealth boats. Mark kept it on course. Casey had told Mark where the escape balloon was, if it was needed to get Jack out immediately. Casey and the team got an invite, so they were off training in the jungles of the Dominican Republic, awaiting Jack's arrival.

Jack got up with the reformed Carlos, as the two of them went to the rail to see his country's lights of Havana, as Carlos pats him on the back to say, "You'd better get some sleep, I have a whole week's worth of stuff planned, you me and the men, while all the women will enjoy the beach."

"Your right, I'll turn in" said Jack as he made his way inside, then up the stairs to the wheelhouse, and knocked on the door, it opened and Jack was pulled inside and the door was locked shut, inside it was Alba and Alexandra who stripped off Jack's clothes, with his help, as he was taken to bed, while Sara was on one side, and the other was a more open Maria, also carrying a baby, Jack had his way with Alex and Alba, as they participated in his new sport, with each receiving full pleasure till he could go no further and slept in between Sara and Alba on the left side, while Alex and Maria were on the other, it was a night of doing it, to all of them, all four hours worth.

Next morning all was quiet, even the engines were shut down, as Jack awoke to see land and the dock, as he sprang up, quickly dressed, and went out, and closed the door.

Jack was on the deck as most of everyone was either on the beach or up at the village, Jack saw all the elders, as they came to him, to thank him, and give him hugs and kisses, they led Jack up to the village, only to see Carlos and all the men walking the other direction, to say, "Were going scuba diving along the ship wrecks, do you want to go?"

"Sure" said Jack, as they all got into this tram of sorts, as it towed the trailer around, Jack was in the back, along with Timmy, across from him was the boisterous Red, but was low key as he saw how many agents were around as he recuperated from his wounds, as for Jack, he was a quick healer, and the best doctors in the world assisting him.

They arrived, as Carlos said, "Now, listen up there are three groups, the first will have me and Jack, in it, the next group will be his support team, and lastly it will be what makes up the family.

Four gorgeous girls strolled out, all in about equal size and impeccable shape, Carlos had a thing for this sharp looking brunette, named Dana, she introduced herself as, "My name is Dana Scott", who was the obvious leader, assigned a super hot brunette, Cami Ross, from Arkansas college, ready for work, and Julie Parsons a lovely blonde, that wowed young Timmy, as Greg equally was absolved with as well, Amber Green another blonde took the support team, although it was Mike and Mark who took the lead, as all others were somewhat familiar as Red was in their group took a liking to Amber, who had only eyes for one person, as she went through a safety class, while Dana took a different approach, as she led Jack and Carlos into a room to change, Jack took off everything, and had a small Speedo swim suit he put on, then Carlos helped Jack as he helped Carlos zip up and place on the water proof booties, they stepped out, with keys to their lockers, yet a big man stood guard, as the pair went to a tank that Dana had the two tank kits ready for them, with fins and mask. Inside the dive tank was another professional, as both were set up, as Dana explained how to dive, what to do, both Jack and Carlos went into the practice tank, as the others stood, when Timmy spoke up to say, "Why can't we go in there, why are we waiting?"

Amber turned around to say "This is for the VIP only, your all guests, you'll have to wait till there in the water, and then you'll get your chance."

Jack felt comfortable swimming, clearing his mask, and holding his breath., as Jack it was perfectly clear he was ready, so she allowed them out of the deep pool, Mark was there to help Jack off with his equipment, and on his back, he placed a weight belt on, to say, "This will help you buoyancy under water, as a blinking red light could be seen, by all, except Jack, who was given a bottle of water, and Dana and the girls led Jack and Carlos to the boat. That's when it became weird, a dark haired girl, who said her name was Kelly and a hot blonde said, her name was Carrie, said, "Take the next boat" as she pushed Mark away. Who stood on the dock as the tiny boat took off.

Mike met up with Mark to say, "What's going on here?" "What do you mean?" asked Mark.

"How come we didn't get on that boat?"

"Did you see the size of that thing; it barely fit five people on it."

"What about Jack?" asked Mike?

"I don't know."

"Come on buddy, we need . . ."

"Look what is coming," said Mark, a huge boat, sprayed their position as it came to a halt, for the guy to say, "Were here for Jack and Carlos, is that you two?"

"Do you see what I'm talking about" said Mike, as they all boarded, but Mike felt better, when the guy said they had a VIP boat, as he made the call to say, "They are on it."

Jack adjusted in his seat on the ledge, across from Carlos, next to him was the dark haired lass, Kelly who was all smiles at Jack, and next to him was the blonde, both suited up, the pilot came to a stop, Jack saw he was about a half mile from the beach, and another boat was anchored, to hear the guy say, "This is how it works below us is a sunken ship, follow Dana in, she will double back and then around the wreck, there is an oyster bed, near there, if you want you can use your knife, to dig out a dozen or so each, attached to your belt is a bag, to collect shells or whatever you want to collect the dive will take 30 minutes min, up to one hour, any questions?"

Jack looked at Carlos, for Carlos to say, "Let's go", and he jumped off, Jack followed, as the guy said, "Aren't you girls going to follow your guys?"

"Oh yeah, as Kelly pulls a gun and shoots the pilot, the gun fire echoed all around, as Mike took over the boat, and kicked it into high gear, as the boat was bearing down on the little boat as the two girls dove in, minutes later the small dingy exploded.

Jack was next to Carlos following Dana inside the huge ship, Jack was amazed by how the sea has taken it as its own, it was calm, and serene.

Behind them was two girls on a mission, however, a minute later, Mark dove in with tank, and knife in hand, these were shallow waters for octopus and shark, sting rays and migrating jelly fish, Mark was equally on a mission, easily catching up with the two killers, Mark sliced the calf of Carrie, who turned trying to get her knife, as Mark pulled her mask off, and cut her breathing tube, a quick move, and the blonde was dead, as the knife slit her throat. The other one was ready for him, as she had her knife ready, as behind him sharks were feeding, by all the blood, Mark kicked it into gear and rushed her with bad intentions, and sliced his way in, this all-purpose former special forces expert sliced once sliced twice, and knocked the knife out of her hand, thought about what Jack would do, so he turned the knife around and hit her on the head, enough to get behind her, to cut off her breathing, he swam backwards. Surfaced, Mike and the others were down below, as another boat was on scene it was Amber, Julie and Cami identified themselves as part of spy club, the black haired girl was hauled up, she was taken down, stripped of her scuba gear, as a plane came over, and a package was dropped, it parachuted down, as Mike and Mark positioned under it, as it landed close by, Mark hauled it up, quickly, he opened up the package, and placed the harness on Kelly the spy and Mike inflated the weather balloon, as the wire was taunt, as Mark positioned the boat, as the plane picked up the weather balloon, and off she went.

Meanwhile, Jack and Carlos, saw a few sharks, but kept following Dana, Jack saw a huge conch shell, and went to the bottom, he picked it up, and placed it in his bag, until Dana motioned "No", and Jack pulled it out and set it back where he found it, as he caught up with them, as she led them to the oyster beds, it was beautiful seeing how structurally engineered, they were placed.

Dana was showing them were to take from, by using their knives, then the sign of ten minutes to go.

Jack saw a few sand dollars, and a starfish, then he pulled up what looked like the tooth bed of a shark, he lifted into his bag, he looked at her, she gave the thumbs up, as he continued to look around, just as a large barracuda made its presence known, then a shark came, as the barracuda took off, Jack saw Carlos was done, as they surfaced, to see the two boats, even the smaller tied up boat was gone, as they swam back to the large boat, Mike and the three girls helped them aboard, as Jack took off his mask to say, "Where is everyone?"

"Well the others are further south of here, how was it for you?"

"That was fun, I'd love to go back down there" said Jack.

"Yeah, I'd like to go again" said Carlos.

Amber says to Dana, "I'll take them around the cove to the coral beds, and take Julie with me."

She shook her head, that it was alright, Mike helped Jack as the girls helped Carlos into a new tank, as Cami said, "Why don't you let them double up their tanks, then you and I can have some fun."

"Sorry I don't roll that way" said Julie. "You're gay?"

"Nope, I just don't roll that way."

Mike helped Jack and Carlos off, as Amber and Julie went in. Dana went below, to change, as Mike watched his tracking device, as Cami was all over him asking him questions, as Dana came up to say, "What's the big deal anyway."

"My job" said Mike.

"What do you mean, there is another level to all this" asked Dana.

"I really don't know what you're asking?" said Mike. "Well you're watching Carlos right?"

"Yeah, so what do you want to know?"

"Well down here he is known as a womanizer."

"So what if he is, it's really none of anyone's business, is it really, we do a job were asked to do, and if we get a chance to help them out it becomes a fringe benefit, if not, then there are days that we wait."

"Wait, go back to that next level" said Dana.

"Well you just need to impress who you're assigned to guard, help or whatever your role is." "Really are there positions open?"

"It's not my place to say if there are any spots available or not, why do you have any special talents?"

"Like what, you mean sexually?"

"Nah, like communications, martial arts, pilot, scuba diver take shorthand, and anything to help out someone?" said Mike, as he saw the other boat reappear with Mark at the helm, to pull up next to them. For Mark to say, "Where's Jack?"

He went again with Carlos."

"Oh", said Mark looking at the girl who was getting suspicious.

Jack and Carlos surfaced, with the two other girls, and onto the large boat, as Mike took off, and Mark followed.

As they docked, a crowd of people had formed, as Jack and Carlos walked through them, as they were looking and gawking. Jack made it back to the room to change as did Carlos, in a bag Jack stuffed his clothes and gun and holster, and knife, he went out, as Carlos was nowhere to be found, so Jack, went along the beach, to find a chair on the beach, he sat, under a huge oak tree, to sit back and relax, as time went by, yet his phone was ringing constantly, Jack pulled it out of the bag, that was in his shirt pocket, to open it up, he began to open his e-mails, some he erased due to the graphic scenes, he saw their were updates from Lisa, from all over the world, as countries have requested his service, he marked save on the top ten, and placed them in a file, to realize his phone was a portable computer, yet he didn't ever remember when he plugged it in, to recharge the battery, he rolls out his contacts to see Jim's name, so he dials him up, he answers to say, "Hi, where are you?"

"I don't know on some beach, by the marina, anyway why I was calling you, how do I charge this phone?"

"You don't, it's powered by your heart, energy is absorbed by its beating sensation, it may even act as a pacemaker, in the event of catastrophic events, but listen you need to get back and surround yourself with Mark and Mike, and we got word that two known assassins are heading your way."

"Are you sure it's not the two British girls earlier?"

"Nah, one was captured the other neutralized, the one we captured said that two of her associates were down there and you were there target."

"Ain't I always, what's new, as Jack continued this insightful conversation, while Carlos, was looking around for his friend, when Dana appeared in his life, her bright smile, and beautiful complexion, easily had Carlos forgetting about Jack, to say, "Thanks for the lesson."

She lingered on a bit, playing coy, for Carlos to say, "Did you want something else?"

"Well now that you say that, what would it take for me to join your team?"

Carlos looked at her, for him it had been a while since any girl had thrown herself at him, thinking, "Did Jack do this for him" as he went along with it to say, "Really nothing, you just have to be willing to put out, as she touched him down there, for him to say, "To put out the information, necessary for us to complete the mission, specific task", Carlos looked around, waiting for Jack any moment, as she went down to her knees, as Red turned the corner to say, "Hey Carlos, oh sorry dude" he smiles, as Dana gets up, for Red to say, "What's wrong you need not leave on my account."

They both laughed, as the bare cheated Bounty Hunter, only knew of Carlos, the two looked at one another, and then Carlos took Red with him, for a drink and a smoke.

Kate and Debbie were invading the Marina, along with Jen and Monica, while Alex and Alba were on jet skis, only Sara and Maria were resting on the boat, with their security detail in place.

A boat comes to the side, with two men in it to say, "Ahoy, may we board, we have a message for Sara and Maria?"

"Identify your self's?"

"I'm Elliott and this is Bramwell, were with the FBI."

"What's the FBI doing down here?" said Curtis, then pauses to pull out his glock.

"Whoa wait a minute, you got this all wrong", as the two placed their hands up.

"Tell me what you want to tell her, or I will scatter you all over this place."

"Calm down bodyguard, we don't want trouble, as Bramwell, was searching for something, as Elliott, was ready to dive as they stalled.

"I'm going to count to three, out with it, one"

Both were jiggery.

"Two" said Curtis.

As in the background their patrol boat, caught a glimpse of what was going on.

"three", both men drove off their craft into the water, Curtis held the rail, as it was a Dominican Republic surveillance boat, complete with divers, as it made a wake the Commander said, "What's wrong Curtis?"

"Two men wanted to board the boat."

"No problem", then spoke in his native tongue, as four men went into the water, moments later, they caught the two men, and pulled them into the boat, for the Commander to say, "No need to worry, there on board and we will take them back at home port, then we will have fun with them, take care."

The boat zoomed off, as Sara came out onto the deck, to say

"Curtis is everything alright?" "Yes Miss Cash it is."

"I was wondering if you wanted lunch."

"Sure that would be nice" he said, but turned to see that she was gone, next time he knew to keep his mouth shut.

Jack saw Mark to say, "Hey you saw Carlos?"

"Yeah he and Red are on the veranda", seeing Mike, the two were talking when Dana appeared to say, "This isn't about Carlos, you're all here for Jack Cash, the Bounty Hunter."

"And so we are" said Mike looking at her in his cocky way. "Well at least you could be honest with me" said Dana, as Mark steps between them to take her arm and say, "All you are is hired help, yes we know you're in spy club, and we know Jack is the founding member, but he is here to relax, rest and not worry about some girl who wants to join his team, look around you, there are beautiful women everywhere and lots of them."

"Yeah because the Miss World beauty pageant is being held here." Said Dana.

"What did you say" asked Mark.

"Some 300 of the most beautiful women have been flying in all day."

"Carlos", said Mark, under his breath and caught up with Mike to say,"Let's go see Carlos." "Wait" pleaded Dana.

Mark stopped in his tracks to say, "Wait, is right", looking at Dana to say, "How would you like to help us out?"

"What are you doing?" asked Mike.

"Go with it, watch, so you want to help, why don't you get your friends, Amber, Julie and Cami together and participate in the event."

"We could do that, it starts this coming weekend."

"Good that will give us enough time to get Jack out of here and ring Carlos's neck" said Mark, as the two fled her, as she had a smile on her face, with a low sinister laugh.

Jack reached the veranda, to see the two drinking and smoking cigars, to hear Carlos say, "Ah Jack have a seat and admire the view, place your bag down, as Jack took a seat next to Carlos's right, to see what they were looking at, throngs of gorgeous women, all circling around in the lower end of the village. Jack got up and left, moments later Jack was surrounded by all those lovely ladies. As he found hands on his shoulders as Carlos laughed, to say, "Look around my friend, do you know what this all about?" "No, a festival."

"No Jack, this is my wedding gift to you?"

Jack looks at his brother to say, "What are you talking about?"
"It's simple my friend, there all here for you."

"What are you saying, you're whacked out."

"No, no, no my friend, this is the Miss World beauty pageant,
however, it's really an audition for those who want to enter our
marriages."

Jack just looked at him, like he was crazy, Jack began to walk
off, when Carlos and Red caught up with him to say, "Listen my
friend, I'm serious, you and I are judges, for this weekend, so let's
go mingle around, as Jack carried his bag with him, as he made it
back to the Marina, where Dana was cleaning up, as Jack saw her
to say, "Do you know if there is a taxi available, to go to the region
of Monte Christi?"

She looked up at him, to say "No, there is really no taxi, but if
you want I could drive you, it's about ten minutes away."

"Great, I'll wait over there."

"I won't be long" said Dana, as Jack took a seat, on the stone
wall, while she washed up, and placed the tanks away, closed up
and locked the doors, as she came by to say, "I'm ready now, ready
to go."

"Sure" said Jack as he fell behind her, out to her car, as she led
the way, then she unlocked the door for him, as he got in, just as
she slid in, Jack looked over at her, to see the brown hairs on her
arms, as she caught him to say, "What are you looking at?"

"Oh nothing" said Jack as he was looking the other direction,
as Dana said, "I'm not worried."

"What do you mean" asked Jack. "Oh nothing "said Dana.

"Alright out with it, what do you want to know?"

"Well funny that you asked, you're with Carlos, and I'd like to
join his team."

"Really, why do you want to do that?"

"Because he has all these agents around supporting them, and I
like to be one of them."

"I think you're mistaken, but if you must, and want to join his flock, I'd could put in a good word for you, what you have to offer me?" asked Jack, looking at her.

"This ride."

"Oh I see, sure, do you have a cell number, I can pass onto him" asked Jack.

As she said it, he programmed it in his phone, to say and your name is Dana, as his phone rang, as they approached the village, Jack got out as she stopped to say, "Thanks for the ride", she drove off, with a smile on her face, as Jack made it to the dock, and got into his smaller boat, and took off, out to his bigger boat, tied it off, and went up the ladder to see Curtis to say, "How was your day?"

"Not bad, a little trouble here and there."

"Why don't you take some time for yourself, Sara and I need some time together."

"Sure thing boss."

Jack watches as Curtis takes the boat in, to call up Lisa to say, "It's me, what do you have?"

"we uncovered where Annabel Ryan is, you know Miss Margaret's daughter, however the officials won't allow anyone to go in there except you, it's also confirmed she was brained washed and living as a wife to a prominent Doctor named Lester Graham, of Mercy hospital in downtown Brussels, we could pick you up by flight at 0600 hours, with your team in place and on board."

"No, just the immediate crew, it's just a pickup and delivery?"

"Yeah but it's also an extraction of the doctor."

"Alright have Paul and Rick on board." "Will do, tomorrow at 0600 pickup."

"Oh one more thing, I need info on a spy club girl named Dana, I met scuba diving what do you have on her?"

"She is the top agent we have down there, why is she misses number six?"

"Maybe, and about Samantha, I'm bringing her mother with me, so whatever you need to do."

"No, don't worry about it; she and Sara are both invited.

"Thanks" said Jack as he slid the phone shut, and went into the galley to see his lovely wives Maria and Sara hard at work cooking, a seafood stew, Sara saw Jack to give him a big hug and kisses, while Maria did the same but in a more reserved way, as they ate, Jack heard a boat, and went out to see it was Curtis, to say, "Ah your back, I need you to lie low, I'm leaving tomorrow morning for a quick three day trip, watch over Sara and Maria, while I'm gone, my support team is on the ground, if Mark or Mike needs to know then tell them."

"Yes sir", said Curtis as Jack went back in, finished his supper, then went to bed, with Maria and Sara, at 0500, Jack arose, as did Maria and Sara, who were dutiful in their attention to him, as He told them he was off on a short three day mission, dressed and well armed, his blue watch a staple of his tools, he had a hearty breakfast off poached eggs, buttermilk pancakes, hash browns and sourdough toast, with freshly whipped butter and strawberry jam, a cup of black coffee, and an orange juice. Curtis ate with them, as he was the only one allowed in, to share the moment with them. Jack with Curtis's help, pulled out the harness and helped it onto Jack, then Jack twisted the balloon, it inflated and was launched, as it soared upward, as he held onto the rail, as the alarm went off, and Jack was gone, Jack soared upward, what a rush, he felt, as the two big wheels, wound that cable up, to a platform below the plane, as Jack got to the rail under the plane, the platform raised, and Jim unhooked the line, and helped Jack up, to see Debby, and Brian, Paul and Rick, two that were unexpected was Trixie and Mitzi, who led Jack into his room, and closed the door.

Jack slept the entire way as the rest awaited the landing at Brussels' International Airport on the outskirts of the city; they were cleared to land, and placed in hanger three, to come to a stop.

Jack opened the door, to see all was waiting, as a customs officer was there to check everyone out, and as a council member, once he saw Jack he handed him the official paper, to say, "Welcome misour, Cash, our country would like to extend its thanks for you visit and the President asks if you may join him tonight for a celebration, for the absolution of those behind the abduction and slavery, and at this banquet, you will be honored, shall we say two of you?"

As Jack looked around at his candidates he choose Mitzi, who accepted, and he wrote her name down, to say "Now, we know your vehicle, it carries diplomatic plates, as for assistance all of our agencies are at your disposal, here is my number, and we expect to see you around six tonight."

"Yes, you shall", said Jack graciously . . .

As Paul and both Rick looked on, as Jim herded them away, then doubled back, to talk with Jack, to make sure he had everything. "Black tie event, I don't suppose you have a suit for me?" said Jack.

"Of course you can thank Debby for that" said Jim. "Oh yes, Debby how is she working out?"

"Well she was the one who came up with the whole balloon idea, and how to do it safely, she is an asset." "I should have taken her."

"Nah, she doesn't like the lime light, but Mitzi does."

"Can you place the suit in the car, along with taking anything out of the trunk, so I can store a couple of bodies?"

"It will be done" said Jim, as Jack turned the corner to see Debby, making herself at home; he came up on her to whisper "Thanks."

She turned around, somewhat disappointed, yet was nice, to say "This maybe my last mission, I'm more of a ground girl, but thanks for the chance."

"Your welcome", as Jack collected up Mitzi, who held onto a nice evening gown, set it in the trunk, with some shoes, to say, "I'm ready to go."

"Paul, I'll let you know when I need you, Jim can you get Paul some wheels."

Jack and Mitzi got into the Mercedes Mac Laren, and it roared to life, and off they went.

CH 8

Annabel Ryan
the Damsel in distress

J ack and Mitzi sat in his car across from the apartment
where Annabel was suppose, to be at, the stately manor was
spectacular, the tinted windows, hid them and all the dog
walkers, three hours till the dinner, Jack was deciding to go in or not,
he carried a satchel, and within it was an antidote, and serum kit.
Just as the doors opened, a doorman, let her out with her Springer
spaniel, to do his business, Jack used his professional digital camera,
to take pictures of her, as the Identification, appeared on the screen,
of a perfect match, as she went back inside, while Mitzi was on
the phone to Lisa. Then an odd thing occurred, a car whose driver
looked like the doctor, drove past, in that bleep of a second, Jack took
the shot, he was unrecognizable. Jack turned, and opened his console
to put the camera away, as the images from the laptop were down
loaded to his phone, as they waited. Jack was ready to make contact,
when out on the balcony was Annabel, and her man, as Jack went
back to his console, it was too late, they went back in.

Time was running out, as Mitzi reminded him, "It was only an
hour." Then Jack said, "Twenty minutes, according to my clock."

"Yes, but we need to change and be ushered in", he heard in his
ear piece.

"Your right, Jack started the car, and told the car stealth mode, fast."

Jack laid back and let the car do all the driving, and manipulations of the light changing, to favor them, meanwhile behind them stuck in traffic was Annabel and Doctor Lester, trying to get to that same function, with little or no success.

Jack was right fifteen minutes later, they parked by the side entrance, and then went in, with their clothes, into a private bathroom, as Mitzi locked the door, Jack sat on the tub's edge to watch."

"It's not like you haven't seen me naked before", she said as she pulled off her top, to reveal a black bra, and matching panties, to say, "and you're wearing a white dress that is nearly see through?"

"What it won't be that bad."

"Really be my guest" said Jack as she slipped it on, and it was evident she would have to lose the bra, as she said, "What do you think?"

"I can see right through and they stand out like the American flag."

"What do you think I should do?"

"I could trade you and let you have mine, or go without."

"No thanks I'll go without", as in one fatal swoop, she pulled them down, as Jack got a nice view, to hear her say, "How does it look now?"

"Better, you can hardly tell." Said Jack with a smile. "Come on let's go" said Mitzi.

"I was trying to be a gentleman."

"What to watch me get naked and then what?"

Jack stood up and pinned her to the door, as she said, "Finally your giving a girl what she needs, as he opened the door and he pushed her out, to say "I'll be there in a moment, try not to get yourself into too much trouble."

Jack dressed quickly, and as he was ready, he slipped on his holster and gun, then his tuxedo jacket.

Mitzi stood waiting for him, as he approached her, he turned away from her and out to his car to deposit his other clothes., then he went back inside, to see his date, who slipped something into his inside pocket, then wraps her arm around his as the two walked into the main dining room. In the middle were round tables, and then up above was a long table Jack assumed it was for royalty, he led Mitzi in, to see a porter, who said, "State your name, Sir?"

Mitzi spoke up to say "Mister and Misses Jack Cash", she said proudly.

"Yes, right here, your one of our VIP's and takes a seat on the left side of the table please, cocktails will be served, everything is all paid for, but if you like a donation plate will be offered later." Jack followed the man in through the empty tables as they were one of the first's guests, Jack pulled out Mitzi's chair for her, she sat, as he pushed her in, he saw the sign for restrooms, to tap on her shoulder, to say "I'll be in the restroom".

Jack walked the hallway, to see the cut crystal entrances, then around the corner, was a door, he looked out to see, a parade grounds, as a huge limousine pulled up, then people begin to exit, so Jack back stepped to men's restroom, he slipped inside, to see the stalls, urinals, and sinks, he washed his hands, as another man came in, as he exited, he came to the end of the hallway, to see, the place was filling up, on his left was Mitzi, his table had doubled in size, Jack took his seat, as Mitzi gushed all over him to a lady next to her, then a gentleman bragged he was rich, and for Jack and Mitzi to come to his jewelry store and buy her some gifts, as Jack whispered in her ear, "Keep an eye on our target, when she gets up to use the restroom, go with her, as she comes out distract her and I will administer the antidote."

"Yes sir" she said loudly.

"Do you obey what your husband's says to you" asked Gloria, the older lady.

"Always, he says, I do." She said smiling at him. "Really you sound like them, are you part of the Oasis society?"

"No, I just believe, that I'm my husband's servant, who is this Oasis Society?" asked Mitzi, while she was making small talk with the other's at the table, as Jack surveyed the tables, in front of him, when his phone was ringing, he pulled it out, to lower the volume, to read the mail, he opened it to read, "Gloria thinks were with the Oasis Society, is it related to this case?" asks Mitzi in a text to Jack. Jack texts,"Who is Gloria?"

"Over there, she said her name was Gloria Thomas some record producer, or something like that?"

Jack forwarded it to Lisa, and then sent it. And then began to scan his messages, from all of his wives, then he saw one from Devlin, his former dead partner, he hit the translate to written word, from voice, to say "Congratulations on your marriage to a strong and giving woman, I spent the day with her, your quite a special man, and never realized what you mean to others, and from this day forward you can count on me to having your back and protecting you from evil, if you give me another chance to take a shower with you, I will make it up to you, Jack I love you."

Jack muttered to himself "That was nice, a partner I'll never forget, to hit save."

Jack slid his phone shut, to see Mitzi place her hand on his arm, lovingly, as Jack noticed Gloria was on a non-stop talking mode, as Jack placed his hand onto Mitzi's back, as Annabel, past them by. Jack rose, to help Mitzi up, as she said her goodbyes, then catches up with Annabel, to go into the restroom, Jack stood in the hallway, he opened the small case to pull a pen, in position, the door opened, as Mitzi blocked the door, Annabel was forced into Jack, as he struck her bare forearm, releasing the antidote, for her to say, "Hey Mister, you stuck me."

"Sorry Miss, I was just trying help my wife out", Jack raised his hands, to allow her to pass. Into the restroom, then re-emerged to see, Mitzi embraces Jack to give him a long smoldering kiss, as Annabel watched, then returned to her table.

Jack broke off the kiss, to say, "She is gone, you can stop." "It wasn't an act, I like kissing you."

"I like feeling your boobs."

"So what's stopping you, go ahead I don't care" said Mitzi. Jack led them back to their seats, only to hear Gloria going crazy over that kiss, she watched, till Mitzi say, "Yeah, wait till tonight, he'll get that and much more."

Jack tuned them out to see a meltdown was beginning to erupt, as Jack tapped on Mitzi shoulder to say, "Better go get your girl" said Jack, as the two were off, first was Mitzi there to console Annabel, telling her she was a friend of her mother Margaret Ryan, as Jack hoisted up the Doctor, and the two were led out, the other direction to his car, out the doors, Jack held the doctor's arm behind his back as he came to the trunk, it opened on his command, inside was a zip ties, Jack zip tied the doctors wrists, and one for his mouth to suppress his tongue, he hoisted him into the trunk, then zip tied his ankles, a quick search revealed a soft cloth and a small bottle of chloroform. The girls got in, as Mitzi calmed Annabel down, to hear his phone ring, Jack sat in the driver's seat to answer it, it was Lisa who said "Oasis Society is an offshoot of this group, can you take pictures of all the girls you suspect to be part of this, and get a face recognition, I've notified the police to assist you."

Jack slid the phone shut to say, "Can you drive them to the airport" "Not in this car?"

"What do you mean?" asked Jack.

"This car is yours exclusively, just like your gun; we have been told under no circumstances can we drive this car." "Alright, let's get out."

"What's going on?"

"The mission has changed, Oasis Society, may have more girls under duress", as Jack gets out, with towel in hand and a dab of Chloroform, and out went Annabel.

She dropped to the grass, as Jack picked her up, the trunk opened, as he set her inside there, Jack hesitated, then decided to zip tie her mouth, wrists, and ankles, to hear, "Your really going to traumatize her now."

"That's the least of her troubles, come on, I need your help." "Really what do you have in mind?"

"Remember those collection plates?" "Yeah."

"Well, you speak German right, so you speak, it and ask for a donation, I'll hold the plate, and take a picture of both couples". Jack held the door open for Mitzi, as she walked in, Jack pulled his phone, to set it in the picture mode, in one hand, and in the other was the gold plate, he swiped off the end table, as Mitzi caught on, and led Jack to each table, as his motion picture camera caught all their faces, and the donations, four tables down, Jack motioned to two other girls, at different tables, as an announcer Identified Jack as a usher, and that ensured Jack went to every table, the plate was bounding over with cash, as Mitzi changed out it with another, then at the last one, Jack was at his table, as music was played, they sat down, as Jack sent the streaming video feed.

Prime rib was served, along with lobster and fried artichokes, the rich guy, uncorked the champagne, to pour it off for his new friends Jack laid his phone down on the table, while he looked at the tower that butter has melted under a candle, several sauces were on a curved plate, using a spoon he sampled each one, a sweet marmalade, a white hot creamy substance, a black fluid, and a creamy Brussels sprouts, as it said on a plaque, Jack sampled the prime rib, as his wrist watch, had no colors to distinguish if it was poisoned or not, so he tore into the meal.

Mitzi was on the gossip train, barely eating. As Jack's phone hummed, he slid it open, a list of eighteen girls were confirmed missing, against the data base, he then forwarded it to Mitzi's phone, to add in the text, "Lure these girls into the women's restroom, I'll take care and we will use a limo to get them out"

Mitzi stood up, and went to the girl furthest away, as Jack got up, he slid the phone in his coat pocket, to pull out the chloroform towel, as Jack stood at the women's restroom, to divert other women to the other bathroom, across the dining room, then one by one, he chloroformed the girls, then zip tied their wrists and mouth's over the next hour, for all eighteen girls, then with Mitzi's help, he carried them to a limo, as Mitzi got in with the girls, Jack drove the huge, limo, he stopped by his car, popped the trunk, and pulled out the sleeping Annabel. Jack set her in the front seat.

Jack drove off, onto the tiny streets, making sure he dented half a dozen expensive cars, as he got out onto the highway system, to the airport, he slowed, to see the same gate guard, Jack flashed his badge, he was waved in, down to the hanger, Jack dialed up Jim, who answered, Jack saw the hanger door go up, as he drove in, as he parked, there was Brian, and Debby ready with Jim to help offload and carry the girls in, Jim comes out to see Jack holding a young blonde, girl to say, "Where's the car at?"

"I left it behind."

"You can't, was it in a residential area?"

"Yeah, oh shit I forgot I got someone else in the trunk, how about, I take Brian with me, and Mitzi . . ." "And all the girls?"

"Keep them in my room; can you come up with more antidotes for the rest of them?"

"How long will you be?" "Maybe an hour."

As Jack carries Annabel, in, binding cut off her, to lay her across the already crowded bed, to say, "Round up Brian, and were going back I got a plan."

Jim stood at the door, and then allowed Jack to pass, as he spoke with Brian to say, "You drive, Mitzi in the middle."

Jack turned to say to Jim "Say how come Mitzi or Brian can't drive the Mercedes?"

"Because there not you or I, but I may take it under consideration, for a change."

Jack slid into the passenger side seat, as Brian, backed up the limo as the door opened, and Brian swung the big rig around, he drove it like a pro, as Jack explained his plan to Mitzi, "We will go back inside, and one by one, lure the gentlemen into the men's room, while Brian, you stay in the limo, while I will bring them out for you to take back to the hanger, any sign of trouble just get out of there. Jack was telling Brian where to go, as this time the place was crowded, as Brian took several tries to get that huge limo onto the parade grounds, to park next to other limo's, Jack and Mitzi got out, they went in through the backdoor, past the restrooms, to see the King and first lady was there all were still eating, Mitzi took her seat with Jack to get a earful from Gloria, as it looked calm, so Jack motioned her, to their targets, then one by one, Mitzi was on a roll, as Jack had eight down, and zip tied, when all of a sudden, it all came to a crashing halt as city police and the corruption flowed in as the place became a shooting gallery, Jack, waved Mitzi off, as she ran out only to see the police coming at her, she was caught, as bodies were flying around, Jack didn't hesitate, and pulled his weapon, he took shots to clear a path, the commando's went down, with eye shots, as Jack got to Mitzi, as several commandos tackled Jack, Jack lost his gun, and at that moment the black colored pistol, was picked up by Mitzi, she held it firmly to squeeze off two shots, before the pain threshold was going too far and tossed it to Jack, who took it, and finished off his two tacklers, Jack pulled his phone to take pictures of his dead commando's, as the King and queen, were whisked away, Jack shot at those who were following them out, as the King got into his limo, as it drove off, Jack stood outside, watching the limo leave as Jack was locked outside, as he tried the back door, Jack pulled off his belt, took a strip of plastic explosive and a blasting cap, he coiled up the belt and put in his pocket, to sync up the transmitter, he went against the wall and blew the lock, Jack emerged, to see four commando's down, as the shooting was still in good form, as Jack drug the bodies away from the entrance, as he looked around the corner, to see a new force had arrived, dressed in all blue, from the way his car was, Jack ducked into the Men's restroom, to see all of his men in a row, Jack pulls out his belt, pulls off the rest of the plastic explosive, to roll it out, he made an X on the outside wall, by the window, set the blasting cap, he dialed up the phone and the soft wall blew outward, as Brian looked on, put the limo in gear, and went to the explosion, as Jack was pulling out a guy, Brian opened the rear doors, as Jack tossed the first one in, Brian went in, to help out as a commando say Brian, only to see the commando drop, as Jack passed by Brian, to pull in the commando, and lock the door, as Brian, and Jack carried the six remaining men out, Jack watched Brian carry the last man out, while, Jack, opened the door, to crawl into the bloody hallway, to see that on one side was the commando's on the other was the police, and as Jack peered around to see Mitzi, behind a table, on its side, he pulled up a dead commando as protection, as he felt the bullet slamming the dead, man, as he dove on the stage, and then he became the target, Jack paused to curl around, he shot back and commandos went down, while they retaliated one hundred times the bullets back, as Jack inched closer as all around him he was getting pelted, he kept his head down, as both the commando's and police were firing at him, as he slipped down on the far side, he saw Mitzi, he also saw the dead diners all caught in the crossfire, Jack motioned to Mitzi to come to him, as he knelt down and shot all that were firing his way, she leapt up and out the doors, followed by Jack, as the doors, shut, was the limo, and Brian, as Mitzi got in, as Jack waved them off, as Jack watched them head off across the parade grounds, to the other side, as he inched along the wall, only to see his car was trapped by all the police cars, looking it over, he got in the first one, and moved it back, then another one forward, seeing a path, Jack slid in behind the wheel, to say "Start, stealth, go."

The car took off, and across the parade grounds, he exited, as he was hands free, as the car went into extreme top speed, as it zig zag the narrow streets of Brussels, and just like that he was already at the airport, as it slowed and stopped at the gate, to hear, the airport was on a lock down basis, "Sir no one is allowed in."

"Diplomatic plates exclude that, I'm flying out." "Sorry sir" said the attendant.

Jack pulled his weapon, and the gate went up. To say, "Allow the limo right behind me in, or."

"Alright I get it."

Jack drove over to the hanger, to dial up Jim, to see the hanger go up, as he drove in, around, and up the ramp into the plane, to park into the wheel wells. Jack got out as the car shut off, to see a lab all lit up, to see Jim still at work. To say, "You should really think about enclosing that in a room"

"I'll take that under consideration."

Jack went down the ramp, to click open the hanger, to see the limo drive in, and park, both doors opened, as, Jack went to the rear, as Mitzi was in Jack's arms, kissing him, as Brian, was on the other side, pulling men out as Jack extracted Mitzi off of him, to say, "Go inside and help with the girls."

Between the two of them, they off loaded the eight men, in the cargo, while Brian went forward, to the planes controls, while Jack activated the ramp to come up, but Jim said, "Stop were not leaving till I get done with this antidote, let Brian know, will you."

Jack went to Brian to say, "Jim wants you to secure the cargo before we go."

Brian and Jack worked as a team, to set the men in pull down net bunks, Jack even pulled out the Doctor, and then they secured the car. Jim finished, seeing Debby, from the room, to say, "How are the girls?"

"Resting, we have them on the floor in blankets and pillows, what can I do to help?"

"Can you fill those syringes with that fluid, while I get us going?"

Jack took a seat across from Debby watching her work, while the plane moved, Jack watched her move around, so he got up and help brace her by holding onto her, as they heard, "Prepare for lift off."

Debby leaned back into Jack, as he placed his arms around her, for her to say, "It's about time we get close."

"All you have to do is ask" said a smiling Jack.

"It's that easy?"

"Yep, I liked you the moment I met you."

"And so did I, so know what, we do it right here."

The plane took off, out of the hanger, taxied, and then thrusted upward, into the skies above Brussels.

CH 9

New team, New tactics

J ack held onto Debby like he meant it, firmly around the waist, while propped in the doorway. She was grinding into him, to say, "It would sure be nice if we could just do it."

Jack whispers, "Where and when, you name it, but you name the place."

"If you like, although this looks like a laboratory."

"Converted, use to be the cargo's bathroom, but I asked Jim, to make it into a lab for disease control." "What about the troops we carry?"

"Really there shouldn't be, you're our only cargo, that's why the room was enlarged, a super massive bed was put in, I guess we have twelve girls on it, however all eighteen girls were once on there."

The plane leveled off, at cruising altitude, as Jim looked left and right as two American F-18 Hornets escorted the plane over the Atlantic.

Jim went back to see Jack and Debby finished the syringes, as Debby went into Jack's room, with the tray, as Jim said, "If you like come into the cockpit, I have our bunk you can have, our flight is eight hours, back to the Dominican Republic."

"Where else could I go?" asked Debby, looking confused at him.

Jack followed Jim back to the cockpit, to see that Jim, pulled out a bunk, as Jack sat down, only to see to peer forward to see a fighter aircraft as an escort. Jack went back to the bunk and sat down and put his head into the pillow, and was out.

Mitzi thought about Jack while she and Debby attended to the girls as the serum was taking a hold and the girls were coming out of their stupor. Then one stood up to say, "I know you you're the one who lured me to the bathroom, where is the guy who gave me this headache?"

"Sit down, relax, he is gone, you're on a flight home." "What do you mean?"

"You're on a plane and were taking you home."

"What of our husband's, captors, oh hell I don't know what it was, like I was trapped in a nightmare."

Other's also came around till all was sober, for Mitzi to say, "Listen up, each of you were kidnapped and forced into slavery, drugged and sent to Belgium."

One raised their hand, who clearly was an instant leader, to say, "Who other than you is our savior?"

Mitzi composed herself to say, "His name is Jack Cash, International Bounty Hunter."

All the girls became quiet, looking at one another as they all rushed the door, only to hear Mitzi whistle, to get their attention, to say, "He is not on this flight, he took a private plane out, so lie down and get some rest, use the bathroom as needed, but your all staying in here, till we land."

Debby helped some, while Mitzi stood guard, as all went back to sleep, Mitzi motioned to Debby to watch over them, as Mitzi slipped out. Mitzi entered the cockpit, to see Jack, to gush over him, by pulling out the top bunk, to hear from a ruffled Jim to say, "What are you doing?"

Mitzi stopped what she was doing, to step forward, she leaned in, to whisper,"Have you lost the real purpose of why we are here?"

"I know your purpose, but this is our space," said a miffed Jim.

"According to protocol, you work for me, and you can be replaced, is that what you want?"

Jim looked at her to say, "Are you serious?"

"Ah that's it isn't it, you're in love with Debby, aren't you, what did Jack make out with her that's it isn't it, does she know you like her?"

Mitzi stepped back to begin to laugh, as she stripped the top bunk to hear, "Go ahead, and tear up that bunk that is mine."

"No Brian, this bunk, this plane and all that is in it, belongs to him", as she placed the pillow, and sheets and blanket on Jack and turned out the upper light, to say, "So Jim what is your plan, are we flying to where you want to go, Washington or Dominican Republic?"

Jim turned his head, speechless he stared at her, stuttered a bit, to say "Back to Dominican Republic." "By whose authority?"

"Well I talked with Jack?"

"Yes but did you talk with me, or Lisa, what about the passengers on our flight?"

"That's my point, just like you said Jack is the very most important person on this flight." Jim turns his head to see she was gone, to say to Brian, "Keep us on course." "It's on autopilot" said Brian smartly.

Mitzi was refilling the coffee, when Jim approached, to say, "Look I'm sorry for what I said, I'm just a little frustrated, that he likes her, and he is this spy who is such a humanitarian."

"Had you thought that he is being him, this is what he does, and pardon me if I like to help him out, just ask Brian, who himself is just grateful to be a part of this, I know you live in your own world, but either your with us, or I'll send you home and get a pilot who will take risks, and one more thing Mister, whoever Jack chooses to be with, its either going to happen or not, and you'll have no say in it whatsoever."

Jim backed away from Mitzi, knowing a battle was brewing, and he backed off to go in to the cockpit to see Jack, then Brian, who said, "Who's the boss now?"

"Shut up" said Jim. Taking his seat next to Brian.

"You know, she is right." "How so?"

"Well we all work for someone, I was in the armory for the eighteen months, and several Commanders later, we get wind of a super guy was coming, then we were all getting excited, the place was cleaned from head to toe."

"What is your point?" said Jim.

"For that we were in the support role of possible greatness, but we, you and I are living the excitement."

"Yeah I see your point, maybe I lost sight of."

"Hold on I'm getting some chatter on the world feed, do you want to switch on the satellite feed?" asked Brian.

Jim turned on his console, to see across his screen, then a live feed, from Belgium, where a reporter, was speaking.

"Turn it up said Mitzi handing the two some coffee.

"That's right the King of Belgium, narrowly missed an assassination attempt this last evening, when a planned attack occurred, unbeknownst to the attackers, American Super Spy Jack Cash and his wife, were present, as you can see from an earlier footage, caught on several cell phones, twenty four commandos stormed the fundraiser, only to go down to the Super Spy, of the World, it was a lineup of three of the top spies of the world, Thomas Jones, British secret service and his wife, Dana Jones, and from the Russian side, Vladimir Putin, and with him a girl of younger, by all accounts the three of them took down eighteen, and saved the King, and his party, as their awareness averted a major coup attempt, this explosion caught on tape was one of two events, that signaled the beginning to the end for the Commandos. Then the police arrived with UN advisors to confirm all the dead."

"Spokesman for the UN, Gene Garp from South Africa, said, he sanctioned, the use of force, to take down those terrorist, avert a coup, and for the real reason, all of this took place, and he later refused more specific details." "For the Atlanta News, this is Natasha Rogers."

Jim turned his head back towards Mitzi to say, "I'm deeply sorry, I didn't know."

"Sorry about what", snapped Jack as he sat up, as he answered his phone."

"I'm sorry I didn't know," said Lisa, who went on to say, "The phone call I placed was intercepted by the militants."

"No, It wasn't, they had a VIP on the inside, or it could be either the British versus the Russian, whom were there as buyers, check the name Richard and Gloria Kendall, they own some Jewelry store." as Jack scanned his video file, to mark the pictures and then said, "Here they come."

"Why haven't you answered your phone?"

"I was tired I'm sorry to you, from now on contact Mitzi." "Her phone is off, she won't respond."

"Then contact Jim, oh I think he wants out, anyway."

Jim turned his head not looking good, to hear Jack say, "Contact Debby, I'll see if she wants your job." "What are your plans?" asked Lisa.

"I don't know, Jim said he was taking me back to the reception?"

"He did" screamed Lisa in the phone, she calmed down, to say "I'm sorry, he isn't your boss, according to your flight plan looks like you'll be there in two hours, the government of Belgium, has credited you with twenty four commandos, and what do you have of cargo?"

"I think nineteen girls, and nine men." "So that's fifty two million."

"The nineteen girls, is a gift."

"No they are not, you're not in a position to give gifts, the only gift you give is that your still alive, these covert operations, you undertake, needs some more support, from now on I'll have Black Ops on board, how does that sound?"

"Fine, just put two women on that team, as well."

"You got it, you're the boss" Jack slides his phone shut, to say to Mitzi, "Where is your phone?"

She looked around, feeling for it in her pockets only to say,

"I must have dropped it back . . . . "

She was cut off to hear a strange noise, and then Jim answered his phone; he was calm as he listened, as he was getting chewed out, as Mitzi said to Jack, "Are you hungry?"

"Sure what do you have?" said Jack getting up to follow her into the galley, to say, "I like what you have done to the place."

"Really, it is all Debby; do you want to pick up where we left off?"

"Nah, I'm a bit worn out, but thanks for the offer" said Jack taking a seat, as she unfolded a table, she placed a silverware rolled up in a dinner napkin, as she set out four carton's of milk, two whole and two chocolate, the microwave went off, and a steaming plate, was pulled out as she said, "Roast beef, twice baked, mashed potatoes, buttered corn, and a slice of cranberry sauce." Jack smiled up at her, to say, "Thank you", she then placed a small cup of hot coffee, in a holder, to squeeze a bit of lemon. She looked up to see Jim, his whole face and demeanor had changed, as he said, "Here use my phone, is now yours, do you want to fly into the airport or."

"Parachute in?" asked Jack. Looking up at him, in between bites.

"We can do that, again I want to apologize, for my behavior to both of you."

"No problem" said Jack, but Mitzi just looked at him, to watch Jack eat.

"If you're so in love with Debby, then telling her, I don't care, it's like we never did anything, and I just like her and think she is an asset to the team." Said Jack to Jim in between bites.

Jim leaves as the conversation was over and it was becoming weird, as Brian stood at the door, to say "Jack when you're ready I have a harness and two chutes ready, Jim said he was going to drop you at a low level, it that alright?"

"Sure whatever."

"Well are you going to drop in that tux?" asked Brian.

"Nah, I have my clothes in the trunk of the car, I'll be there in a moment" motioning for him to get lost. Jack ate while Mitzi was on the phone with Lisa, she closed up the phone, to say, "We will drop you off, then go to Washington, then come back with Black Ops group and some candidates, girls."

"That's fine, but I have a few I'd like to add." "Go ahead I'll type them in", as she was ready.

"Her name is Dana Scott and Julie Davis; on second thought can you make Dana my personal assistant?"

"Sure whatever you want," said Mitzi as Jack finished the platter, to say, "That was delicious and very good, is that how all the food will taste?"

"It will for as long as I'm making them."

Jack looked at her as he got up, went around the corner, to see the trunk open, on the starboard side, he saw all the captors being held in net cages.

"That's so that they don't move around", said Brian. Jack saw that his clothes were folded very neatly, to say, "You didn't have to do that."

"It was an honor, besides whatever I can do, to help you I will." To add, "This sure beats being in an armory cage."

"From now on you're staying near the plane, you're too valuable to me, to get you involved, but thanks for helping out, unlike Jim."

"Oh I don't think you'll ever have a problem again with that, sometimes we all need some attitude adjustments, even I, or our ego's would get the best of us."

"Your right about that" said Jack as Brian helped, Jack undress and redress in his clothes as Brian was careful around Jack, to say, "Don't worry I don't bite."

"No but your gadgets do", said Brian, keeping his distance. "Really, so I'm a walking time bomb?"

"No I didn't say that, actually I've said enough, do you see I placed your clips and rounds vest, are you out?" I guess I forget to save the spent mag"

As Jack pulls his holster off, then pulls his gun out, unloads the clip, empty."

He saw that he did in fact slide them back into the holster, to set all three empties down, to reload, and stick two new in, to say, "Do you reload all of these?"

"Yes, individually, over in that makeshift lab."

"Maybe you guys ought to expand that out to be the size length wise of the room", said Jack walking over to a place by his room.

"Good idea, but it's up to Lisa to have that happen." "Not anymore, I will take care of it" said Jack as he re-holstered and then placed his wind breaker back over, and zipped it up, as Brian had the harness, laid out for Jack to step into it, then as he adjusted the straps, he hooked the parachute on, and hands Jack a helmet.

Jack waddled with Brian to the ready position, as he said "I'll lower the ramp, and you jump out to the left get your bearings, as it will be north is your land zone, Curtis has activated a light beacon, on your boat.

Mitzi, saw Jack, and then knocked on the door, as Debby let her in, to close it to hear" so we want to see him now?" "Who?"

"Jack Cash." "He isn't here."

Just then the air variance in the room changed, then it equalized, as the girls swamped the door, only to open it up to see Brian, for some of them to say, "Are you Jack Cash?"

"No, he just left."

Jack released his first chute, it opened as it was expected to do, as Jack paraglide, he maneuvered the glider downward, through the clouds to see the boat as dawn was about to break, he slowed his air speed, as he made his final approach, and then Curtis was on deck, as Jack was caught by him and the two pulled the rest inward, Jack shredded the paraglide, for Curtis to cleanup, and went into the boat, up to his cabin, he opened the door, closed and locked it, to see Sara and Maria fast asleep, Jack quickly decided to take a quick shower, then slid into the bed, next to Sara.

Mark was shaking his friend who opened his eyes to say, "What is it, is it my turn to watch, leave me alone."

"Get up and look and see."

Mike opened his eyes, to see the television was on, as Mike saw it, he went to the window, then said "Nah we would have known, where's Mitzi, Trixie?"

"That's just it, neither is picking up, besides I think Trixie is in Virginia, helping out Samantha, and Mitzi last I knew she was flying around with Jim."

"Yes, but how did he get out of here?" "Probably by that weather balloon deal." "Nah, you're crazy, who helped him?" "Probably Curtis."

"Well we won't get any info from him, he guards Sara, and she hasn't left the boat."

"I guess we will find out that beauty pageant begins in two hours, if he is here or not."

"If he was the one who was there, I'm just sorry we missed it," said Mike.

"At least you're not in the doghouse like me."

"Cheer up Mark, for you your family comes first, besides you were hand selected by Lisa herself."

"Yes, but you were selected by Jack."

"So what, we need to get back in this game, you know it's pretty shitty to be left out of a covert mission", said Mike as he looked down at his phone was dead, as he tosses to Mark, who says, "Yeah mine too, as soon as we left the water, mine was dead, we need backups."

"Or waterproof phones" said Mike, shuffling through his bag, to see his sat phone, to dial up Jim, a sweet voice answered it, for Mike to a say, "Jim."

"Nah, this is Mitzi, who is this?"

"Its Mike and Mark."

"What have you boys been up too?" "Oh you know, watching the boat."

"While we're off to Belgium, I've been trying to get in touch with you all last night before we left, Trixie is in Virginia, with Samantha on her last leg, so we took who we had, as a result of not being able to get in touch with you guys, the plane will have a strike team aboard at all times, now and forever more."

"Our phones went dead, honest." Said Mike.

"You know better than that, there are no excuses, the mission goes on regardless of your lack of communication, between the two of you, keep a phone safe, I'll bring you both back two new waterproof phones, from now on, I'll keep you guys informed, but I hope it doesn't happen again, this is like spy club, another mess up like this and you will be out and off to the club." She hung up on those two idiots, as she scrolled Jim's phone, then closed it up, as they made their approach to Quantico, they landed, and into a special hanger, where the families of the girls were being held. Lisa presided over the event. As Jim lowered the ramp, and stood to see the girls run off the back of the ramp to their awaiting parents arms, even Miss Margaret and Major John Lincoln, helped Annabel, the noise calmed down to hear Lisa speak over the bull horn, to say "On behalf of the U S Government we would like to say how sorry we are for this in-convince and that the girls need to go next door, for a safety screening and blood tests."

One man spoke above all else by saying we are going to sue the government for the treatment of our daughters, look they had straps on their head, cuts on their wrists and ankles."

The rioting calmed down as the Black Ops strike team made their presence known, men dressed in all black and mirrored visors, they stood in a military line as Lisa came down to the floor to address their issues, to say "Now mister what are your concerns?"

"I'm concerned the savage way in which, my, our daughters were handled."

"Really how so" said Lisa as the strike team moved in closer.

"Your suppose rescuer, Jack Cash binded the girls wrists and ankles and their mouths, we have the right to sue, for damages."

"Play the tape, look at the video, I didn't need to show you this, but this is what your daughter's narrowly missed, terrorist attack on King Leopold's life, you see Mister . . ."

"Andrews."

"I know, our man here as you see, goal or mission was to extract one and with his own initiative saved eighteen, before this happen."

Brian stood next to Jim to say, "Ain't that something, you save someone's life, and someone else is finding a way to make money off of that."

"No, the worst part is the guy isn't even grateful for what Jack just did" said Jim.

"It still isn't right, whatever the costs, do you hear me!" said the man who placed his hand on her shoulder to get her attention, as the strike team placed their weapons up at him.

Lisa turned to them to say, "Stand down, mister Andrews, who has an issue with us, so let him be, usually means he has something to hide, so you go do that, sue us, as she bent in to whisper to him to say, "See that man on the screen, he just saved your daughter, let it be. You're a disrespectful man, and I'll just call Jack up and let him visit you, you see we can't touch you, but he can", as she stepped away from him the guy, who was ready for action.

Lisa spoke up to say, "So we'll see you in court then, here is the card of Jack Cash's attorney, her name is Erica Meyers", as Lisa leaves the man looked at the soldiers, who stared back at him, as he gets up, only to see his daughter came to him as he hugged her. The soldiers and the families saw the replay of the battle, then a unexpected word came from the King of Belgium, King Leopold, spoke, "Dear Mister President, from your intelligence you realized how important was for you to have your top agent present for my protection, and safety, although some were hurt and some had died, but my flee to safety will forever be remembered, and would like to honor this agent named Jack Cash, please allow him to visit us when it is convenient, thank you, sincerely King Leopold the Third."

Jim looked around to realize and said to Brian, "Yes you're right we do have the best job in the world, so what did Jack say to you?"

"Oh he said something about having a room for us and an armory"

"Yes I was thinking the same thing, call you're contracting teams; I need a word with Lisa." Said Jim.

"You got it." Said Brian.

Jim past the soldiers, to go into the admin office to see Lisa speaking to some families, namely a hot looking African American famous looking girl, as she past by him to say "Hi, who was that, she looks famous?"

"She is the super model Lisa Connor; she wants a personal meeting with Jack to show how much she was grateful for what he did, as also ten others, what I can do for you." Said Lisa.

"Can I have a moment with you privately" asked Jim.

"Sure come on in" as she placed her hand up to Ramon her bodyguard. Lisa turned on the light to say, "Have a seat."

"I'd rather stand, if you don't mind" said Jim. "What is it; I've been up all night over this." "Well Ma'am."

"Wait; just call me Lisa, what is going on here, Jim, out with it?"

"Well about what happen on the plane."

"Enough, I already got the details from Mitzi, do you know why I hired you?"

"You needed someone to mentor Jack." "Precisely and when is that going to happen?" "I'm working on it"

"That's not good enough, you're an excellent technical guy, you take orders well, you're just not a people person, but for what you do is excellent, as far as I'm concerned you work for me, forget about Mitzi, she is a control freak, but we need that, it creates a check and balance environment, if you want to help out more, that's great, but I won't expect it, we realize now that you have some hidden agendas, and in the end, if Jack gets wind of it I'd say your days are numbered, do you hear me now."

Jim just looked down at her, to say, "Although I'm sorry, I'd like a more communication plan."

"What, communication plan, how about you telling our agent, to go back and get his own vehicle, that is your job, I'm beginning to think, the Pentagon was right, replace you."

"Whoa, wait, I've given great service."

"Good at best, come on retire, and allow someone younger, more enthusiastic, who isn't a gawker of women."

"I'm sorry."

"That doesn't cut it anymore; we need dedicated people ready to do what Devlin did for Jack, take a bullet for him, and are you ready to do that, Jim Bannister."

He looked up at her solemnly, to say, "Yes I will."

"That's coming, it's the when and where it happens, were all scrambling to learn how all this works, we still don't know how to shadow Jack, with getting him in situations that could get him killed, your main job, is to support him, you work exclusively for me, but if Jack asks you of something you do it whole heartily, as for Mitzi, well there are changes on the horizon, plus there is the United Nations council on spies coming up, so I need you, and Brian, Jack wants him involved, so he works for you, teach him what you know, he may be your successor, as for Debby, she is the fleet manager, of the planes and ground equipment, as that is what she is so famously known for, and we just received notice that her whole award winning staff, will join her, here on this base, lastly, the strike team, Paul and his crew will be your ground force, that travels with all the planes you fly, in addition, they will be the planes support force doing whatever you ask, just before you came to me, Jack sent this via his phone fax, is a detail of what he wants on the plane" she hands it to Jim.

Jim, who looks at it, to say "Can I be honest with you." "Of course, you're out there, in the field."

"Well I agree about an armory for Brian, now that we have troops, and on one side, then on the other, we could make a lab out of it, but I'm not going to reduce Jack's room, just for the sake of troops, the whole idea of the room was a totally enclosed self contained sound proof room, would be a place for Jack to rest, regardless of who is along for a ride."

"Alright I follow you that are his room, so what if I rode." "Well you would be an exception, but look at the shooting, he was dirty, he needed rest, those girls were so dirty, that room is in a state of stench, Debby told me a couple pissed in the bed, a five thousand dollar custom made bed wasted, who does this?"

"Alright your right, when you take the plane out, you are the plane captain regardless of who rides, if you say that room is for Jack only then that it will so be."

"Hell, Mitzi doesn't share her hot meals with anyone?" "Did any of the girls get a hot meal?"

"No, not that I was aware of, that's because she told me she makes them herself."

"Actually she does, then flash freezes them, that is right, well I guess that what we lose sight of, who is the very most important person, and all else just deals, thanks Jim, I needed that, really, when you get back on that plane, it is yours, do what you want, spare no expense and get it done, oh before I forget, that weather balloon idea is just brilliant, can we have that tool with our troops, on the ground, and in all vehicles, especially in his car?"

"Wait that gives me a good idea, what if, I place a two hundred foot cable, remote active, a self inflating balloon, as we catch it, the sides veer out to stabilize, as we set the winch in motion, it retracts, under the plane, we install a magnet, on the plane and the top of the car, controllable." Said Jim, getting excited.

"That's brilliant, get it going, but if you're working on that, you'll need a pilot to fly."

"That is true, you know someone?" asked Jim.

"I know of a pilot, I'll send him your way, in the future, let's not tell him what to do, is all I ask from you?"

"Yes Ma'am, I mean Lisa".

"That's better, now off you go".

CH 10

The day that the men had court

J ack awoke, with his hands on Sara's large supple breast, he let it
slide down, her firm body, to her leg that she split apart, so that
he could slide his hand in, he liked how she felt, she turned, to
use her belly to push him away, she smiled to say, "You seem tired,
what have you been up too?"

"Oh you know, out rescuing people and saving lives."

"We saw your handy work on the world satellite feed, you're
getting sloppy, who was your wife, and it said your wife was
with you?"

"It was Mitzi."

"Oh I like her, she cares about you, if it has to be someone, I'd
prefer her or anyone who will give you some protection, and does
your phone ever stop ringing?"

"Nah, it has ten phone numbers so who knows, I need a
personal assistant who know how to use that thing."

"Oh I'm sure there are plenty of candidates, come closer
sexy man."

The two kissed, as she held his cute goatee in her fingers, to
part their lips, to look at each other, for her to whisper, "If you
want take me from behind."

"I would but I'm exhausted, I'm supposed to judge some event
in a couple of hours, with Alex and Alba."

"What's it with you and pair names."

"What do you mean?" he said as he played with her breasts. "Well there is first me, then Samantha, then Alexandra and Alba, now we have Maria, is it gonna be Mitzi?"

"I don't know I never thought about it, but doubtful." "Why not, you ever have her?"

"Well yes, but what is a suppose man to do."

"Slay as many women as you can and marry those you can't, said Sara."

"Ha, Ha, funny, little girl, nah I'm done with this whole marrying deal, how about just mistresses from now on."

"Maybe for now, have you seen the women going to be at this event" asked Sara.

"What, what do you mean?" asked Jack.

"Turn the light on" said Sara.

Jack leans over to click the light on, as Sara pulls a magazine out to show him, to say "I circled those I think it would be nice, you know I talked with Carlos yesterday when he came and visited us, here." Jack looked over, the pages to see that six were circled, to say

"So they all look like what I already have, that one looks like Maria, this one looks like Margarita, then Alba, this Swedish girl, too innocent, I don't know maybe, hey you know what I was thinking was what I was supposed to do before we wed."

"What sleep with all my bridesmaids, well you had your chance, but because you lost your partner, I may give you a pass, how about on our one year anniversary, I invite them out on the boat, and we recreate that night" said Sara.

Jack just looked at her naked body exposed to him, to say "You look like you got a lot bigger, since . . ."

"Since when, I have been eating like a pig, oh guess who flew in?"

"I don't know your cousin's."

"No silly, Tabby and Leslie, they both felt guilty and returned your money, also Glenda just called me to say she wanted to be more involved, so she will be here later tonight, she asked if she would receive Sam's portion of her compensation?"

"I don't know, it's up to Lisa, or I guess the President and his staff."

"Really she kind of creeps me out" said Sara.

"Well her concern was all the medical bills, which I paid off, or the government did, but your right she is money hungry." Jack tosses the pamphlet back on the bed as he gets up to say "Should I stay and lay with you?"

"No, you need to go, or Carlos will be here to look over us, if you know what I mean, go get ready."

A knock on the door, to hear, "Honey, it's your Mom and Sister." Sara motioned for Jack to get something on, as he found yellow swim trunks, a t-shirt, a shirt vest, his holster and windbreaker, and flip flops, to hear "Honey the door is locked?"

"Hold on Mom, Jack is here."

Jack grabs her baseball cap, and a pair of sunglasses to hear "Hey that's my hat."

He leans in to give her a kiss, as he broke away from her she said

"Hey after our child is born, I want my three days of total seclusion." "You got it" said Jack as he opened the door to see Heidi and Kate, each gave him a hug and a kiss, with Kate lingering a bit longer, to hear "Hey Sis leave my man alone."

Everyone was laughing, as Jack left, out onto the dock to see Curtis to say, "Hey can you help me pull off a jet ski?"

"Yeah sure, don't worry; I'll get it, just hold on."

Jack watched as Curtis, was quick on the crane and hooked up the jet ski, and it was in the water, as Jack held the lead line, Curtis was on the deck, as he took the lead line from Jack, as Jack stepped down onto the Jet ski, Jack fired it up, as Curtis threw the line to him, as he wrapped the rope up, and secured it in the front cargo hold. And speed off, he felt better on the calm harbor, as he easier to handle, he slowed down at the city port, to the community beach, as a guy on the beach to help hold the jet ski as Jack threw him a rope, as he help Jack beach the jet ski.

An island native helped Jack up onto the beach; to walk up first to meet up with was Mark, who said "Hi how was the mission?"

"It was good, how was your trip?" "Good"

"Hey do you know where I can get some breakfast?"

"Yeah the event has sponsored an elaborate buffet inside." said Mark pointing to the large auditorium, as Jack walked across the warm sand; he sees another familiar face, to say "What's up Mike?"

"Oh you know nothing not-a-thing." "Are you coming in?"

"Yeah, right behind you."

Jack went through the side door to smell all that was good a huge buffet line, where women and men mingled, Jack fell into the line, to pick up a plate, silverware, eggs, three ways, he scooped up some scrambled, then some potatoes, as Mike and Mark was next to him, Jack waited for a business man looking dude, who was slow and deliberate to proceed, Jack saw the huge fruit compote and took two scoops, then four chocolate milks, in cartons, there were pastries and ice creams at the end and a big old island girl manning a register, the guy in front paid five US dollars, she looked at Jack as she looked at the wall, then looked at him to wave him on, to say "No money for you, move on."

Jack sees Carlos in a VIP section, to see all the girls step aside for him. Jack sat and began to eat listening to Carlos wager with the contestants as they listened to his tall tales, he noticed one of the girls Sara circled, she was from Spain, Jack noticed Carlos had a program guide, is what they were all laughing about, Jack went back to eating.

Meanwhile in Tampa, a law firm of Fancier, Alister; Caldwell, James; and Thomas, Jim, convened, as the lead partner Alister, spoke, "Come in and take a seat, we have a new case, let's get everyone on who it is and what we can expect to get, "James explain."

James Caldwell stood to say,"As of this moment our war chest is 150 million, we found out that this guy were going after, gets a million per each assault and capture, so were asking 100 million in damages, he sits to allow the last partner to stand to say, "I'll handle the lead, and I'll take Brandy and Carol to sit at the table, for you two and the entire staff, we need to search out the menace's true name. A hand went up to say,"Who are we looking up? Isn't true we just go after the government, not an individual?"

"That is true, Drew, (A paralegal), but what we're looking to do in this civil case is implicate a specific person rather than for a specific act."

"What if he has immunity?" asked another. "Immunity isn't for everyone, this is a defection, that explicitly shows neglect, and all were looking for is for him to confess?"

"Who is he?" asks another.

"He goes by the name of Jack Cash, International bounty hunter."

Everyone looked around to each other, as Drew stood up, to say,"Yeah, that guy is famous, so what you're saying the guy who rescued all those girls in Brussels Belgium, you're going after?"

"And what are you saying Drew, you're scared?" Everyone was laughing.

"No, but like I and others, who saw that dramatic footage of 20 plus Commandos attack a King, and only one man stood in his way, they failed and he won."

"Sounds like you're a cheerleader, Drew", stood James, to add, "Come on folks this is what we do, go after those in the military that do wrong, and they should pay for their actions and the government should pay for their actions to the victims."

Jim stood lastly to say, "Uncover the secrets this Jack Cash has, Monday I'll file the briefs in federal court, that will be all."

The room cleared out, as the three looked at a familiar face to say,"Thanks for coming, what do you think, I think we have a big one this time?"

The man moved to face all three to say,"I don't know, I think your making a big mistake?"

"How so, he committed so many crimes, I have someone who wants to sue for a wrongful death, and another they were assaulted to death, all punishable to life in prison."

The man looked at them to say,"This one may get complicated."

"How so, everything we do is a risk, but on a sure thing, we can't lose."

"That's not it; allow me to make a call, to get a better perspective."

"Alright, we'll listen."

The Man dials the phone then places on speaker to hear it answer, for her to say, "This is Samantha Kohl, how may I help you Francis?"

"Listen. Me and my partners are building a case on one of your agents, and would like to know your insight?" "Alright sure, who is it this time?"

"The guy goes by the name of Jack Cash, do you know him?"

"Yes, he is a colleague."

"Fine, can you tell me if that is his real name or not?"

"I don't righty know, he just works with Lisa Curtis, at CIG. "What do you think if we went after him?"

"I don't see why not, if you think he committed some crime, bring him to justice."

"That's what we wanted to hear, thanks Samantha Kohl." "Well if you're going to say it that way, I may object" the line went dead for the man to say, "Well if she is on board, I'd say you have the green light."

Back in Virginia, Lisa picked up a call, to hear a frantic voice on the other end, saying, "This is bad, Samantha took a critical turn for the worse, they want to go in, and I told them no, Miss Curtis I need some direction here", said Joe Javier.

"Calm down Joe, put the doctor on" said Lisa, looking at her watch.

"Yes this is Doctor Thomas, is this Miss Curtis?" "It is, so what is the prognosis?"

"Grim at best, maybe twenty four hours."

"Alright, I want you to pull out any non-essential equipment from the room, under no circumstance, will you take that baby out until I tell you so, I'm on my way, let me talk with Joe, please." "This is Joe, what do you want me to do?"

"Stay put, I'm on my way, under no circumstance will the doctor touch Sam, is Trixie their?"

"Yes, she is waiting to receive the baby." "Put her on please."

"This is Trixie, yes . . ."

"How is it going there?" asked a frantic Lisa, scrambling to get things in a bag.

"Well not as bad as what Joe has made it seem, he is so protective of her, they brought in a cat scan machine, now it's gone, she seemed to have stabilized out, according to Mitzi, she said the numbers match up to what is appropriate, so I feel were in a good place, for right now."

"Time wise?"

"Could be a week, month or year, as you know she is terminal, if Jack wants to see her, now would be the best time, she is conscious, and asking for him."

"And the baby?"

"It's ready to come out, anytime, but I'm not the expert, that is what Mitzi told me, is Jack coming?"

"He is now; prepare the way to receive him, and the family."

"Yes Ma'am."

Lisa slid her phone shut, to get up, opened up her door, and see the plane hangar was wide open, on a semi hot day, loud noises were blaring as music played even louder, she went to the side of the plane to see Jim to say, "I need you to fly to the Dominican Republic and pick up Jack and his party, and bring them back up here."

Jim slides out to see her; he wipes off his dirty hands, to say, "Right now."

"Yes right now, the secondary plane is ready?" "Always, but it doesn't have the pick-up barrel on it."

"No need, just fly to the airport, he will be waiting, with Mike and Mark."

Jim yelled down to the guys saying, "I gotta go, weld the hinges, and install the magnet, but wait till I get back, Brian."

Lisa watched Jim with a jump in his step and fire in his britches, running out of the hanger, she sees Brian, dirty as well, come out of the plane to see Lisa, to say "Hi."

"Hey have you seen Mitzi?" asked Lisa. "Yeah, she is in the kitchen."

Lisa walks past all the noise, to pass through multiple doors, to quietness, except for the aroma of fresh cooked foods, she swung open a door, to see a sea of chef's working, and Mitzi in the middle of all of it, to say "Mitzi could I have a word."

Mitzi and Lisa walk into the quiet room, to say "Do you have a catering business I don't know about?"

"Nah, these are for the planes meals." "That's pretty obsessive of you?"

"No not really, just doing my job, what can I do for you." "Well this is a bit sensitive, Jack is flying in today, and I'd like to know if you want to go replace Trixie on point?"

"Sure I could do that, where is he staying while he is here?"

"I don't know, hadn't got that far, any ideas?"

"Sure there are those captains' quarters above the admin offices."

"By the river front?" asked Lisa. "Yeah, I think so."

"Can you take care of that, and then meet me at hanger thirteen; here is a card for you to get in."

Back in Washington DC, an attorney was on the phone.

"Mister Andrews, this is Attorney Erica Meyers, I was calling you to inform you of a hearing on Monday Morning at ten O' clock sharp, at one constitution avenue, floor 33, room one."

"How did you get my number?"

"You're in the directory, I wanted to save you a trip back to Florida, before your case is heard, and do you have an attorney on retainer yet?"

He was quiet, and then spoke up to say, "Yes, well his name is Arthur Jackson."

"From the famed Jackson, Johnson and Hostetler, of New York."

"Yes, how did you know?"

"I did a search and twelve years ago, you hired him to represent you against the government, and you won, looks like a sizeable judgment in your favor, 450,000 dollars, well you're in good hands, so do you want me to call him or I'll let you do that?" He looked at his phone as it went dead. She hung up on him.

He dialed up his friend, waited, and then heard, "Can I call you back I'm in the middle of a meeting."

"I have a hearing on Monday."

"Really, don't worry about it, I'll get a continuous, so who is the attorney and who is suing you?"

'Well it was something I said."

"I'm listening; I'm in a private office now, so explain."

"Well I threaten to sue the Government."

"Yeah, so what I do that every day, who is representing?" "She said her name was Erica Meyers."

There was a pause, and then he said "Did you say Erica Meyers?" "Yes, that's right, what's the big deal, do you know her?" "Well let's say, this there are two female attorneys in the federal court system, one is in the appellate court, and the other is in the Supreme Court, where is your hearing?"

"She said One constitutional place, floor 33 room one, at ten O 'Clock sharp.

There was a long pause as he said "We will have to be there, can you gather your witnesses, and have them there at 07 o'clock, so that we may go over your stories."

"Your voice is different what's wrong?" asked Mister Andrews.

"Sounds to me like we may be in front of a Justice of the Supreme Court, I have it here, she is the Chief Adjutant General that works for the Supreme Court, as its chief general counsel, as I look at her profile, for her age, she has a doctorate from Harvard Law, no worries, I have this weekend to get ready for her, who are the one you are suing?"

"His name is Jack Cash, some Bounty Hunter."

"Now this is something, I can dig my teeth into, what did he do?"

"He used some type of drug to subdue my daughter, then placed a plastic tie around her mouth, and tied up her hands, at her wrists, and then her ankles."

"Did he sexually assault her, or physically touch her in an inappropriate way?"

"Yes the ladder, I guess he put his hands all over her, no she remembers him picking her up."

"Tell me, these bindings did they cut her?"

"Yes, they left gauges as to where they were too tight." "Wait, you said he was a bounty hunter, was he the one who kidnapped her originally?"

"No he was the rescuer." "Wait what?"

"Yeah, he went in and took her away from the kidnapper, and brought her back."

"So how did the government get involved?" "What do you mean?" asked Mister Andrews.

"Just that, most bounty hunters work for a specific agency in a roundabout way, but not within the government as I know of, hold on I have another call I must take."

"Yes this is Arthur Jackson, who is this?"

"Hi Mister Jackson, this is Erica Meyers, I was letting you know that your client Mister Andrews had made the intentions that you were representing him, is that true?"

"Well yes."

"Then I was calling you, and sent you my brief, via e-mail and same day travel, there should be a U S Marshal there for your signature, we are counter suing your client for National security reasons, any questions?"

"No, "he said with a deep breath, to hear "Then have a great rest of the day and we will see you in court on Monday morning." Mister Jackson, looked up to see the marshal, who tapped on the window, he opened the door to hear, "Are you Arthur Jackson?"

"Yes Sir."

"The Supreme Court, request your presence, at 10 o'clock sharp, on level 33, room one, the address is listed in this document will you sign?"

He did, as he held the document, as his main partner, came to him to say, "What's up with the US Marshal, do we have a good case, hey do you have a moment, there is something I want you to see." do.

"O Kay", as he followed him in to see.

"Alright play that back" he motioned for another colleague to The video played, as a court TV reporter came aboard, to say this miraculous recovery and safety of the King of Belgium was foiled by one man International Bounty Hunter Jack Cash, killed eighteen of twenty four terrorist, to rescue this woman, as the two fled."

"Wow that was amazing wasn't it, that guy was the one who they sent in?"

"What do you mean sent in?"

"Where have you been, this guy, is our newest sensation in terrorist destruction and capture, he is I guess what some call a Super Spy."

Mister Jackson looked down at his official wrapped document, to raise his hand to say "I must go, give me a few moments please", he went to his desk, to sit down, carefully he used his letter opener to slice the package open, carefully he pulled the document out, he was sweating, as he saw the official Supreme Court seal, and as he scanned the document the signature was by the Chief Justice Holt, he went back up to read from which the counsel was, under her name bore Executive Branch, General counsel, he scanned down, to see the words, detriment to national security, and the word Treason, to an agent of the U S Government, especially the President of the United States of America, Mister George White the third.

His mind was racing, to think," Where's that gun at?" "Hey Jacks, what's wrong, what is that?"

"My death warrant." "What are you saying?"

As his partner came forward to look down at the document that is as powerful as a sword, through their hearts, for him to say "Who are you defending, from the looks of it, he must be a mass murderer, look on the bright side, you have been there before, with that tobacco case and won."

"I was on that team, your right it can't be that bad", said Art, gaining back his confidence.

"Wait, I thought you said you were defending a client, this say you, are suing Jack Cash."

Back in the sunny skies and hot temperatures of the Dominican Republic, Jack sat with his two beautiful brides, Alex and Alba close by, as each young lady passed by his booth, he had his own scorecard, and wrote as he felt, as he was getting bored of all this, but the rest was a welcomed sight, his phone rang, gave him a distraction, it was Mitzi, for which Jack said,

"Hey you, you got your phone back?"

"No, this is a new one, but listen, I wanted to give you a heads up, Jim is on his way down there via plane to pick you up; Its Sam, she has appeared to become conscious, her breathing tube is being removed as we speak, so we will see you in a couple of hours, sorry this was so unexpected."

"Yeah it is, but it was expected, it's fine, thanks for the heads up."

He looks up to see the harried Mother of Samantha, for Jack to say, "Looks like you got your wish, your daughter is awake." she walked past him.

Jack sees Curtis drive by, he returns with an ATV and trailer. Sara's mother Heidi and Sister Kate was helping Sara pull it off and along, off the trailer. Jack joined Sara, and the pair rode up the hill, as it made its way up the hill, Jack stood up, to say "Take over for me, I need to get going."

Jack walked out into the middle to see he was joined by Mike and Mark, as a plane flew over, landed, and turned on the tarmac, the ramp lowered, immediately troops disbursed to secure the plane as a refueling truck came forward., behind Jack a tap on his shoulder he turned to see Dana, for Jack to say, "How can I help you?"

"You mentioned something about allowing me to help out?" asked Dana sincerely.

"Oh yes, wait a minute" said Jack as he scrolled through his phone and all the missed calls, he checked his E-mails, to see a confirmation, for him to step forward to say "Alright, you and Julie come aboard, I'll have Mitzi, well I mean, get your stuff, and get aboard, the ATV with Sara past by them, to see Jim was helping Sara onto the plane, up the ramp.

Jack made his way over the shrubs and onto the grass, to the ramp of the plane, he saw the troops scattered about, he made his way up, to see a wide open plane, to say "What no car?"

"We were in a bit of a hurry" said Jim hurrying about as Jack followed him to add, "You're not the Jim I know, where is that cranky pants I know."

"He is gone; he went by the way of the dodo bird."

Jack just looked at him to see that the plane looked the same to say, "Any changes?"

"Yeah didn't you see the jet engines instead of the props?" "No not really, why is that important?"

"It's all about airspeed, the jet engines makes the flight down here faster, three hours than four in half, that's why we use the prop plane for pickups, were currently, designing the car, to be picked up similar to how we can extract you."

"That's nice, any changes to the inside?"

"Why would you care, well I didn't mean it that way, look this plane is still the same, the only proposed changes is a lab and armory is taking away from the cargo hold."

"Hey do you think we could put a jet ski in here?"

"I don't know, I'll take it under consideration, next you'll want a boat."

"Nah, maybe a rubber raft with a jet engine" said Jack making a statement, as he went to his room, he opened the door, to see, Sara was in the huge bed, her sister Kate and her mother, Heidi by her side.

"I guess it's time we get off?" said Heidi kiddingly.

"Nah, you can come with us, you know where were going?" asked Jack.

"Jack honey, I told them about our dear friend Samantha." "Yes we approve, both Greg and I, we know all about what you do and we support both of you one hundred percent, you're our Son now."

"Well, I will tell you that as passengers, you will have to check in with Brian, he is the manifest officer."

"That's not necessary" said Jim behind Jack, who turned to see him, to hear, "Things have changed."

"I'd say they have, said Jack to add, "Mitzi's not aboard and you're a changed person."

"No it's not that, were doing things a little different now."
"Alright I guess you don't have to check in, I need to talk with Jim, if you will excuse me."

Jack stepped out to close the door, to say "Come on, what is going on, are you retiring?"

"Why are you" said Jim smiling. "No" said Jack confidently.

"Then you answered me, take it for what it's worth, let me say, said Jim, "I gained a new found respect for who you are, especially from the last mission, but that's all your getting from me, if you like you can sleep in my bunk if you like, hey I have someone I want you to meet, you know Debby is off the plane now, she and her whole staff, now run a portion of Quantico, so Jack I want you to meet our new in flight hostess, her name is Nicole Lange."

"Any relations to Tim?"

She turns to smile and say, "He is my father."

"Alright welcome aboard."

"In our family we hug not shake" she said as she embraced Jack, she stepped back to hear, "Hey I didn't get that type of welcome", said Jim.

"You're not, Jack Cash," she shot back. Then turned to say

"I know about coffee with a lemon, but anything else I should know?"

"Nah, I don't require much."

"That's what Mitzi said too, she packed four trays of food for you, shall I serve them to you in an hour or so?"

"I don't know, but thanks, he said to Nicole, to speak to Jim by saying, "Do you know where Brian is?"

"Yeah he is in the flight tower, he said he has a friend here or something like that", said Jim.

"You really have changed and I don't know if I like this new Jim." alive."

"Trust me Jack you will, my sole job is to keep you safe and

"Alright, I still don't know if I like it, hey I have a couple of female passenger."

"Of course you do."

"What does that mean?" asked Jack. Looking at him weirdly.

"Nothing, sorry, what do you have?"

"Well, these two girls wanted to join the team, I did a background check, and a preliminary test, but they're going to see Margaret Ryan, to see if their eligible, and also my wife's mother will also be on this flight, can you make up a provisional room for her."

"Well she can be in your room." "No she really can't."

"Oh I see, I got you buddy, I'll take care of it."

"Now I'm your buddy, what is going on here", said Jack.

"Nothing I swear, just leave me alone" said Jim. "Now that's the Jim I know."

Jack enjoyed the playful banter, but realized he was getting annoyed, as he went into his room and closed the door.

Jim went down to the ground from the ramp to see the plane was refueled, and water replenished, and the trashes removed, Paul got his men back in order, as they were the right choice for the ground crew, he held the manifest clipboard, to see Brian, ran back towards Jim, to say, "Thanks, I needed that."

"It was that short?"

"Nah, my buddy is in the flight tower, told me that Carlos and Jack have this whole village to themselves." "What about all these people?"

"He said their some sort of agents" said Brian.

"Wow, hey Jack has three more guests to board, I wrote down, as you can see "Jack, his wife Sara, her sister Kate, and her mother Heidi."

"How do you know that?"

"Their on the other side of this wall inside his room" said Jim. "Who did that?"

"Who else his mom."

"What, who is that?" asked Brian. "Mitzi."

"Oh yeah, sorry, I'm just stunned by all the pretty girls down here and look at what is coming."

"I'd not stare if I were you, if their Jack's friends have them seat up by the crew."

"Yes Sir."

"Men board" said Paul, as he steps aside to let his men aboard, he stood to wait for the two girls with bags in hand for Brian to say, "Names please?"

"My name is Dana Scott, and this is Julie Davis, were with the CIA special agent division, as she shows her badge, Brian writes it down for both.

"Do you need a hand up?" asked Paul, being sincere. He helped first Dana, then Julie, to hear, from Brian, "Paul can you show them seats up front by cockpit please."

"Yes Sir."

Paul led the two girls to their seats to say "This is our attendant her name is Nicole, if you need anything, don't be afraid to ask."

Paul sees his men in the cot bunks, resting as one says "Who's the two hotties."

"Nobody to you, Sergeant Lawrence, gather your gear, and place it on the end, you're out."

'What, what did I say?'

'This job is one of privilege, our only mission is to protect and serve Jack Cash, if he has guests, it is just like having the President's own, so respect that."

Lee Paul stands up to say "Lighten up; he was just being a guy."

"I will not allow disrespect, on any level, this is all business, they turned to see a short stout man, who threw his pack down, to say "Is this place taken."

"Nah, be my guest" said Paul, looking at the guy who was smartly dressed.

Then two more men boarded, to take a seat by the outcast Drew.

"Are you guarding the ramp" said Mike.

"Can you move down, to let him have that seat" said Mark. Drew moved closer to Paul, to see an older lady with silvery white hair, kind of spiky. Then the ramp was raised, as Brian, went up to the door, he knocked, Jack opened to say "Is there a white box here, for my gun, or do you have a cleaning kit for it?"

"The box is in the drawer, with a change of clothes, as for cleaning your weapon, I don't know, even that is top secret."

Jack closed the door.

Brian went to the cockpit to say, "Were all secure, hey Jack wants to know if he can clean his gun?"

"No it's not necessary, just recharge, no need to tell him, I'll tell him via intercom."

The plane took off, and quickly leveled off, as Paul stood up to say "Drew your on the pack, when we get back your going through sensitivity training."

"Why don't you send me back to my unit?" "You don't want to do that dude" said another. "Name's Drew."

"Whatever, there must be a reason that has put you here now, so seize the opportunity."

"Who cares" said Drew.

"You do, why did you join the service in the first place?" "To serve my country."

"Well that's what you're doing now." "What do you mean?" asked Drew.

"Well all you're doing now is protecting one man, right, do you even know why you are here?" asked Curtis.

"NO."

"Oh, hey Paul, is that your name, are you in charge of this soldier?"

"Yes, what is it?"

"This soldier has no idea, why he is even here, do you?" Paul stood in front of them to say "Sort of, were here to give support for the planes welfare, and its passengers."

Curtis gets up to say, "No, that's not it at all, do you know this plane's sole purpose is to transport one man, this is Jack Cash's plane, he is why we all have jobs, our existence is all because of him, what you do affects his performance, either through you actions, your speech, his comments, and behind you there are hundreds of others, I'd love to be in your position, rather than mine, you need to embrace this as if the President of the US was the passenger himself, that's right, that man in that box carries that power, if he has a guest, they are treated as if they are his first lady or men, you guys need to become tight and as one, because in the near future that and all this will be compromised, and you will be thrown into chaos."

"Can I ask who you are?"

"Sure, I'm a bodyguard for Sara, Jack's wife." "Come again" asked Paul.

"I'm a Government trained operative chosen to guard, Jack's wife."

"How did you get that gig?"

"I was chosen, that's how it all works, someone sees you, and if the person thinks you could fit a role, and then you get the job, believes me someone is always watching."

"How long is your term?" "Could be any time to forever." "What is the pay like?"

"Does it matter, enough to live comfortably?"

Back in an undisclosed location, deep underground, was a complex, which, Samantha was now a guest of.

Mitzi reviewed the medical documents, as she saw Samantha was breathing a bit better, color had returned to her face, she was even smiling, as she approached her side, to grasp her hand to say "He will be here soon, rest peacefully dear." Mitzi looked up to see Lisa, in the observation room, with John Lincoln and Margaret Ryan, who looked down at her. Behind Mitzi was Joe, the fiery Cuban hot head, who was rushing about, Mitzi pulled away from Samantha's warm hand to see Joe, to confront him to say "Joe, you need to calm down, everything is fine here", as she pulled him in to hug him, to add "It will be alright, you just need to calm down, especially in the presence of Jack." wait."

"Yes your right" he said humbly.

"I know it's almost over, there is nothing we can do now, but Up in the observation tower, from behind, Ramon, hands her the phone, to say, "Lisa the call is for you." to hand her, her phone, for her to say "Yes this is Lisa."

"Its Erica, the problem is handled, however Jack will need to be present, dressed professionally."

"Time and place and he will be there." "Supreme court around nine."

"Your office?" "Yes"

Lisa slid the phone shut and hands it to Ramon to say "Do not bother me, unless it's Jack, or the President," "Yes Ma'am."

Jack sat in the only chair, thinking what he wanted to do, either seeing his beautiful wife who was sandwiched in between her mom and sister, or thinking could I possibly join them, to his thought of who surely loved her." he thinks as a knock on the door.

Jack gets up to open it up to see it was Nicole.

She looked at him as he looked at her, for him to say "Yes, what do you need?"

"I was thinking you needed something?"

"Nah, I'm fine, probably for the rest of the flight."

"Alright she said as she lowered her head, but Jack stepped closer to whisper, "Listen, if you feel that you want to bring me a cup of coffee, a snack a meal whatever, you just do it, I won't say no, but if you ask me, I'll just tell you no, just food for thought for the future, but I don't need a thing, actually I'm going to take a shower, so thanks anyway, I'll see you when we land" said Jack as he closed the door.

Nicole, feeling better, walked around only to hear "I could use something to eat" said Glenda, as she past by her, into her galley, she was cleaning up, when behind her she felt something as a hand touched her shoulder, as she turned to see Glenda, for Nicole to say, "Yes."

"Didn't you hear me? I'm hungry what can I have?"

Nicole shook her head, to say "Nothing."

"What there must be something in there for me?"

"She said there is nothing" said Jim in a booming voice, to add "Go back to your seat, and leave Nicole alone."

She turned to see Jim, an average looking man, with a scruffy beard, to say "I'll talk with Jack; he will force you to let me have something."

"First off you don't know what you're saying, this is my plane, and your only getting a courtesy ride, just like Jack, whatever food that Nicole has is for emergencies only, is this an emergency? you may if you like have a cup of coffee, but as far as I know there is not any food, so please take your seat."

"I will, but I still think you have some food" she said in a huff. Jim filled his mug back up, and realized he missed Mitzi, she would have put that woman in her place" he thinks.

Jack finished his quick shower, quickly dressed; Jack hit the intercom button to say "How long before we land?"

Jim sat back down, to plug in as he took Brian's direction, to say "Oh about forty minutes."

"Alright can you let Nicole know I'd like something hot and some milk?"

"Will do" said Jim.

"I'll do it" said Brian, who slides back and gets up, to step out to see Nicole sitting to say, "Jack would like a hot plate, just pull a platter, uncover and in the microwave for three minutes, let rest one minute, he likes four milks two whole two chocolate."

"Ah ha you do have food" said Glenda, right behind Brian, who turned to say "Miss I'd advise you to sit back in your seat, that food, regardless of the quantity we have on hand is for only one person, and that's it, if Jack asked me to feed you I would, but he hasn't mentioned it to me" said Brian.

"Well I will just go ask him."

As she went for Jack's door, when Brian yelled, "Paul I need your help?"

Glenda knocked on the door, as Jack opened it to see her to say "What is it?"

"Sorry Jack" said Brian.

"That's alright, what do you need Misses Smith?"

'Well I was hungry, and wanted to get something to eat, may I have something?"

"It's up to Brian, I don't know what they have, is that all?" Jack closed the door, as Paul physically held the arm of Glenda, to say "Miss Smith you need to take your seat, as he escorted her to a jump seat, he took a seat next to her.

"You don't have to sit there" she said as she wiped some tears away. For her to continue to talk, "Why do people do this to me, are you listening to me?"

"Ma'am, it's not my position, I was asked to guard you, so if I were you I'd keep quiet when we land you can get all the food you need."

"What about you and your men, aren't you hungry?" Paul was quiet as she kept talking, so he made the decision to answer her, as he said "Lister Ma'am, where were going is private, and you really need to be quiet, your right, I could eat, but this is not my place to ask for food, all of this plane is for Jack, whatever happens, you need to respect your surroundings" he looked over at the very pretty girls who kept to themselves as one spoke up to say "Maybe she doesn't know who he is?" said Dana.

Paul shot back "What does that have anything to do with?" silence fell on them as Paul went to the door, to help Nicole, Jack opened the door, the smell of that food was intoxicating, as Jack took it to say "Thank you Nicole, oh also can I get a pot of coffee, seems the refrigerator is empty?"

She put her hand to her face; to say "Oh I'm sorry, I forgot to fill that" said Nicole.

Jack closed the door. As Paul took his seat by Glenda.

"What a jerk, who is he to talk with her like that?"

"Your misses Smith, my name is Dana, I'm a CIA operative, what is your relations to Jack?"

"What do you mean?"

"Well, everyone on this flight is connected to someone, like Julie and I are with Jack, as is that man; you look like you don't know what is going on here?"

"That is enough" said Jim, to add "As I said before, you're a guest, regardless of who you are, shut up and keep quiet." "You can't talk to me like that, I'm Jack's step mother." "Then why are you not in that room with the rest of the family?"

Everyone was quiet, except Dana who was shaking her head, to look at Glenda, to speak softly to say "I know why now, too bad for you."

Nicole past by them, to knock, as Jack opened the door, and took the coffee, to see Glenda, who was crying, to say "Glenda could you come on in."

She jumped up, as went into the spacious room, with a nice sofa, she took a seat, she was smiling, to stand in front of her, to say "When you first met me, you said that I disgusted you, you're the woman, whose husband left her, a daughter whose accident limited your way of life, I came along and paid off all the medical bills, plus I gave you one hundred thousand in cash, for which, you called me a drug dealer, in which you called the police, well I wasn't arrested and nor am I a drug dealer, you just couldn't accept any man for your daughter, even me."

Heidi, smiled, to past by Jack towards the restroom, when all of a sudden she slapped, Glenda on the face, to say "You ever disrespect my son, I'll have you taken care of."

"Stop it" said Jack man handling Heidi, to see her move along, to say "I guess she gave you something to cry about now, I wanted to tell you, while your among people I work with I'd rather you not speak with them, I have a reputation to uphold, if you don't know by now, I'm what they call an International Bounty Hunter, I go into countries to extract those who have been kidnapped, for that I'm paid one million dollars per person, rescued, captured or killed." Glenda looked up at him with a different perspective, as he continued" your daughter was on her way to the end, as things occurred, we all think she will be giving us a present that her body can no longer give, you should celebrate her, instead of being bitter about her leaving you and us, she isn't your little baby girl, you need to let her be a wife, mom and friend, as far as Sam goes, Samantha requested that Sara adopt him as hers, so if you want to see and be part of his life, you may want to get along with her mom, Heidi, her sister Kate, and Sara who will be her primary mother, even if you hate me, I totally understand, but you better be nice, especially where were going, if your disrespectful, you will never see the day of light ever again, listen up ladies be nice, I need to take care of some business", Jack opened the door and stepped out to see Paul, to say "Thanks for helping out, she will be alright, she will be in the room till we land, Jack sees Curtis, to say "Didn't know you would be traveling with us, as seeing Mike and Mark, listen can you get close to Misses Smith, and guide her around, will you do that for me?"

"Yes Sir" said Curtis.

"Mike and Mark, come with me."

Jack went into the cockpit, with the other two, to say "Sara her mother and sister is here, between the two of you can you both watch over them?"

"Of course, you can count on both of us." "Men prepare were going to land "said Jim.

CH 11

The Supreme Court

The players from the law firm of Fancier, Caldwell and Thomas, were on the fast track to getting this case going, so they decided to file the case in Federal court seeking damages from, Jack Cash that was until a paralegal uncovered Jack's secret truth and raced into Jim's office to interrupt him, to say, "I have it Mister Thomas." He places down his phone, to hold the receiver to hear."

"I have his name."

"Out with it, what's his name?"

"Gunther Schecter, of the famed family from Bonn Germany, he has a mother Sophia, and a sister.

"Alright let's add that name to the motion, good job" said Jim. And e-filed the motion, to stop to take a look, that there was a specific motion, already for one Jack Cash, he reviewed the motion, to see that it was addressed "The Supreme Court", and said "Oh shit, got up and ran into the spacious office of the lead partner, those that saw Jim, said, "Calm down what do you have boy?" Frantically, he calmed down to say, "I think we may have a problem?"

"How so, we know all about him now."

"Turn on the news network" as Alister, clicked it on, it showed some weather, some commercials, and other stuff, for Alister, to say, "What is the trouble?"

"He already has a motion, against him, Jack Cash." "Excellent, who is on theirs, and let's combine the cases, this is getting better than ever." Alister said, until, his excitement calmed, as the news serviced reported, On Monday morning, at 9 am a show down will occur here at the Supreme Court, when it takes on the hearing between, Jack Cash, and mister Ron Andrews, who is suing Jack Cash, for cruelty in the attempt in rescuing their daughter, Jack Cash, the hero, in the eyes of the government, say, "There will always be haters for those that try to save others, what he is trying to do is point the finger at the savior and not the ones that really did it, so we will find out today on how he fairs."

Alister clicked off the monitor and sat down, to say,"Now we're done."

Zero nine fifty five, Erica stepped through the door, with Jack in tow and all the Supreme Court justices rose. On the right side was a small group, two young girls, that looked at Jack, but did not smile, only turned away from him, and the man that accused Jack smiled at him, as Jack past behind Erica, to stand next to her and seeing all eleven Justices looking back at him, and to the countless others that were at their seats, that reselms a jury.

A Mallet rang out to hear, "Here, here, the Supreme Court will now here the case of Mister David Andrews versus The United States of America, as specified International Bounty Hunter, Jack Cash". Chief Justice Holt the one in the middle says, "Begin Mister Arthur Jackson, this hearing is to either establish the validly of your accusations against the United States Government and specifically Jack Cash, who let the record state is present, Now according to Miss Meyers, she gave you the articles of exemptions, for all of Mister Cash's action, so why are you perusing to take this to court?"

"If I may approach the bench?"

"Why would you want to do that, whatever you have to say, in front of Miss Meyers and Jack Cash, so what do you want to say?"

'Well Chief Justice, I was unaware I would be presenting in front of the entire Supreme Court, I'd like a continuous." "Why did you not have enough time?"

"Well not really" said the stuttering attorney. "Miss Meyers are you ready for this hearing?"

"Yes Chief Justice, we are, I have seventeen statements to read, and Mister Cash has agreed to tell his side of the story." "Excellent I see no reason, not to waste anymore time, says Chief Holt, to add, "Miss Meyers did you present the articles of exemptions to Mister Andrews, and how did he take them" said Chief Holt to Miss Meyers.

"He still exclaimed he wanted some money in return for something?"

"So he wanted a bribe, is that true mister Andrews?"

Mister Andrews stood to say, "Well No, your Chief Justice." "If you're lying to me, so help your god."

"Ask them why then they don't want him to testify?" asked Miss Meyers.

"Why don't you allow him to testify?" spoke another Justice. "Yes, why doesn't your client want to testify?" asked Justice Holt.

"He isn't the one who did anything wrong?" said the attorney.

"How did you come up with that theory, do you know who drafted the articles of Exemption?"

"No, not really Chief Justice, I had not really even seen that document, before."

"Humor me, take your best guess?" as the Chief Justice was having fun, only to see Jack looked at his watch.

"Well Chief Justice, I imagine it came from the JAG office, but the last case I tried against the government the soldier didn't have this letter."

"You tested a case in federal court, what was the case?"

A fun environment, quickly changed to a very serious tone as Para-legal's frantically pulled up the case, to give to the bailiff, who gave it to the Chief Justice, as he passed it to the second in line who had a mean scowl on his face, as each member received a copy, he was dead serious as he said "State your case, against Jack Cash, begin please."

A door opened in the back as twelve US Marshal's entered, to take up presence, as the attorney began, as he stepped out in the middle to say "Chief Justice, and Justices, I bring to you the following allegations of miss-conduct of that man, Jack Cash, for neglect, cruelty and abuse to my client's daughter, Cheryl Lynn Andrews, and another, her name is Alice White, with these pictures, he hands them to a projectionist, who flashed up both girls gagged, bound and hands tied, and ankles, in bra and panties only, the Justices were looking in disgust, and the attorney was smiling, to add when I'm through I will prove that man's guilt", he points at Jack Cash in a show boat stance.

Erica was about to stand when the Chief Justice, gave the sit down sign, she whispered to Jack "Something's up, just run with it", Jack nodded, as he undone a bottle of water, to drink it slowly, to hear,"Mister Jackson call your first witness", said Chief Holt, who said something to the other man next to him, as the attorney, said "I call Cheryl Lynn Andrews, to the chair."

"Go ahead Miss Andrews" said Chief Justice, motioning for her to take a seat as the bailiff, informed her of her rights, she said "I will."

"Now Miss Andrews what you say, in this court is now of public record, we have decided that this hearing is of a criminal nature, instead of the civil as first requested, so begin, so think about how and what you say" said the Chief Justice.

Arthur Jackson, was caught off guard, as he paused, the game was over, it was serious, as he turned, to see the Chief Justices all stand, as did Jack and Erica, as the President of the United States, George White, the third, emerged from a side wall, to take his seat, with his emblem, in place, as almost all the aisle were filled behind Jack Cash, as he sat, so did everyone else. words.

"Were waiting, Mister Jackson, who was careful to place his Meanwhile back at his prestigious office, U S Marshal's and federal agents seized, and arrested all his employees, and all of their records.

Mister Jackson looked at the President with a huge smile, to say "In your statement you said "Mister Cash touched you all over, can you be more specific?"

"Well he touched my breasts and my legs down there?" Mister Jackson was picking up momentum, to say "Tell us how he abused you?"

"Well he grabbed me from behind, with his arm around my breasts, then he tied my wrists together, and laid me face first on the bathroom floor, he bound my ankles."

"So you could say you couldn't move?" "No, I wet myself" as she began to cry."

Mister Jackson waited to see the audience reaction, only to see a couple of Judges and some of his arch enemies, to hear "Mister Jackson do you have any more questions for your witness."

"No your Honor, I mean Chief Justice." "Miss Meyers, would you like to cross?"

"Yes, Chief Justice, I would, now Miss Andrews you said, "My client, how do you know it was Jack, wasn't it true you were drugged?"

"Yes, I felt sluggish, but I know he was the one." "When you laid face down, were you told anything?" "No, my mouth was gagged."

"That is not my question, what was told to you while you were on the ground?"

"I don't know?"

"Was it true you were out?" "Yes, that's it, I was out?"

"Do you remember the limo ride, where you rode on top of the others, and the thirteen hour plane ride?" "No" she said and started crying. "That is all, Chief Justice Holt."

Mister Andrews stood up to begin, as the Chief Justice says "Call your next witness."

"What about a cross?"

"You had your opportunity to get out the facts; I believe were close to deciding if this is going to trial or not, so please continue."

"Well my next witness is Alice White."

"I will warn you Mister Jackson if this is an identical statement I will not allow it, proceed carefully."

"It won't be, it's about the cruelty, like the limo ride, and the plane."

"Then proceed, please, Miss White please take the chair."

The bailiff moved in to have her take the oath, for her to say "I will." "So Miss White tell us all what you experienced when you awoke, in your captors hands."

"Well I felt two hands on my breasts, as I was drug backwards, then I was laid down, the door opened, and I saw other girl, as I went in head first, hitting another girls knees, the ride was fast and we were tossed about, till it came to a screeching stop, then different men, touched my breasts, as I kicked back, till they threw me on a bed, as other girls were laid next to me, several girls were laid on me, as two women cut off our hair."

"Stick to just what happen to you, the rest is hearsay, be careful Mister Jackson" said the Chief Justice.

"I was released, I hit one of them and I was sedated, I woke up in my own pee, then I asked for food and water, and I was made to drink out of the sink, when we landed we were told, the captor was freeing us and we wanted . . . ."

"Again, I asked you to state what happen to yourself exclusively, the next slip and I will hold you in contempt of court, do you understand?, proceed" said an angered Chief Justice.

"Well I wanted to see who my captor was" then she changed her thought, then for the first time in six month's I could see clearly and then when I was released from the room, I raced down to see my parents, who said, that they were being held."

The sound of the mallet, several times, to say "Alright Mister Jackson, your witness crossed the line, Bailiff, take her into custody", she wept as she was led down for the Chief Justice to say "Wait, I have a few questions for her, but first do you have anything to say, Mister Jackson."

Arthur Jackson looked at his notes to say "I would like to summarize the conclusion."

"I have to say "Its best you sit down, Marshal's please", three Marshals' took their place by each prosecuting person, for the Chief Justice was going to say something as Jack rose, as did the Justices, and the President, as Jack raised his hand.

"Yes, Mister Cash did you want to say something?" "Yes, if I may, clear up some of this confusion."

"I think it is not necessary, as he looked over at the President who shook his head, to go ahead, as the Chief Justice, took a deep breath, to slowly say "Alright I will allow, this but only if Miss Meyers asks the questions."

Jack helps her up, as he passed her to take a seat, he raised his right hand, and read the oath to say "I Will".

As Erica with a page of notes began, while Arthur Jackson and David Andrews, were listening, to say "State you name and official title and who you work for?"

"Alright, my name is Jack Cash, I'm known as an International Bounty Hunter, but I Guess I'm also called a Super Spy."

"Who do you work for?"

"Well I thought it was the President of our United States, but really I work for the Supreme Court."

"That's right Jack Cash; you're the representative of the Supreme Court of the United States."

"What is your interpretation of the articles of exemption?"

"It gives me the power, to capture, detain, or in some cases even kill anyone I choose necessary, to defend the United States of America."

"That is right; the articles were drafted and ratified, in 1914, right after the First World War, to allow an operative to operate as they see fit, to carry out missions around the world.

Erica looked over at the attorney and Mister Andrews, to hear, "So with this power you are armed right now?"

"Yes, as Jack opened his jacket, to show its butt, of the weapon.

"Tell us or better yet, if you would provide this video from the surveillance camera's given to us by the King Leopold of Belgium." She pressed play, as Jack spoke, "Here myself and my pretend wife, were asked to locate, and extract, this woman I'm talking to her

name is Annabel Ryan, I took a photo of her, for confirmation
of target, I sat at the VIP table, and took a picture of that man,
Rich and Gloria Kendall, who signaled the Commandos, once I got
confirmation, I injected Annabel Ryan with a serum, to counteract
the drowsy state she was in, she went wild, so I subdued her and
the others in fear their loud aggressive behavior would expose us,
having the foresight, I learned my lesson, and carried her out,"

"Hold on, do not say anything except in the video please", said
Erica.

"Alright, I searched the husband of Annabel, to find a cloth
and chloroform, so I thought what would he use that for, you
see me standing there, looking around, to see something just
wasn't right, I got on my phone, and my contact required a video
confirmation on those that were kidnapped, and she told me to
get their faces on camera, so you see me walking table to table
with a collection plate, getting donations, at first it was just those
I thought were involved, but as you can see I hit all the tables,
then sat down, to catch Rich speaking Armenian, to realize, that
something was up, but not confirmed as his photo came up empty,
but eighteen kidnapped girls did, so I asked my wife to lure them
into the women's bathroom, using the chloroform, it put them out,
yes they are bounded, but it was easier to carry, and it not on the
video, they were set in a limo, that could carry all nineteen girls, as
I told my wife to come along, we took off, and then, had to come
back to pick up my car, I entered, at the end of the dinner, and
the King was present, to begin to taking out the men who had
imprisoned the girls."

"Are the two women any of the person's here?"

"Yes, here on my phone, do you have a e-mail to send it to"
The bailiff, hands Jack a piece of paper, which he does, it flashes up
on the screen, for Cheryl Lynn to scream out "That's the man who
assaulted me."

"Enough or you too will be held in contempt of court, proceed
Mister Cash."

"From here, you see the Commando's enter weapons blazing,
I left the men's bathroom, and began to shoot", as the video rolled

for the very first time, clear head shots, as ten Commandos went down, as Jack jumped onto the upper level to push, the King, and his wife off, to the side door, and just like that, they were out, and the door closed shut."

There was a bit of laughter, as the outside camera showed Jack kicking the door, trying it, then over to the locked glass door, off went his belt, and placed a bit, blasting cap in, he radioed it, it blew inward, as Jack pulled out another four bodies, to make his way back in only to have all the guns pointed at him, and"

"Stop the tape" said the Chief Justice, to add "There were over five hundred rounds, in that area shot at you."

There was silence, as Jack was motioned to continue, "So I was forced back in the men's bathroom, and seeing my prisoners, I thought, as an explosion outward continued the video, and another limo pulled up, as that person and Jack loaded them up, it showed Jack had enough, and went head hunting as five more went down, as the countries police was on one side, the commando's on the other, as Jack jumped back and was working his way over to that lady, bodies were everywhere, as he grabbed her hand and out the door he went, to the limo she got in, and it sped off, as Jack met with the Commander of the police, for Jack to say "It was all clear inside, all Commando's down, so I asked the police to move so that I could get my car out, the video ended and everyone stood up to applaud even the Chief Justice and his colleagues.

"Mister Cash, I believe we have all the information we need thank you for giving us some of your precious time, please go your wife, she is critical."

Jack stood, to say "Thank you for the opportunity to hear me out, it is an honor to serve you all."

All the Justices and the President stood, to motion to Jack to come to him."

"Erica approached him to say "I'll finish these proceedings, thank you for your service, looks like the President wants a word with you, see you soon."

"Whenever you like" said Jack with a smile. Just as Cheryl Lynn rushed Jack, Marshal's subdued her, to hear her say, "I just wanted to show my thanks and give him a hug."

Jack went through a passageway, to have the door close, and into a room with the President, who said "Have a seat, you just won me a re-election, thank you, and the numbers are just pouring in, is there anything you would like?"

"What to drink" asked Jack comically.

"No, sure, what I meant anymore support, other than the incarceration, and I'm looking into that?"

"I don't know I was asked to start up a spy academy, I don't know a billion dollars a year that is really up to Lisa."

"That's what I was afraid of, listen Jack you need to be a standalone guy, and limit your relations with her, she is with the CIG, and not exactly looking out for your health, she got wind of some Intel that there was going to be an attack, that's why she had you where you were at, there is a woman I want to have you get in touch with, she can be trusted, her name is Claire, she heads up the NSA, a very tight ship, she will stock a dynamite team for you, it was a good idea, from Miss Meyers to have me there, it gave you creditability and me a another four years, with misses Linda Jackson, who thinks highly of you, here are five stars your now a five star general, in addition to that pay you'll receive monthly, you still will get one million a capture, the King of Belgium, would like to know if you would come to his country and train a body guard force for him, could you do that as a favor for me?"

"Sure, when and where just let me know?" "What about this school? Where I could teach them, in the meantime I know a few agents I could send there to help out."

"Excellent, I'll pass that on to him, he also wanted to know what he could give to you."

"I don't know a chateau with some land, that way it gives me a chance to visit maybe something overlooking the sea, or a lake, I like lots of goats, goat cheese is good, oh I don't know I like wine too."

Jack went and raided a refrigerator of a pop, to say "You want one" "What do they have in there" asked the President.

The court room, still sat in silence, till the Presidents marquee was taken off, for the Chief Justice Holt to say "Miss Meyers has given me 122 charges against you, you both will be bounded over for trial on Monday of next week, and looking from the damages occurred to the plane a sum of 22,550, will be paid, then there's the matter of professional services, Having sued the President of the US, is a million dollars, taking up mister Jack Cash's precious time, his wife is on her death bed, awaiting the arrival of their first child, is one million dollars, and of our time is one million dollars, and according to this document, you sued the government and won, to have your son released from active duty claiming he was the sole surviving son, which, when he joined as a supposed adult he waived that right, so I will vacate that judgment and that amount will be paid back in full.

"Starting on next Monday, I need to see three million, four hundred seventy two thousand and five hundred dollars in cash, divided into three separate bags, hearing dismissed."

Jack rode the same elevator down as the President, for him to say

"I'd like to come visit you from time to time?" "Absolutely, I have nothing to hide" said Jack.

"I know that's what I like about you, you're a team player." Jack received a text, "Go ahead answer it maybe Sara?"

"Nah its Jim, says to meet him in the back." "Hey that's where I'm going."

The two exited, to a mob of secret service and spy club people, each falling in to support the other, as the President shook Jack's hand to say "Your doing a great job, keep up the good work, expect a bonus for Christmas, that is, because I got re-elected."

"Your doing a great job" said Jack as he saw Jim, who led him to his car, to say "I took it out of the shop, there must be fifty thousand people out front, so I sent Brian home, we will let the President go first and then you can slid in."

"Aren't you coming" said Jack seeing Jim stand where he was at.

"It's your car."

"Get in; I'll give you a ride back."

Jack got behind the wheel to say, "Oh that is different,"

"Yeah were changing the steering wheel, to add some new features, in addition Mercedes is handcrafting a one of a kind, later I'm flying over there to work with their designers to create a new super car, exclusively for you."

"That's nice."

Jack drove off, and into the column of the president's caravan, till the highway, where he got on, hit his plate button, to say "I noticed Virginia plates, do we still have diplomatic ones?"

"Of course, hit it twice,"

Meanwhile back at the courthouse, each man took a different path down, as Arthur Jackson was read his rights of ethical misconduct, and disbarred, Mister David Andrews and daughter Cheryl Lynn, took the elevator, it stopped, on the twentieth floor, a single tall man got on board, he hit the garage button, to say "I've been asked to guard you."

"We don't need your help, were getting off at the lobby." "Don't say I warned you, you have till Monday to get that money to the courthouse, try to run, and we will hunt you down", the doors opened to a new reality, thousands of angry men were pounding on the glass as Marshal's armed held the line, for David to have a change of mind to say, "I'll take that protection now."

Down in the garage, was three black vans, Norse man pushed David in to say "I hope that wasn't too cruel of me, wait till we get on the road, HA, HA, Ha, he laughed as all three vans took off, the Giant drove to a luxury private grounds, called Pine Acres, as the sign said, he drove into a garage and parked, a man slid the door open, so that David and his wife June, and son, to hear the Giant say, "Go inside relax, my boss is waiting for you."

All four went into the living room, where Kelli Bridges of the CIA stood, a tough looking chick who was fierce, to say "Jack Cash asked me to help you out, for a family sue crazy."

"Is this what this is all about, I had death threats on my phone, Scott has to hide out as he was booed, this morning and will miss the playoffs, what have you got us in" said June angrily.

"Enough of the games, I will tell you this, if it weren't for the President's re-election, I imagine all four of you would be six foot under, as the Giant appeared, his hands alone the size of their heads, to continue, you'll be safe on this base, as long as you stay in the house and lie low, but I will tell you this there are friends of Jack, that is far reaching, like some of the most famous assassin, who would pick you off for trying to discredit Jack Cash's reputation, even himself, but we all know he is way too compassionate to do that, that is why he has all the power and no one else does, so I will leave you for now, make your arrangements for that money by phone fax or e-mail, and I will see you on Monday."

Next up was the Tampa firm, led by Jim Thomas and staff, Brandy the paralegal, through the doors of the federal courthouse in Tampa, to the awaiting room, they checked the docket, it read their firm against the United States, specific Jack Cash, they were allowed in, to an empty room, to the front, on the defendants side was a huge TV set. Jim and his team assembled they were half hour early, and so waited, till the bailiff, spoke up and said, "All rise the Honorable, Miss Hendricks presides, which put a smile on Jim's face, to see that she appeared, went up and sat on the bench. She hit the gavel, to say, let's start the procedures, are we online?"

"Sorry your honor", spoke Miss Meyers, as Jim and the others looked over, to hear, "So I see here you filed this brief a week ago, but updated it last night, to state that this was an emergency filing, why was that?"

"Your honor we felt the defendant Jack Cash, was a flight risk, and wanted the order to keep him here."

"How did you come to that conclusion?" asked the Chief Justice Hendricks.

"He has two names and has his own plane, and lives in Germany."

"According to these papers, he lives in Mobile, so why didn't you file in the state of which the defendant lives?"

"He also roams on a boat that currently resides in the Dominican Republic so at this time, he was stationed at New Port Richey, and he uses different names."

"I got that Mister Thomas, and from the documents Miss Meyers filed, to counter your claim, stipulates, that Mister Cash, or Gunther Schecter, are a property of the Supreme Court, so I must sign off on this civil complaint, and send it to the Supreme Court in Washington DC, is that suitable for you Miss Meyers?"

"Yes your honor", she said.

"Mister Thomas, how about you?"

Stunned he looked at the Justice, then over to the screen that was turned to face them by the bailiff, to hear," Mister Thomas, it is, my name is Erica Meyers, I represent Jack Cash, or Gunther Schecter, and from the declarations, it says your suing him for 100 million dollars, but I don't see your bond of 100 million are you sure you know what you're doing?" she waited for an answer, while they scrambled to confirm that, she continued.

"As of this moment, I believe we have a criminal case, I've instructed the IRG, you might know them as the Internal Revenue Group, to inform me that you don't have the 100 million retainer to file, which constitutes a fraud."

Jim nodded, when he received the news, he spoke up to say,"What is our alternative?"

"Well from this point on, you don't have one, as your probably aware of, your group was the one who filed the motion, regardless of the money value, your goal was to detain my client, which constitutes terrorist activity, and as you already know, we as a country won't tolerate that, so next Monday, at 0900 you'll appear here in Washington DC to defend yourselves on fraud, first, then the Supreme Court we evaluate and make a ruling on your case, any questions?"

"I believe we are close to that number?"

"It's not about being close, you stipulated your concern of the class action suit, which would award that group the asking price of 100 million dollars, as your aware, you need to cover that settlement amount, just in case, you lose, which according to these records you never have, well that is until now, you see from this point on, any case you try on the federal level, you will face me, my specialty is contract law, and procedural protocol, which ensures correct ethics, and I was surprised when I read your motion, that you didn't reference the 1914 ruling that protects spies foreign or in our country of any wrong doings to anyone, person, place or thing, especially, if they are known, to be such, under the instruction and ratification of the world council at the UN as such placed on January of 1915, to protect those from liability therein."

Behind them, Marshal's handcuffed Jim and his team, took the prosecutions witness's, even Bridgett's once jubilant face was now screaming, over her anguish. They were led out of the court room, down the elevators, as all the while the two paralegals spoke, on how and why and what they were going to do, for Jim to say, "Shut up, they are wired, don't say another word, they will use it against you."

Meanwhile at the firm of Fancier, Caldwell and Thomas, it was business as usual, that was until a courier arrived, to the receptionist, to say, "I need an official to sign for this."

She looks at the package, to say, I'll need a partner to sign, can you wait?"

"Yes", he said and took a seat, while she got up and went back, past a sea of paralegals all working hard, past them to the large offices, and to the lead partner, it read "Alister Fancier." She knocked, he waved her in, through the clear glass, she entered, and placed the package on his desk to interrupt him and some strange looking black guy, he was big, and had massive hands, but had a distinct look, she looked up at him, to hear Alister say, "Tina it's not nice of you to stare at Mister Tyrell."

"Sorry", she said as she looked down, as he signed the electronic pad, she took it back, as he said, "As you were saying, you won't have to worry about customs, we have court orders we can throw at them."

Tina made it back to the front, to hand it to the gentleman, who said,

"Thanks", and left.

Moments later, a swarm of men came in, and took them all by surprise, and in that moment, everything stopped, everyone in the paralegal pool raised up their hands, and those in the big offices, were told to come out and keep their hands up, and then a man, stepped in, he showed them who he was, only to fall away, to allow a man in a wheel chair, to appear, to say, 'My name is agent Henderson, I'm with the FBI, and your all under arrest, you too Mister Tyrell, and take them?" he knew he caught a big fish, but now it was even bigger, they got the number one bad guy; Tyrell Scopus.

"On what charges?" screamed out Alister Fancier.

"On conspiracy to fraud the government and to protect and help that of a known terrorist."

An officer held Alistair's head down on his table onto of his new document, for Agent Henderson to say, "Make sure you take that legal document with him, he signed to ensure the fraud. The FBI led the entire office out into the parking lot, where the FBI took them all into custody, and in went the investigators.

CH 12

Sam is on the fight for her life

The plane landed, taxied, and into its hanger, turned around, Brian was lowering the ramp, the troops went out first to secure the surroundings, big door closed, as they went to work, refueling, Lisa, stood at the foot of the ramp, she smiled as she saw Dana and Julie, to say, "So you're the two who want to join us?"

"Yes Ma'am, My name is Dana and this is Julie."

"Well welcome to Quantico, Virginia, wait over here, you're both from the CIA." "Yes."

"Paul, can you escort these two to the Admin office, just as Curtis, drives out an ATV and trailer, to say "You won't need that, let Paul use that."

"He can have it."

Inside the secure building Jack and family await to see Samantha. Paul and the girls take off, as Jack and the women with Mark and Mike, helping Sara, for Lisa to say, "You're quite along, since I last saw you."

Sara smiles, for Lisa to say, "Come follow me."

Jack was behind her, then Sara, and Mike, Kate, Heidi, and Mark brought up the rear. All fit into an open elevator, Lisa punched in a code, the doors closed and it went down a couple of levels, as Jack stood by Lisa, and Sara, the doors opened, as they all stepped out behind Lisa, to a door, that read "SECURE BY PERMISSION ONLY."

Lisa turned to say, "Agents to the rear, Jack, and Sara only, the rest wait, please." Lisa pushed the door open, to darkness, as nothing could be seen, Jack helped Sara, through the darkroom, as Lisa held onto Jack's arm, to another door, it opened to a heavy lighted room, to see Ramon, and she said, "Ramon will escort our guest through the secure room".

"Sorry about all this, but this is the fastest way to the south part of the hospital, there is the viewing window, she is down below, for your privacy she was moved against the window side, down those stairs you can go down, as she motioned to a big guard to help Sara, as he moved in cautiously, as he walked the slow pace Sara walked till Jack said, "If you can get the door."

"If you don't mind sir, allow me, it will be an honor", he said very respectful.

Sara nodded in agreement, the Giant guy placed his hands carefully under her knees and across her back, holding her arm, she went up easy, as Jack opened the door, and they went down, at the bottom, he set her down, and stepped back as Jack helped her across the small space, to the open door, where a lab was situated, and two men and a woman dressed in all whites, first helped Sara get dressed, she looked like she had a tent on, as Jack began to crack up at her.

"Hush mister, that's not funny."

With booties on her feet, and a mask to wear, and a cap on her head, she stepped into the sterile environment, to pass through a plastic curtain, to see Mitzi, who went to her to say, "Come here dear" As Mitzi, helped Sara to the side of the bed as others watched above. Sara grasped her dear friends hand, as she woke to see her, Sam smiled, as Mitzi helped her with a stool to sit on, as Samantha spoke, "Nice to see you."

"Me too, I Love you, how are you feeling?" asked Sara, as Jack stood at the door, watching the two.

"I'm not sleeping anymore."

"I will miss you" said Sara as tears were streaming down her face. As seen through the visor.

"Stop it; you need to be the strong one."

Sara just stared down at her friend.

Upstairs was a little different, as they all were peering down, seeing only portions of them both as Miss Smith suddenly began to get agitated to say, "When can I go down and see my daughter?"

As Mark was trying to calm her down, she snapped at him to say "Get away from me, don't touch me" as she pushed Mark away, when the Giant, emerged from the elevator, Bacchus, was coming at her, for Miss Smith to say, "Hold him back, and you stand back, your testing my patience." She said to Mark, ready to seize her.

"If it were me I'd had them throw you off the plane, while in flight", said Mark, somewhat out of place.

"That would be murder."

"No, that would be peace, everyone would be happier" said Mark, trying to defuse a situation, as now it was Ramon, also moving in on her.

She sees Lisa, to say, "After my daughter dies, when will I get her compensation?"

Lisa just looked at her to say, "No, never, that money is not yours, all you are is her biological mother, who is estranged, I'd watch what you say, from now on, or I will let Norse Bacchus, have his way with you."

"Oh, you're just kidding?"

"Yeah, you caught me, I was kidding, go ahead go down and see your daughter."

Lisa spread her arms to say, "Give her room", and then turned to see Heidi and Kate to say, "What are you two waiting for?" "Well were not immediate family" spoke Kate.

"No you're both not, but you're both doctors, and Jack thinks of you as his mother and his sister, in my book that is family." "He said that" remarked Kate.

"Hush, be respectful" said Heidi, her Mom and ads "Thank you Lisa."

"Yes that is fine, oh before I forget; can you stay on, to see this through?"

"Absolutely, were here for Jack." They said in unison. "That's nice to hear, I was going to leave to allow your family to have some privacy."

"Thank you" said Heidi.

The two were escorted down by the Norseman, giant Bacchus. Jack continued to stand by the door, watching the two laughs, as her mother dressed in protective gear quickly, and went to the other side, of Samantha, while Sara held onto both of her hands, to hear, "Hey baby, it's your mom, you sure hit the jackpot on this one, and how are you doing?"

Sam broke the grasp of Sara and motioned her mother to come closer, she bent over so that Samantha could whisper in her ear, she said, "Mom, get-the-fuck-out-of-here, I hate you bitch." Samantha leaned up and then down with that big deep breath, as her eyes was bugged out.

Miss Smith wobbled back and then staggered against the wall, she was crying, she dropped to the floor, as Jack went to her, gradually, pulling her up, as she was crying uncontrollable, two guards appeared at the door as Jack, led her out of the room, for her to hear, "Miss Smith, come with us, we will take you out."

She pulled herself away from Jack, she was pulling everything off, that she put on, as one man pulled on her, as the other slapped on cuffs, to say "You're under arrest."

"What, what did I do?" she said still reeling over what her precious daughter had said to her.

"The government is charging you with abuse to your daughter."

Jack turned to see her being led out, then sees Margaret Ryan, step down to meet up with him to say, "First thank you for rescuing my daughter, and secondly, some of my talks with Samantha was discovered, that, her mother is the reason, she caused the accident that put her in the wheelchair, but it was because she wanted to die, because of the mental and physical abuse she endured, we discovered the abuse, from the cat-scan, her jaw had been broken over twenty times, the only good thing that ever happen to her was that you showed enough interest in her that she felt like she had hope, but the damage of her body was too great, I'm sorry."

"As for Misses Smith, you're free to do whatever you want with her life, she is being held, just let me or Lisa know."

Jack just looked at her, it was as if she wanted to hug him, so he allowed her in, and she hugged him, as Heidi and Kate heard all of it, had tears running freely, as Jack held Margaret, as she continued to say "I'm sorry, over and over again", Jack neither held her harder or not as much, but as a support for her. Moments had passed by, till Jack felt several more hands on him, as three women were all emotional, and he continued to support them to hear, "Come on ladies, let's let Jack, alone and go see his wife, as three emotional women stood back to let Jack alone. Which was said over the intercom? Jack passes Mitzi to say, "Thank you."

Jack entered the room, to the other side of Samantha, to touch her hand; she grasped his with authority, as Jack bent down to hear, "I love you."

"I love you too, darling" said Jack.

'Who is that behind you, honey, is that my doctor?"

"Jack turns to see Kate and Heidi, hugging the wall, to say "I guess they are."

"I'm not blind, I can see them, and can they come in?"

"Of course, Jack turns to wave them in, they both came in past Jack for each one to give a hug Samantha, while Jack went around to be behind Sara to hold her as he places his head on her shoulder, and places his arms around her, to touch Samantha's other hand, Samantha's smile lit up the room.

Samantha spoke slow deliberate words of praise, to all of them, but as Mitzi saw Samantha was tiring out, to say "Alright I hate to break this up, but now I must ask, that one at a time spend with her, as Jack fell back first to say, "I think Sara should go first."

Everyone else agreed, as Jack went out, carefully taking off his outfit, he gave it to an assistant, as he saw Lisa, up in the observation tower, which he took the elevator up, got off to see Mark, who seemed like he wanted an embrace, but held his position. Jack saw Lisa to say, "It's nice you're here, do you have time to go over things?"

"Sure, let's go" said Lisa, as she led him through the secure room that was lit up for him, looked like a computer storage facility, as they made their way into the elevator, both stood apart as the doors opened, as she led him to her office, for her to say, "Have a seat do you need anything?"

"Nah, I'm fine, but what is that smell?"

"It's the kitchen, where Mitzi and her crew make the meals for the plane and us on the ground."

"Well maybe, I'll take you up on that" said Jack, as he watched her take a seat behind her desk, as Jack sat on the sofa.

"So let's talk about you, I'd sure thought you would spend more time with her than that?"

"You know me; it's hard for me to see her like, in that state, for me it's over quickly." Said Jack as he wiped away a tear.

"Miss Meyers has told me that you're asked to re-appear in court on Monday, as Mister Andrews is returning to pay off what he owes, and you are being sued, for cruelty and abuse to some Bridgett Carpenter and some others all told sixty eight infractions, during your last mission."

"Sure, that's fine; will I have the same attorney?" "Yes, she is there for you for life."

"Sounds nice, what else?"

"Well I like the two girls you just recruited, what did you have for them?"

"Nothing really, hasn't decided."

"Alright how about you let me have them and you can have . . . ."

"The giant Norseman, Bacchus." Exclaimed Jack. "You'll trade the girls for him" she asked earnestly. "And I want Ramon."

"Wait what about Bacchus."

"Fine, I wanted someone as a personal assistant, can Alba does that?"

"No, just wait were training those girls, you once had." "And how is that going?"

"Well to tell you the truth, it's not, their dropping like flies." The only bright spot is Debby, but she is past her prime."

"What thirty, is past their prime, what does that make me, a senior citizen?"

"No silly, you're ageless, but those around you need to be young."

"Who says, you're crazy if you think you can find or build a make believe agent, half the girls you have don't even have half of what Debby has, if it were me, I'd make her my partner." Said Jack.

"What about Blythe?" asked Lisa?

"Will I ever see her, again?" asked Jack. "Depends if she passes the final tests."

"How about, I help you out and stage some type of qualifier, call them the spy club games?"

"You would do that?"

"Sure, anything to help out" said Jack. "Sounds like we have a deal."

"Now what have you got me into?" asked Jack.

"Well, were all making a transition, and anything you could do would only help us out, said Lisa pulling out a map of Quantico Virginia, to point out places and points."

"Sure I'm all in for that, is this the area we have? asked Jack." him?"

"Its east of the airfield and south to the boathouse." "So it's official I get Norseman, for Dana and Julie?"

"Well I didn't really say that, what are you going to do with

"Have him join the strike team."

"I don't know about that, I guess we could ask him?" "Alright, I can see you really don't want to depart with him, so I'll take Tami."

"Tami, where did that come from, you mean the girl from the spa?"

"Yeah, for my assistant, you have had her, what a couple of months?"

"Yeah you're right, alright I will have her here tomorrow morning, is that soon enough?"

"Will she be able to access my phone? also help to keep on top of all the calls and e-mails I get?"

"Interesting, have an assistant to answer the phone calls and e-mails, maybe I could have her do that for me? too." "I guess were done here?" said Jack.

Jack stands up, to walk to the door, as she says, "Where are you going? says Lisa."

"Mitzi just texted me that she has a space in Quantico ready for me."

"Where is that at?"

"She said it was by the boat house"

"Oh alright, I'll see you tonight for dinner?"

"Sure", said Jack eyeing her as she, to say, "Let's talk about missions."

"Well that's tricky, because I'm really not your boss, but you need to know what the President wants, or needs I guess."

"I'll I need is clarification, for instance, take this last mission, I went out there to expose a mole, namely the Commander and it worked."

"That's what I'm saying, you really don't need a specific mission, and trouble just finds you."

Jack looks at her, to say,"I like that plane, can I have it?"

"Sure, but the government can't justify having a pilot on hand while you lounge around there in Mobile, here in DC or at the new base in Quantico."

"Alright how about this, you let me continue to go after the top 100, as my needs are met, and as my desires for resources' are fulfilled, I'll get them from you?"

"Of course, that's why it would be nice that you were here, we could talk, instead of you living in Mobile."

"How about, after all this settles down, I'll give you an answer, and if I do move out here, I'll need a place that I can protect my family, rather than on this base."

"On that I know of a place, that has some acreage, and we can place all of our technologies to make it safe, what else? she asks.

"I like this, rather than me telling you, you just go ahead and make it happen." to show her, he has finally committed to her desires, to add, "Well what is up with the organization of the plane, some have food others don't, I guess where the organization at, Is?"

"That is all about to change, Jim and Brian and Nicole, will be your permanent flight crew, your assistant will have a place on board, and she will coordinate with me, where the plane goes, as for the strike team, I just received word that the 82nd airborne division, has decided to send a component up here, to begin training Special Support Ops, for your plane, grounds etc, etc, so by the time you get here there will be major construction, and over a thousand man force, training, there is a Marine I know will join your team, his name is Major John Lincoln will always be in charge on the plane, but he will have the best of the best, their new call sign is SSA, it was a play off the British commandos."

"Shall I ask what it means?"

"The SSA stands for Super Spy Agents."

"Clever that was original, what about other implements?" "Like what do you want?"

"I like that ATV, how about a motorcycle? a rubberized stealth boat?"

"Does Jim know of these Ideas'?" "Possibly, I don't know."

"Alright I'll have a talk with him, but as far as any equipment you need, it's his job to perfect it, before it goes into service, anything else?"

"How about a crew cabin?"

"Sorry we just can't, I know all about that one, where you slept in the cockpit, and allowed the girls to have your room, do you want to see the bill?"

"What do you mean?"

"Yeah, little miss innocence's, soiled the mattress, sheets and platform, one even etched the inside glass, with her initials, which compromised the whole capsule"

"What was that? a capsule where?"

"Well actually both planes are equipped with escape pods, in case of the plane is shot down, over the sea, is a ball, water proof, with a beacon, once activated, virtually indestructible, look here it is, see the monitor, she clicked it on to show him, it rolled it showed, the test taking place and all the action, as it was taking place; off the coast of Alaska, fifty miles off the first time, you sit in a frame and the ball rolls on the surface, the other time was two hundred miles, during a storm, and the volunteer, was blown another three hundred miles, he said it was like a roller coast ride, there is the capsule carried by all the coast guard, it doubles as a small boat lift."

And the other one is the room, you're in, in the event the plane is shot out of the sky, the crate you call a room, is a self contained unit, that recycles the water, and wastes, and then it is a survival box, complete with tracking devises, the cabinets should have enough rations for a month, and inside is a crash seat, that is stored under the bed, the water supply, lines the inside, the crate itself, went through missile testing, and survived, only drawback is the igniter is in the cockpit, and once released, the crate is hurled out the back end."

"What about a parachute for the car?"

"Good question, I'll talk with Jim about that, I don't think we thought of that going over the scenarios, but we will, anything else?" "Nah I think that covers it, see ya."

The next few days flew by on the base of Quantico, as Tami was still not there, and each day Jack would see that Brian and Jim and a new pilot, Jeff Larson, "Lars", were near to completing the car pickup, to say that they would test it on another car, before using it on the Mercedes, Lisa got her new assistant, recalled from school, it was Dylan, who seemed a bit flirty, with him. Sara and Jack visit Samantha, who has since declined in health; it's been sixteen hours since his last visit to Samantha."

"I'm supposed to be in the courtroom, in four hours, its five o'clock, Brian, said he would take me in his GTO, so I've changed into a suit, with a pink tie, so says Sara, its October the cancer awareness month, whatever that means, this journalizing is for the birds, he tosses the journal aside, to leave the room, and pull the door shut locked, down the stairs, out in the morning. A Green

GTO, souped up was parked, Jack ran across, he was ready, slid into the passenger seat, and Brian spun the tires, and off they went, for a short one hour ride into Washington DC, to the new address of the new Supreme Court, one constitution avenue as they parked, it was seven or so in the morning, Jack got out as Brian said "I'll pull around and wait for you, if you like?"

"Nah, go back, If I need a ride, I'll call" said Jack, and took two steps at a time, the huge skyscraper was brand new, inside was a guard, Jack pulled his badge to show the guard, who asked "Do you have a weapon?"

"Yes I do, but I'm not going to let you have it." "I'll have to call my supervisor?"

Moments past, then Erica showed up to say, "Allow him to pass, please, he is my client."

"Go ahead this time" he said with a smile, now knowing who he really was.

Jack walked through the most sophisticated electronic machine in the world, nothing, it was black, as Jack said, "See ya."

Jack was rising at viewing this very beautiful woman, the way she walked, was mesmerizing, then she opened the door, he walked in to see literally one hundred associates, all scrambling around, but gave way to Erica and Jack as she led him to her office, for her to say, "Have a seat."

Erica shut and locked the door, and closed the blinds, to come around to face him to say, "Your older than I expected, you're doing some fine work for the government, so well that the current President should win reelection with no problem, why you're here, well you don't need to be, that's what I'm here for, to represent you, will you take the stand, hold on", she began to wave herself to cool her down, she went and got something to drink, to say, "Would you like something?"

"A cup of coffee, with a squeeze of fresh lemon?"

"Sure hold on a minute, as she unlocked the door, and went out, then came back to say, "It will be here momentarily."

"Is everything alright" said Jack looking at her pace around and was talking incoherently, for her to say, "Will you sleep with me?"

Jack just looked at her as she said, "Strike that, you have to bear with me, but you're the, It right now, your all over the news, and the thing about it is you have the ability to take anyone's life, and for no reason, yet for safety reasons, you gag and bind those nineteen women and save their lives, all by yourself, how did you do that, that was probably the most incredible thing I have ever witnessed in my entire life, then you, help the King of Belgium escape, then go back in and blow the door, to rescue eight more hostages, but take out nineteen commandos, they should have given you a medal for your bravery, instead some smuck sued you for brutality and abuse, and now we exposed a mole, and another firm is after you, at some point all of this has to stop., and all I ask you is; How do you plead?"

"Guilty as charged" said Jack.

"No, you're not Guilty, and I will enter the plea, your only sense of guilt is you going back in there and trying to save more lives, I know your married but would you consider screwing me just once?"

"Are you on top, or do I get you from behind?"

"You'd consider it, strike that, I just got married, I know I will have this guilt hanging over me forever, would you consider if I got a divorce, would you marry me?"

Possible, does that mean unlimited sex?"

"Of course, what girl wouldn't want a super spy for a husband?"

"You'll have my children?"

"Yes of course, that's what I want, too." "You'll be alright with my five other wives?" "Of course that would be hot."

"Lastly, you'll live under my roof, for the rest of your life." "Wait before I answer this" a knock on her door, she opened it, the smell of lemons was refreshing, for her to take the cup, and hand it to Jack to say, "Can I have a sip?"

"Sure go ahead, were practically dating" said Jack. She sipped it to say, "Darren make me one too, thanks."

She closes the door, to say "What am I doing, do I want to throw away my life with Steve for Jack, some say I should, heck you're a super spy, that alone makes me so wet, and with Steve, well it just isn't there." Jack stood in the ready position, it had been a while, for him, as he went to her, a knock on the door, she opened it, to receive the coffee, she drank it down quickly, and she closed the door, locked it down, turns to him and said, "Just fuck me."

Jack held her hips, as she pulled her panties down, he slipped on a condom, she was right she was extremely wet, as she was in for the surprise of her life, as he was big, and she felt it, and it was too much as she exploded, as she kept quiet, but it was no use, after thirty minutes, everyone in the office knew what was going on, she began to sweat, as she said "Are you going to finish up?"

"You don't know that much about me, I'm into this new sport called Sport Fucking, know what that is?"

"No, but I'm getting the idea, how long does that last?"

"Oh some say four hours" said a confident Jack who was getting a firmer control. Jack continued the stroking to say, "What time is the appointment for? "As he slowed his pace,

"Oh nine o'clock, thanks, as she began to pull away, Jack was ready to go again, as he darted back inside of her, for her to say "A second time?"

"Oh I'm good for three or four more times, and at least four hours."

"Yes, then I will marry you" she said in a wave of euphoric feeling, just allowing him to have his way with her.

Inside the Chief Justice chamber sat eleven powerful people, aids have come and gone, to clean up breakfast, for Chief Justin Holt, to say, "Let's talk about our most current case, as he got everyone's attention, to say, "Is it constitutional for the victims to sue a rescuer, just because he uses force to extract them?"

"and older man speaks up," in my time, force was force, and those spies were told to put a bullet in anyone who disagreed with them?"

"That's fair BS, but these days the days are changing to find out why someone does the things they do, and that is why this agent we have is our instrument."

"If he is our agent, why doesn't he do what we want?" asked another.

"This is the tricky part, we don't know what to do with him, or how to direct him, his boss is the President, as we oversee him as well, just as long as it pertains to the constitution, and the 1914 decree covers all of Jack Cash's actions, and if that isn't enough, the UN's World Council has said, they would gladly take Jack off of our hands, in exchange to wipe out our current debt."

"That's one trillion dollars?" said another.

A woman spoke up to say, "One person is worth the entire countries debt?, I'd say, we better go at great lengths to make him feel very welcome and ensure he stays on our side, so what is the case before us" said Alice.

Jack and Miss Meyers rode the elevator up to the 33rd floor, where three lines were, with each a x-ray machine, and for Jack and Erica they took the VIP route, and was ushered straight in, on the left was the entire firm of Fancier, Caldwell and Thomas, and at the front table sat the men, closest to them, was Alister, then James and then finally, Jim, dressed impeccable, as Jack and Miss Meyers took the right, and not a single person on his side.

The bailiff, stood to announce, "Please rise, and wait till all the Justices, take their places, and thus the Chief has struck his gavel, to take your seats, understand?" as if waiting a response, for Jack to say, "Yes Sir", everyone looked at him, as did the bailiff, to say,

"Number eleven, John Cooper, former Maryland DA, he walks the plank to the last chair on the right, in direct face to Jack, for the Bailiff to say, "Next to him, is the honorable, William Booth, former NY police chief, was the commentary of Erica whispering to Jack, to hear, "Next is one of the youngest, girl, her name is Connie Williams-Stupor, inside to the left of her is Ronald Smith, a young eighty one years old, he is the last of the old stalwarts and old guard, along with BS, to hear, Next is Margaret West-Campbell, second in command, and a fiery red head, and at the head of the table, is the Chief of the Justices, Mister Justin Holt, he is fair and true, you'll get a good shake with him, that side is the strong side, usually the foes, and those on his right are the voice of reason, usually the opposes, led by, "Next to the Chief is Gregory Wilson, a former professor of ethics at Brown University, that

African-American persons opposes everything, and leads his group at the table with the "Next, to him is the oldest, welcome, Arnold Baden-Sowell, he is from Arkansas, and he himself had expressed his delight in what you did for that state in your last big round up, the other Justices call him BS, for short, if you know what I mean, but really he is a fun guy, Next to him, is Alice White, she is the current's President's selection, as being the current Presidents distant niece, she has a strong background in the field of politics, some say it was her election, to this seat that got him re-elected, this is her first major case, Next to her and by the door is bathroom break, Roger Johnson, former senator, who's weak bladder, has him leaving during the process, so don't be alarmed if he just gets up and is gone for periods of time, and lastly, Mister Wayne Rogers, he is fair he is what they call a wild card, he is a flip flopper, even if he likes the issue he will be the only one fighting to the end, so who knows how all of this will go. She stop talking to see all the Justices were standing and facing them, to hear, We have one more guest, please welcome our President of our United States, Mister, George White the third, he came in, went behind, several other Justices, to a seat next to the Chief Justice, and an emblem, was placed behind him, as with the others, for the President to say, "All sit", but they waited for him, as he still stood to say, "Allow the record to show, I will proceed over this hearing, you may begin, Mister Fancier", said the President as he took a seat followed by all the Justices.

Mister Alister stood, to say," Mister President, Chief Justice, and the other Justices, I'd like to apologize for not having everything in order, our bond has been paid, 100 million as requested, I'd like to start out by saying, this man Jack Cash, isn't who he says he is", Alister stands firm at his table to realize, he needed to cut the crap, and get on with it, to say, "As I was saying, Jack Cash is Gunther Schecter, the famous east German spy, anyway, he has inflicted the damage and cause to my client, in the terms of her losing her husband to his neglect."

The Chief Justice, slammed the gavel down, to say, "Will you allow me your honor, Mister President?"

The President nodded, for the Chief Justice to say,"We all read your motion, are you aware of the articles of the 1914 Decree, issued in September eight weeks after the assassination of Archduke Francis of Austria, that thrushed us into World War one, its design was to protect the spies, and set some sort of exchange program, in the event they were captured, so as you can see its still enforce as it was back then.?"

Alister looks up, from having that letter in front of him, to say,"Yes." "I don't mean now, Bailiff, Johnny, place it up on the screen" said the Chief Justice.

It flashed up on the wall, for all to see, all that were there read, some pretty legal jargon, but the just of it read, those that are chosen by the President, for the President, may be his instrument in the country or on foreign shores, to do whatever it takes to accomplish his (President) intentions, via one persons action, this so person, will be covered against any liability, here or there, from the action and beyond, no such strangers shall challenge or indict them for those such actions, or themselves shall be treated as an conspirator and charged as such, and made aware to that agent, to see what he prescribes to be of the action, they may confer with the highest court, or even the President himself, but the action, is always left up to the discretion of the agent."

Everyone had continued to read, but for Jack he saw his authority and responsibility all laid out for all to see, and the justification, of his actions, were constructed, not recently but over a hundred years ago, now it all made sense, the call to duty, as he saw the position was only open to two, one was Ben Hiltz, as it said west coast, and the other was Jack Cash, above their names were only about twenty total. The screen went blank, the Chief Justice said,"So I say to you Mister Fancier, what you have to say?"

Alister looked at the Justice to say,"I guess nothing?"

Number nine, spoke up, to say, "Sure you do, tell us about why you were looking up Jack Cash, and found his real name, I'd like to know what his background is?", as the other Justices were talking amongst themselves, to hear, "Well what we uncovered was he comes from a prominent family in Bonn, Germany, he has a living mother, Sophia and a sister, Christina, a son named Jesse Carter, and finally a girlfriend named Natasha Rogers, who befriended him in prison, and that's when she became pregnant and thus produced his first heir, now he is married and with several babies on the way." He said with the utmost respect to the Justices. Each justice looked at one another, as the Chief, said "Allow us to convene and we will render a decision", as the Chief Justice motioned for the President to move first, he got up.

"All Rise." Jack stood beside his sharp attorney. Following the President, the Justices got up, and then single filed exited, into their room and closed the door. The President, talked with Chief Justin to say,"Is our man alright then?"

"Yes."

"Then get him going, I'll take my leave."

The door was closed shut as the President was gone, as the Justices all went to separate areas of the room, to see a young woman of distinction was present, each of them knew who she was, as the Chief went to her first, extending his hand he said,

"So what is our honor to have you here in our presents?"

"Don't you know, as they shook hand and smiled for the Chief to say,"Care to sit in?"

"No, I'm just waiting for all of your answers?"

"For what is the question?" 'asked Gregory Wilson. "You'll have to school your new recruits, Justin, besides what do I always want, and if your all not aware, then I will tell you, it is to have the rights to Jack Cash, and I will tell you this he will never see a courtroom ever again."

"What makes you so sure?"

"He is just like your President, although he is your instrument, he does what policy you put into place, he is the one who actually is the tool that makes it all happen, when your done playing games send over to me and we will treat him like he is really wanted, and surely not by having his laundry aired in front of this court and public policy."

"She is right", voiced up the eldest and only woman on the current bench, Miss Margaret West-Campbell, spoke as others listened as she spoke eloquently and said, "Miss Holstein is right, Jack Cash is one of ours, he should be treated with the utmost respect and dignity, and it will be the last thing we do, is to allow the United Nations to come in here and take our best agent away from us."

"That is the fight I'm use to hearing, but it may just be a matter of time, when eventually he will become ours, it's now or later."

"This may be true but for the moment he is ours and will stay that way, until later", she put up her hands to say,"I think it's time to let them know our judgment and allow Jack his freedom."

Each justice nodded, as they passed by Meredith, through the open door, you could hear,"All rise."

Each Justice took their seat to include two extra women, all eleven sat, as did the court, it was the Chief who passed the document over to Margaret, who struck her gavel, then waited to see their guest Miss Holstein step in, to hear," In the matter of the wrongful death against Jack Cash, dismissed, and for all charges against Jack Cash, they are all dismissed, as those in the plaintiff side were dejected over the news, to hear, "In addition, there are court cost and fee to be paid, as the bailiff, hands her a document, she reads it to say, "The court cost filed and the attorneys fee, and not to mention Mister Cash's daily fee, of ten million dollars you owe the court thirteen five, which is above and beyond that 100 million." She slammed the hammer down, she stood up, to say, "Mister Fancier, I'd advise you to pay that to Mister Cash today, in the event, it is not I will hold you in contempt, do you understand this Mister Fancier?"

"Yes I, we do, your Justice."

"As for you Mister Cash, you're free to go and arrest whoever you like . . . . Without penalty.

"Does this court understand?" looking at Miss Holstein, who smiles back at her as the everyone stood, as the Justices exited. Miss Meyers turns to Jack to say, "See I told you I would take care of you" she embraced him and saw Meredith, and pulled away, to see Alister ready with check in hand, for Jack to say, "I'd prefer a transfer, do you have a pen and paper?"

An aide stepped up, for Jack to rattle off a number, and added, "That ten million I'd like you to match that award", as Jack turned to leave only to have Alister hold onto his arm, to say, "Wait, you said matching, is it not for you?"

"Sure, but of all the money you made from the government ends today, unlike the Justices, who suggest you pay me today, you have one month, upon that time, you'll make a onetime deposit of twenty million dollars to that account, in and on behalf of my name, are we clear, Mister Fancier?"

"Yes."

"You can let my arm go, or you'll be next, oh, and one more thing, if you attempt to run, I'll appoint enough Special Ops men to watch over you, and additionally, I'm vacationing now so I may ask a Destroyer to come sit offshore and point its 20 inch guns at your prominent place of business, do you understand that?"

Jack turns as he is directed out a side door, as it closes, a guard holds Miss Meyers back.

All was quiet as he stood in front of probably the most powerful woman in Europe, who said, "Looks like the Justices gave you swift justice, and money to boot, do you know who I am?"

"Yes, your Meredith Holstein Chief Justice for the World Court council for the UN."

"Good you're very smart, since I know more about you than you know of me, allow me to tell you what I can offer you." "I'm listening?"

"First off unlimited resources', and support troops, and complete Army, Navy and an Air Force, and then there are the wives and children, as many as you like, plus a manned and defended bunker underground facility just for you, it's all for you and then there is the money, think unlimited, as we pull from 178 countries, each has a signed agreement where you go in and whatever happen, happens, but at all times you'll be safe, as for the money, we can give you a billion dollars a year, regardless of your service, meaning whatever you do, and all of it is without tax, what will you say?"

Jack looked at her, only to hear, the door, finally open, and Miss Meyers came to Jack's rescue, to say, "Leave him alone, we know what you want", as she steers Jack out, as Meredith yells, "Think on it Jack, we'll see you soon."

Jack is hurried into the express elevator, as the door closed Jack says" What did she mean by I'll see her soon, that offer seemed pretty good offer."

"The only offer you need to worry about is going back to your beloved Samantha who is lying in wait. Miss Meyers escorted Jack out of the courthouse, for Jack to see Brian did in fact wait for Jack as he slid in, and the green GTO took off.

CH 13

Death becomes her

Jack and Brian arrived, in Brian's souped up GTO, and parked, in the hanger, as Jim instructed him, Jack got out to see a lovely red headed woman, similar to Lisa, who carried a huge handbag, with a smile on her face, to say to him, "Hi my name is Claire, the President sent me."

"How are you doing?" asked Jack.

"Fine, I like you already, so where would you like me?" Jim says, "I'll be over here if you need me."

"Thanks for the car" he says to Brian.

"It's yours; you can use it the entire time you are here."

"So where we at, oh yes the building, I guess they allocated a former SEAL'S training center, hop on the golf cart, I'll take you down there" said Jack, willing to drive.

She slides in next to him, as he drives off, to say "From this main road down, to the south is our area, but I need you to confirm and get it mapped out, in that field over there", as he points, "I would like an obstacle course, with a viewing platform, this is our building", as they get out, Jack, opens the door for her, to see the place lit up, and a very familiar face emerged, it was Tami, the front desk clerk, to say, "Thanks for the promotion."

"Tami meet your boss, Claire, this is Tami, my personal assistant, and I guess you found your desk?"

"Yes, I'm taking the end corner across from your office; next to me will be a receptionist."

"Fine, back here could be your offices."

"That will do" she said as they walked through, to see several individual offices, empty, Jack opened a door, to show a huge quantum hut, to say "This can be used for supply, I already have someone ready for this position, as they will be moving all the stuff over here."

"Where will everyone park?" "What's that?" asked Jack.

"You know where will you park your car, surely not out front?"

"True, true, let's look out back" said Jack leading her out to an empty field, to say "I was thinking we need a kitchen and a lounge to rest."

"Then let's build on, and put a parking garage for all the potential cars, what you're thinking five hundred at a time?" asked Claire.

"Nah, maybe ten" said Jack.

"Oh how about this, along the street, we put in classrooms, to the parking garage, I don't know how about five levels, and over there a kitchen."

"What about the windows, above."

"that's easy, we will create an atrium, here, with trees of a tropical nature, and a food court across, the side, Lisa told me that you like the whole buffet line thing, instead lets create themes, like a bakery, breakfast shop, lunch deli, a BBQ station, and a steak house, to follow up with a afterhours pub, for drinks and food, then this place can double as a nightclub?"

"I don't know about all that" said Jack.

She sensed she might be pushing him to say 'I'm sorry, I was just suggesting, how about I get some plans together, then once your happy you sign off on them."

"That's fine, let me show you the upstairs", as they walked in, to see a set of stairs up, Jack took them two at a time, to the top, to say, I'd like this one, but as you can see its small, can we double the size, and install showers in each one, maybe a kitchen when you first walk in, with a bar for a counter, some table, and a bed and sofa, similar to the plane?"

"I'll have to look at that" as the saw the open squad bay. Jack says "if you could have rooms made, similar to mine, I guess if you want, all across the classrooms too."

"Will do, what is our time table?"

"I don't know, perhaps six months."

"So the first class is April of next year." "That sounds fine" said Jack.

"How do you want me to promote this?"

"Just send it out to all the colleges, police academies, military training, and high schools, full tuition and salary paid."

"Will do boss."

"Just call me Jack, now I need to go, oh one more thing I have a builder, here is his number, his name is Robert Bradley, he and his crew build everything, so give him a call."

Jack went out to his cart and was off.

Claire came in to say, "He is sure a busy man." "You don't know the half of it" said Tami.

"Well he will be here on a regular basis, won't he?" "Probably not, do you even know what he does?" "Yeah he is our new Super Spy."

"True, but he travels every day, to everywhere in the world, so I Imagine a lot of decisions you'll have to make in his absence." "Wait, what are you saying, I'm responsible for all this." "Yes, don't worry I can help you, what were you thinking for a staff?"

"I don't know" said Claire, to see a stunning brunette, walk through the door, to say "Hi, is this the offices for the Spy Academy?"

"Hi, my name is Tami, Jack's personal assistant, and this is Claire, base operations Manager."

"My name is Debby, and I'm the supply officer." "Excellent" said Claire, to add, "What do you think brand new desks?"

"Nah, desks are very useable, I bet I could go to the base depot, and pick up what ten desks for free and chairs to boot." "What are you stealing them?"

"No silly, the base depot, is a clearing house of recycled stuff, the desks we can get used but the computers should be new, and I have a line on that, which system do you want to go with?"

"Sounds like your well qualified, you run with it; do you need help with the desks?"

"Nah I brought help", as she went to the door and yelled

"Alright boys bring it all in."

"So you already had it planned?"

"Nah, this was for my area, but I can go back and get another load."

Jack made it back to the hanger, to get out seeing Jim, who said "Were ready for that test."

Jack raised his hand, to wave him off, to say "It's time for me to spend her last minutes with me." "Oh I'm sorry" said Jim.

Jack made it down, with key card in hand, all the way to the viewing area that Heidi and Kate were in, they both came to him, on both sides, crying, to say I love you individually, as Heidi said "She is failing, the end is near, go down and see her one last time", they both kissed him on the cheek, as he broke away from them, down the stairs, to hear Mitzi and the doctors arguing, but that all stopped, as everyone rushed to help Jack get dressed, as Jack made his way in, her stats rose, as she smiled, she was fighting for her life, as she watched him walk up to her, he bent over to give her a mouth to mouth kiss, as Sara patted her man on the shoulder, Samantha's eyes lit up till Jack broke off the kiss, to sit on the edge of her bed, he put his arms around her fragile body, and held her, as she placed her head upon his shoulder she said "I Love you" and closed her eyes. He felt her body was still pulsating as he moved slightly, she awoke, as he set her back to the pillow, to hear 'I'm so tired." "I know dear", said Jack as he let her rest, Sara had since moved back to allow Jack to be with his first wife. Samantha opened her eyes, she said, "I don't feel like a woman anymore, will you touch my breasts one last time, before I go to sleep?"

Jack was hesitate, as one doctor stood behind him, he turned and waved him back, to focus on her smile, as he undid her gown, he opened it up, to reveal her huge stomach, and her very full breasts, carefully he touched them, just like the way she liked them to be touched, soft, and alluring, her hormones were racing, as blood rushed to her face, she was flush, as she took one hand to place it behind his neck she pulled him in close to say, "Thank you, my love for making me a woman again, for I will always be looking down at you . . . ."

She closed her eyes, as Jack gave her a kiss one last time as the machine was going crazy, and in the background was heard, she has flat lined.

"Let's get the baby out" yelled a Doctor.

Jack was pulled off, as he broke the kiss, and the two doctors went to work, as he ended up on the floor, sitting, trying to pull on Sara. with his hands to his face crying, tears were flowing, and so was the blood, his nose bled, as Mitzi was there to assist him, the sound of a baby boy, let out a whelp, Jack was inconsolable, he knew this time was coming, and now it was here, his beloved Samantha was gone, he would never be able to roll her out to the park, or go on long walks, or just lie with her at night, just then Sara yelled out, "My water has broken, I'm having a baby."

"Get her on the other gurney, in the other room", said one doctor.

Jack still held onto Samantha's lifeless hand, her warmth was leaving as she was becoming cold, he still was crying, from her loss, and was losing some blood in the process, as a doctor came back to the room, to say "it's a girl".

Heidi and Kate rushed the room, her mother instincts went to Jack, as she held him as he continued to cry, she too joined in with him, while Mitzi took charge, and pushed the doctors out, and closed the door, Kate was with her sister, smiling, on a small waiting bed, Trixie, had cleaned up baby Sam, and presented him to her, which she held, as Kate, stroked the baby's face, while helpers cleaned up Chelsea, for Trixie to present to Sara, in the other arm. To say "I'll go check on Jack", as Trixie, went in, to see Samantha hand was still being held, she went over to Samantha, and lowered her head, then covered her up, and dropped her down as far as she could go.

Lisa stood above with Samantha's mom, Glenda, who herself was crying at the emotional event, that just took place, to say "Alright haul this one to jail, and turn her over to the Marshal's."

"Wait."

"For what, I gave you several more minutes; your next stop is the Supreme Court, for child abuse, and neglect."

From her vantage point she could see Jack had moved to place his arms around Samantha as his mother Heidi, Mitzi and Trixie looked on, for Lisa to say to herself, "He may be there forever, so she sees Ramon to say "Will you get Norse Man and have him pick up Jack and bring him to my office?"

She turned and went away, with Ramon, while Jack rested upon Samantha's body; he had pulled the sheet down to see her face. Then in one quick move Jack was riding in the arms of Norse man, the giant easily carried the distressed Jack up the stairs, into the elevator, and to the open office door, to the sofa to where he put him down. As the giant stood above him to say "I will stay here as long as you stay put."

Jack nodded his head, as his clasp a pillow, and the giant placed a blanket over him to say, "You need rest."

The giant pulled out a chair and sat down, to watch Jack fall fast asleep.

Jack awoke to see that the giant was gone, Jack slid up, to sit down, and he stood up and passed back out to hit the floor.

Back at the Spy Academy headquarters, the cackle of girls voice's held Lisa back as she entered to see the three of them, were gawking at the two stoutly men moving desks around, to say "Claire do you have a moment?"

She looked at her to walk over to say "Yes?"

"If you need anything my staff is available to assist you." Claire looked her over to say,"Actually I think we are fine for now, do you know when the planes will be transferred over to us?"

"Why do you need them now?"

"No I just want to make sure, first the appropriate funding is available, and then have the accountability on hand for its support, will Jim and Brian be coming over or do we need to find a pilot and an armorer?"

"No, they're both yours, and they should still get their same pay" said Lisa.

"Absolutely, and same for Jack, as the GAO told me that they would cut the checks to us and then we will transfer the money to cash, as what you do, Mitzi informed me of what we need to do, she just didn't know if she and Trixie, be working for Jack or under your pay, and guidance?" said Claire.

"From what I know is that all those Jack works with falls to your jurisdiction, specifically the Supreme Court and Erica Meyers, who told me she will have an office here to complete the change over, and you'll run the base operations, but have no affect on what jobs Jack takes, or his personnel."

"I know that all we do is support his efforts, I believe it's up to you to support his mission man power, and then this Academy will churn out operatives that you will continue to support, and it will be up to Jack and a panel of those chosen to become a super spy" said Claire.

"I believe we are on the same page" said Lisa with a smile, to add, "Did he authorize all of this?"

Claire looked over at Debby, to say, "This is all free." "Regardless, this is his show; maybe he wants everything brand new, besides he just got one billion a year."

Claire looked at her, as did Debby, and Tami, till Lisa added "I also wanted to give you a heads up, Jack's wife Samantha just passed away", Lisa left on that note.

Claire looked at Debby, who herself became emotional, as Tami said, "Let's go see him."

"Where is he at?" asked Claire. "I don't know" said Tami."

"You're his assistant, don't you think you should know where he is at."

"Yes, the last I heard was he was at the base hospital." "Then let's go up there and visit him" said Claire.

Tami led them out while Debby told the men to off load the rest in the building, to catch up with Claire to say, "You know she is right, Jack is who received this money, and it will be his school, all we are here for is to support his wishes."

"That true, Debby, but I remember him telling me to run with what he wanted, leaving the little details to me" said Claire.

"Then you should be fine, but in all my years in the Air Force, I never bought anything unless, I presented a requisition, and there was a signature, just to cover my butt."

"Yes, I need to do that; can you design a document that would cover all that?"

"Hey I thought you were the efficiency expert?"

"I am, but I never started a federal organization from scratch, especially one that comes from the branch of the Supreme Court."

"Listen why don't we as a three some decide as a team to make decisions, then get Jack aboard, with a call to him by Tami, and then a final approval from Miss Meyers" said Debby.

"Then we better give her that office across from where I was taking mine" said Claire.

"That's fine with me, I'll just take a desk in the open pool, but would like to know, if we could cut a door, from the office to the supply shed?"

"Of course, we can do anything, and not only one, but Jack wants two."

The three of them got to the plane hangars, to see both planes were out and Brian was first they saw to say "Hi Brian, have you seen Jack?"

"The last I heard was he was in Lisa's office resting." "Oh because of" said Claire in a statement.

"No I don't think that is it, he had passed out, and a team of doctors are in there now."

"Really" said a concerned Claire, as she and the two others rushed the hanger, only to stop in their tracks, to see the largest man they had ever seen, the Norse man stepped to the door way, crossed his hands in his arms, to see the three girls, to say "That's far enough, Mister Cash, does not want to be disturbed, "Jim", he shouted, Jim stepped off the ramp, to see him heard, "Get your jet plane ready, the Cash's are flying to Mobile in two hours, have Captain Clark's team ready to go, and dressed in suits."

Jim stood looking at the giant, then looked at the three girls, he lingered while looking at Debby, and then went back inside, and moments later came out screaming for Brian.

Brian appeared to say, "Scrap the test, we got a more pressing matter, Jack is going home, for the funeral, lets load up the jet plane, and get his room ready" he said that over a intercom with Jeff the pilot, for him to turn around and land.

"I'm here, can I help you out?" said Debby.

"Sure, you know what to do, can you make sure the refrigerator is stocked; Nicole missed that one last time. Said Jim. Back in the bunker, Sara walked in a place back and forth, with her Mom on one side and her sister on the other, to say, "What is going on here, I just had a child, and now Jack has fallen ill?"

"Honey calm down" said Heidi, her mother consoling her. "What do you want me to do mom, my husband has fallen ill, this is not what he does, and now the doctors don't know what is wrong with him."

"Sis you need to rest" said Kate, also wondering what is up. "Kate I'm fine, I may go breastfeed my babies, and do you want to come?"

"Sure why not, were not much help here now?"

Sara sat on the bed, as Trixie handed her each baby which fed on her very large breasts, while Kate looked on, to say "You always said you wanted to have lots of babies."

"Oh this is just a start sister, for the next five years I hope we have six children by then."

"Well from what I see you'd better hope your husband makes it."

"Awe he is fine he just needs rest, you know she probably broke his heart, she would have done that to me, if I hadn't been pregnant, it sort of kept me on my path."

"Hush sis" said Kate as a doctor came in to say, "Miss Cash we believe Jack was a bit dehydrated, Miss Sanders assured me, that she and her husband would personally take care of you both, I suggest you both rest."

"Yes Doctor White."

"How did you know my name?" he shakes his head, then leaves as the two cracked up, for Sara to say, "What a goof butt, the guy's a dork."

"Sara that is a doctor" said Kate. "So are you and Mom."

"True, but he is a certified specialist."

"What does that mean anyway?" asked Sara.

"Oh you know a specialist in everything" said Kate, as the two girls giggled.

Back in Lisa's now cleared out office, Jack stood up, and staggered a bit, then collapsed, to the floor, but caught himself, as he tried to clear his head, he had knelt up then stood, to get his bearings, as other's were there, trying to stabilize him, and roll him back on the bed. Some time had passed, as Jack now was fully awake, and asked,"May I see my wife Samantha one last time?"

Jack made his way into the room that the body bags that housed Samantha, as he was heading towards where her head was, to hear "Her head is on the other end, said a guy washing up, to add she is now ready for transport."

Jack just looked at him, to touch the zipper, as the man said "Here let me do that for you", only to see the giant which froze him in place, as Jack could feel the giant in one sweep pick him up, and Jack felt no energy to fight with him, but knew he could take him in a fight.

Jack was taken to a bed which the giant let him down slowly.

After some time Jack awoke, he wiped his eyes and saw a familiar face sitting on his bed, with her hands grasping his, it was the one who looks over him and cares about him deeply, for it was Mitzi. Jack smiled at her to say "Thanks, your there for me."

"Always and forever." "Even after I retire?"

"Well we will talk about it when that happens, but don't say that too loud, everyone is already anxious as it is, so what are your plans?"

"Get some rest and get out of here."

"I agree with that, are you well enough to go now?" asked Mitzi, as she pulled his hand up to her lips as she kissed it.

"Nah, what's the rush."

"Oh no reason, except this might be a good time to get the giant to go."

"What, what are you saying?"

"I saw you when you see a guy you would like to add to the team."

"Nah, you're crazy, I have my team in place, so how is my partner coming along?"

"What are you talking about, you have no partner." "What about Blythe, or Dylan."

"Gone, gone they are all gone, she took them all from you." "Great, that figures, so what is your plan?" asks Jack.

Looking at her still in the resting position.

"Just act like you're in a great amount of pain, you know in your head, and I'll convince Lisa to allow the Giant to go with us." "Alright, if you think this will work, I'll try" said Jack as he saw her break away and go away, as Heidi came out from the room, with Kate in tow, as they came to his side to say, "Jack are you feeling alright?"

"I guess as best as could be expected, how is Sara?"

"She has given both babies three full feedings and we are ready to go whenever you're ready", as Heidi sits on one side and Kate on the other, to hold his hand.

Jack broke his hands free to pull out his phone to dial up Jim, via text message,"Get the jet ready, the Family and I would like to go back to Mobile, in an hour."

Jim finished the last details, of the jet, as Debby came out to say

"It's all set for him, and the crib is also in place, do you want me to go down and get the precious cargo?"

"Nah, I just received a text, to say "Jack is ready, were leaving in an hour, do you know where the boys are at?"

"Last I saw them was with the strike team, loading baggage, do you want me to go with you", she said as she reached out and hugged Jim, to kiss him on the cheek to say "Remember you promised."

"Alright, first mate, help Nicole with flight preparations", Jim left her, to hit the ramp running to see Paul and his men, decked out in full military uniforms, at the door for him to say "This is what I want your guys to do, after Jack boards and is in his room, load the casket in place, tie it down" Jim turns to see Lisa, who says change of plans, I want the entire team on the second plane to Mobile with the casket and the base band, immediately, this is Jack Cash were talking about and his wife will get full military honors." The last of her voice rang out and the strike force was gone.

"Have Brian and Nicole on that plane, and you and Debby on this one, I'll fly down with my group in one, before you take off," as she pulls Jim close to say, "From this point forward, this will be our last mission together, after this you will get your orders from Miss Meyers, and your new administration, I knew this day was coming, but think of it as a promotion."

"It was an honor serving you" said Jim, honestly. "Remember who it was all for, I have a feeling you're going to be doing a lot more, real quickly, as Jim saw the Giant carrying Jack in his arms, to say, "What is going on, is Jack alright?"

"Yeah, I think he is in mourning with the loss of his beloved wife, as the Giant passed by, to see Jack was out, Mark was in the front part of the plane, opening the door as Mike was at the ramp, helping the women, he wanted to help them, as tears were flowing down his face, for Lisa to say "Jim I've never known you to be emotional like this, remember wait one hour before you leave, I want to make sure we have the area secure, as Jim saw Debby, with Trixie carrying a crate, do you understand, you're getting a promotion as well, I gotta go, see you in Mobile."

Jim's mind was wandered, to hear his phone ringing, he saw it was Brian, to answer it to say, "You'll be fine my boy, take her up to thirty five thousand feet, and in four hours you'll, as Jim saw that the prop plane was where the jet should have been, to say "Damn that girl, she tricked us again, where is she at?"

"Gawking at the car."

"That's fine, she won't be able to get inside of it, where is she at now?" asked Jim.

"She went into the bedroom."

"Well go in and she what she is up too, and by the way who do you have as your co-pilot?"

"Jeff Larson, the Marine corps pilot, so I let him fly her out, you knows all about discipline."

"When did you switch the planes location?"

"You know when we were going to test the car this morning" said Brian.

"Oh yeah, I forgot" said Jim.

"Well boss good luck and see you in Mobile."

Brian slid his phone shut to step into the open door to see Lisa snooping around, for him to say "Are you looking for anything In particular?"

"No, but when we take off, where does one sit?"

"On this easy flight pull out a cargo net and climb into it, it will be radio silence the entire trip down, as he watched her."

"You can go anytime you like or are you going to watch me?"

Brian thought about Jack to say "I'd like to say, is would it be possible you won't get the place to out of sorts." "Why, don't you know who I am?"

"Well all I know is that this is Jack's private room, and I know there is some things in here that, well I'd say are booby trapped." "Why would you do that?"

"Well just in case, someone ventures in here and begins going through drawers."

"I'll be fine leaving me" said Lisa.

"As you wish, I just warned you" said Brian as he passed a nice looking man to hear Ramon close the door."

Brian smiled, as he took his seat, up front, as the ramp was lifted, he saw the countermeasures switch, he thought about it, to turn it off or not, to say "Who is that woman anyway, didn't she get the memo, I work for Jack Cash Super spy."

Brian got the clearance to take off, as he flipped the intercom he heard her cussing, to say "Band aids are in the head Ma'am, prepare for takeoff", he clicked off the intercom, and turnoff the counter measures switch, to smile.

Jack laid back as Mitzi had put on music, through the entire aircraft, a fighter pilot, had introduced himself respectfully over the intercom, "Good evening folks this is Commander Bill Billson, I will be your pilot today, our flight time will be just at three hours," as Jim, ensured everyone was aboard, lifted the ramp, went to his co-pilot seat, taxied the plane, a veteran pilot himself, lifted the plane off the ground, easily leveling it off, as Jack slept in Sara's arms.

Jack awoke to music playing, it was like a live band close by, Jack rose up, and went to his window, to see hundreds of people milling around in the light rain, the over cast day, Jack quickly dressed, his mind was racing, as he put his shoes on and zipped up his windbreaker, he put in his badge and saw his gun charging he went through his door, down a flight of stairs, to see Sara's room was empty, and down one more flight, to smell the fragrant of food, out the front door. Jack stopped in his tracks, to see everyone had assembled for him, as the band began to play, everyone he knew was there, Cassandra the tailor, Terri, Marci, and Claire, it was like he stepped back into time, The Sanders clan, this three other wives to include his new brother in law Carlos and his family, and there was Lisa, who orchestrated the whole thing, as she led Jack past everyone, who wore black, even the agents who guarded his wives were there, especially Joe, Samantha's protector, they walked past the people, down the driveway, to the turn where a hoist system was in place, Jack stood, as people filed by, touching his arm, as Lisa held Jack on one side and the Giant was on the lower part, all the well wishers took a spot on the bank, below and above, as Sara, Alexandra, Maria, and Alba, took their places, as the band stopped, as a pastor stood on the wall platform to say, "Bow your heads please, Dear God, we would like for you to clear the rains for a brief moment, as to allow us to say our goodbye's to our friend, family member, sister, mother and wife, of our friend Jack Cash, we ask that you place the confidence to come to terms with her passing, and to celebrate her remarkable life and for those she touched, we ask that you watch over us to see that we do more than what Samantha did for us and that you check in on us from time to time to let us know she is with us, and we ask that you help us all in mending the broken heart that Jack feels for the loss of his beloved wife, in your name we pray", "Amen."

Jack stepped forward to the edge of the mini wall, to lean on the casket, to say "I love you Darling, rest well", then Jack saw the huge marble grave stone, That read;

"SAMANTHA SMITH CASH"
"BELOVED FRIEND, SISTER AND MOTHER"
"1ST WIFE OF JACK CASH"
"I LOVE YOU DARLING, Love Samantha.
APRIL 10,1996-OCT 20,2010

Jack wiped away a tear, as the Giant hoisted him up and set him down, as the rain had stopped, and was clearing, as he heard other speaking, but stumbled, to get up, he was an emotional wreck, as Mark and Mike helped Jack up and walked with him to his door, it opened as another agent held it open, they helped Jack inside, as the door shut, Jack stood, to smell all of the delights, as he turned the corner he and Mike and Mark, was five of the most stunning women in the world all say "Hi", in unison.

Jack made it to a bar stool, to see from left to right a dish from each girl who said "Hi Jack, My name is Kristina, and I'm from the Czech Republic.

"Hi Jack, I'm Lucia, from Spain.

In the middle and the one who wore practically nothing said "Hi Jack, my name is Catalina, I'm from Chile.

A real stunner with huge bags, carried balloons said in a crack accent, "My name is Mafalda, I'm from Portugal."

And in the sweetest voice ever could be said was a girl similar to Alba's size say "Hi, Jack Cash, my name is Camelia, I'm from Columbia, South Carolina, and we're here to cheer you up on the sudden loss of your wife, and if you're willing to consider any one of us or all of us to be your next wife's?"

Mark and Mike patted Jack on the shoulder to say, "This is all you buddy, you won't need us any longer."

"Hi Jack" was said in unison."

Jack turned in his bar stool to see his favorite pairing, the brunette of Jen, and the blonde of Monica, to say, "Yes I think I can get over her passing."

The End . . .